THE
RUNAWAY
KING

Also by

JENNIFER A. NIELSEN

The False Prince

THE ASCENDANCE TRILOGY
· BOOK TWO ·

THE
RUNAWAY
KING

JENNIFER A. NIELSEN

SCHOLASTIC PRESS · NEW YORK

Library of Congress Cataloging-in-Publication Data

Nielsen, Jennifer A.
The runaway king / Jennifer A. Nielsen. — 1st ed.
p. cm. — (The ascendance trilogy ; bk. 2)

Summary: Young King Jaron has taken the throne of Carthya, but after enemies
attempt to assassinate him, and a neighboring kingdom threatens invasion, he finds
that he has no friends in the palace, not even his bride-to-be, princess Amarinda—
and his regents think it would be better for Carthya if he just disappeared again.

ISBN 978-0-545-28415-8 (jacketed hardcover) 1. Kings and rulers—Juvenile
fiction. 2. Princesses—Juvenile fiction. 3. Courts and courtiers—Juvenile fiction.
4. Conspiracies—Juvenile fiction. [1. Kings, queens, rulers, etc.—Fiction. 2. Princesses—Fiction. 3. Courts and courtiers—Fiction. 4. Conspiracies—Fiction.] I.
Title. II. Series: Nielsen, Jennifer A. Ascendance trilogy : bk. 2.

PZ7.N5672Run 2013
813.6—dc23
2012035290

10 9 8 7 6 5 4 3 2 1   13 14 15 16 17
Printed in the U.S.A.   23

First edition, March 2013
Book design by Christopher Stengel

For Dad,

who through the example of his life, taught

me to reach for the highest star, and never

doubted that I could.

BYMAR

GELYN

Eranbole Sea

Half-Moon Pass

Isel's Harbor

ISEL

CARCHAR

GELVINS

DICHELL

Swamp

Thieves' Camp

Tarblade Bay

Borderlands

LIBETH

Farthenwood

TITHIO

EBERSTEIN

DRYLLIAD

Roving River

Falstan Lake

CARTHYA

SPARLING

NAVENSTILL

BENTON

PYRTH

AVENIA

N

A Map of Carthya and Avenia

K. LEFAIVER

THE
RUNAWAY
KING

· ONE ·

I had arrived early for my own assassination.

It was the evening of my family's funeral, and I should have already been at the chapel. But the thought of mourning alongside the arrogant coxcombs who would also be there sickened me. If I were anyone else, this would have been a private matter.

For a month, I had been the king of Carthya, a role for which I had never been prepared and which most Carthyans believed was entirely unsuitable for me. Even if I wanted to disagree, I had no credibility for such an argument. During these first weeks of my reign, courting favorable public opinion had hardly been my top priority. Instead, I had a much bigger task: convincing my regents to help prepare for a war I felt sure was coming.

The biggest threat came from Avenia, to the west. Its leader, King Vargan, had come to the funeral unexpectedly. Maybe his claims of only wanting to pay his respects sounded sincere, but I was not deceived: He'd grieve more for the loss of his after-supper cake than for my parents and my brother. No, Vargan had come to learn my weaknesses and assess my strengths. He had come to test me.

Before engaging in any confrontation with Vargan, I had needed time to think, to be sure of myself. So rather than enter the funeral, I had told them to start without me, then escaped here, to the royal gardens.

This had become my favorite place on the frequent occasions when I needed to get away from everyone. The bright springtime flowers were surrounded by tall, dense hedges and lined with plants of every variety. Majestic trees kept the view from above concealed through most seasons of the year, and the grass was soft enough to make bare feet nearly mandatory. In the center of it all was a marble fountain with a statue at the top depicting King Artolius I, a grandfather from generations ago who had won independence for Carthya. My name, Jaron Artolius Eckbert III, partially came from him.

In hindsight, these gardens were the perfect place for a nice and quiet attempted murder.

I didn't even consider something as passive as sitting tonight. Overwhelmed with conflicted feelings surrounding the funeral, and with Vargan's late arrival, my body was tense and my emotions raw. I needed to climb, to work off some energy.

I quickly scaled the first level of the castle, using the unevenly cut rocks as grips for my fingers and feet. The lowest ledge at this part of the wall was broad and swallowed up in ivy, but I rather liked that. I could fold myself into the dense leaves and glance out at the gardens with the feeling that I was a part of it all, rather than a simple observer.

After less than a minute, the gardener's door opened below me. That was odd. It was far too late for a caretaker to be out here, and this ground was forbidden to anyone else unless I invited them in. I crept to the edge of the wall and saw a figure dressed in black cautiously making his way forward. This was no servant, who would have announced himself properly, if he even dared enter at all. The figure made a quick survey of the area, then withdrew a long knife and took refuge in some bushes directly beneath me.

I shook my head, more amused than angry. Everyone would have expected me to come here for reflection tonight, but they wouldn't have planned for me until after the funeral.

The assassin thought he'd have surprise on his side. But now the advantage was mine.

Silently, I unlatched my cloak so it wouldn't interfere. Then I withdrew my own knife, gripped it tightly in my left hand as I crouched at the tip of the ledge, and leapt directly onto the man's back.

As I jumped, he moved, so I only clipped his shoulder as we fell in opposite directions. I was up first and took a swipe at his leg with my knife, but it didn't cut nearly as deep as I'd hoped. He kicked me to the ground, then knelt across my forearm and wrenched the knife from my grasp, tossing it far from us.

The man caught me on the jaw with a powerful punch that

knocked my head against the ground. I was slow to get up, but when he reached for me, I kicked him as hard as I could. He stumbled back and crashed into a tall vase, then fell to the ground, not moving.

I rolled to face the castle wall and massaged my jaw. The fact that my hand was already on my face probably saved my life. Because a second attacker came out of nowhere, holding a rope that he wrapped around my neck. He pulled it tight, pinching off my air. But with my hand trapped inside the rope, at least I could give myself some chance to breathe.

I punched an elbow backward, connecting with the chest of this new attacker. He grunted, but it took three hits before he was forced to readjust his position and loosen the rope. When he shifted, I rounded on him and reared back an arm for a swing.

Then I froze. In the instant I locked eyes with the intruder, time stopped.

It was Roden. Once my friend. Then my enemy. Now my assassin.

· TWO ·

It had only been a matter of weeks since I'd seen Roden, yet it seemed like months. In our last encounter, he had tried to kill me as a final attempt to get the throne for himself. But I sensed his reasons for being here tonight were even darker.

Together we'd been trained by a nobleman named Bevin Conner, who'd snatched us and two other boys, Tobias and Latamer, from Carthyan orphanages with the intention of passing one of us off as Jaron, the lost prince of Carthya. Jaron's parents had attempted to send him to a boarding school where he might learn some much-needed manners, but after he'd escaped the ship bound for Bymar, pirates had attacked with the intention of bringing about Jaron's demise. Nobody — not Conner, not Roden, not the other boys — knew that I was, in fact, Jaron in disguise. Roden still didn't know this. As far as he knew, I was an orphan named Sage, no more worthy of the throne than he was.

It was a good thing Conner hadn't attempted to pass him off as Prince Jaron, because in this short time he'd changed enough to look even less like me. Roden's brown hair had lightened and his skin was tanner than before. He looked older and certainly acted that way. When I'd last seen him, he had been upset, but it was nothing compared to his expression now. This went far beyond anger.

Dropping the rope, Roden got to his feet and drew out a sword. He held it like an extension of his arm, as if he'd been born with that very weapon in his hand. My knife was somewhere behind him, hidden in shadow. The odds weren't exactly in my favor.

"Get up, Sage, and face me."

"That's not my name," I said. And I wasn't going to get up yet.

"I was with you at Farthenwood. You can't lie to me about who you really are."

Which was exactly my point, if he thought about it. Speaking as calmly as I could, I said, "Lower your sword, and I'll explain everything." I had located the place where my knife lay, but it was too far to be retrieved before he could use that sword. So at this point, I much preferred to talk with him.

"I'm not here for your explanations," he growled.

His sword remained ready, but I slowly stood, keeping my hands visible. "You've come to kill me, then?"

"This fraud of yours is over. It's time you learn who is really in command."

I snorted. "You?"

He shook his head. "I'm with powerful people now. And we're coming for you. I'd rather kill you here, but the pirate king has some business with you first."

Although I appreciated the delay in my death, somehow I doubted any meeting with the pirate king was good news. With a smirk, I said, "So you joined up with the pirates? I couldn't imagine anyone but the ladies' knitting club accepting you."

"The pirates gladly accepted me, and one day I'll command them. They killed Jaron, and when it's time, I'll be the one to kill you."

"You mean they *failed* to kill me. You joined up with failures. If I escaped them four years ago, why would you think I can't do it again?"

Now his face hardened. "I have orders for you. And I suggest you accept them."

I'd take orders from the gong scourer before I obeyed him. But I was curious. "What do you want, then?" I asked.

"I'll be at sea for ten days. When we dock, you'll be in Isel to surrender to me. If you do, we'll leave Carthya untouched. But if you refuse, we'll destroy Carthya to get to you."

On their own, the Avenian pirates were destructive, but Carthya would ultimately prevail. So if this was their threat, then they must have allies. My mind immediately went to King Vargan. Maybe he wasn't here to test me after all. It couldn't be a coincidence that this attack was happening so soon after Vargan had walked through my gates.

"I prefer the third option," I said to Roden.

"Which is?"

"The pirates have nine days to surrender to me. But if they do it in eight, I'll be more merciful."

He laughed, as if I'd been joking. "Costumed like a king, but you're still the same foolish orphan. There's one more demand. The pirates want you to release Bevin Conner."

I snorted again. "So he can join them too?"

Roden shook his head. "I only know that someone wants him dead. Surely you couldn't object to that."

Surely I could. Conner was no friend of mine. He was my family's murderer, and the reason pirates had tried to kill me four years earlier. During my short stay at his estate, he had been brutal to me. However, I would not turn him over to Roden any more than I intended to give myself up. "Conner's death will do nothing for the pirates," I said. "It's only revenge they seek, for both our lives."

"So what if it is? Your life is over, Sage. Accept your fate with some dignity and save your country. Or try to fight back and see us destroy everything. We'll burn your farms, raze your towns, and kill everyone who stands between us and you." He stepped closer to me. "And if you try to hide, we'll take the people you love and punish them for your cowardice. I know exactly whose death would hurt you most."

"Maybe that's your death," I said. "Why don't you go ahead and punish yourself right now?"

With that, Roden lunged forward. I tried to grab his sword, but he kept hold of it and swiped down at me. It cut across my arm, and I yelped and released him. Shouts of my vigils echoed behind us. Finally. I wondered if my cries had disturbed their naps. It was about time they realized I was in trouble.

Somewhere near us was my knife, but Roden kept swinging, forcing me to back away from him. With my next step, I tripped and fell into the fountain. He came to the fountain's edge with the obvious intent to strike, but now my vigils had arrived to help. Without a shred of fear on his face, he began fighting whichever man was closest. I could only sit there, stunned to see how much progress Roden had made in his skills in such a short time. He cut through them as if they were little more threat than snowflakes.

I jumped from the fountain and dove for the sword of one of my fallen vigils. At the same time, Roden wounded another man, who fell backward and tripped over me, knocking me to the ground and landing on my legs.

Roden kicked away the sword I'd wanted. Then, with his blade at my throat, he crouched near me and said, "The decision is yours. Ten days to surrender, or we'll destroy Carthya."

I was only midway through one of my better curses at him when he raised the sword and crashed it down on my head.

· THREE ·

When I came to, Roden and his accomplice had made their escape. Considering the injury to my arm and the thunderous pounding in my head, it was probably a good thing they were gone. However, Roden's threats still lingered in the air. I was lucky he had not carried out the worst threat while I lay unconscious.

Wet from the fountain and bleeding from my arm, I stumbled into the courtyard to see another patrol of vigils running toward me. I singled out one of them and told him to give me his cloak, which he did. They said something about my needing a physician, but instead I asked he be brought into the gardens to attend to the men there. Then I ordered the vigils to keep everything as quiet as possible, at least until the funeral ended.

With a hand clamped over the wound on my arm, I slowly walked to the chapel, where the funeral was underway. I should've gone to the funeral in the first place, rather than to the gardens. The attack on me would have happened anyway, eventually, but at least I'd have paid proper respect to my family. They deserved that much from me.

I had always missed my family while I was on my own at the orphanage, but here at the castle, their absence haunted my every step. I desperately wanted to go inside where I could properly mourn for them. But looking as I did, that was impossible. So I huddled like a spy beneath a small open window to listen, hoping that wherever my family was, they would forgive me.

Inside I heard the voice of Joth Kerwyn, my high chamberlain. He had been my father's adviser and my grandfather's adviser too. Possibly even further back. It seemed to me that Kerwyn had always existed. He was speaking of my brother, Darius, now, and I barely recognized the description of him. Darius was four years older than me, and had been about my age now when I last knew him. Still, if there was any truth to Kerwyn's words, Carthya now had the lesser of Eckbert's sons for a king. As if I needed another reminder of that.

Next, each of the regents was offered the opportunity to speak. Those who did gave predictably exaggerated honors to my family. A few were coarse enough to work in their politics. From Master Termouthe, who was currently the most senior of my regents: "And now we have King Jaron, who will certainly honor all his father's cautious trade agreements." Or Mistress Orlaine, a friend of Santhias Veldergrath, who couldn't contain the ridicule in her voice as she said, "Long live King Jaron. If he leads us half as well as he entertains us, then Carthya has a truly great future ahead."

Even in my condition, I nearly barged into the funeral then.

I had in mind a few impolite words that would've provided weeks of entertaining gossip for the court.

"Jaron?"

I turned, not sure whether to be pleased or embarrassed to see Imogen walking toward me. She moved cautiously, clearly confused about why I was here and not inside.

Imogen had been a servant at Conner's estate of Farthenwood and had undoubtedly saved my life there. One of my first acts as king was the small repayment of making her a noble. It was interesting how little her new status had affected her. Certainly, her clothes were finer and she often wore her dark brown hair straight down her back rather than in a servant's braid, but she still remained friendly with everyone, no matter their status.

Her eyes scanned the dark skies. "Did it rain? Why are you all wet?"

"A nighttime bath."

"Fully dressed?"

"I'm modest."

Wrinkles formed on her forehead. "When you didn't show up at the funeral, the princess asked me to come find you."

Princess Amarinda of Bultain was the niece of the king of Bymar, our only ally country. Because of that, it had been arranged from her birth that she would marry whoever sat on the throne of Carthya, sealing the alliance. This was supposed to be my brother's duty, one I believed he was happy to fulfill.

Now the duty had come to me. The happiness over it had not. Amarinda had made it clear she was equally miserable over our betrothal. Compared to Darius, I felt like a consolation prize, and a poor one at that.

For the first time, Imogen noticed my wounded arm. She gave a soft cry, then moved closer to get a better look. Without a word, she crouched down and lifted her dress just enough to grab the fabric of an underskirt. She tore off a length, and used it as a bandage to bind my arm.

"It's not so bad," I said as she wrapped the injury. "The blood makes it look worse than it is."

"Who did this?" I hesitated, and she said, "Let me get the princess."

"No."

Imogen's eyes narrowed. "This is important. You have to talk to her."

I'd talked to Amarinda plenty, with every polite phrase I'd ever learned, such as "That's a nice dress," and "This dinner tastes good." But we'd both avoided any of the things that really needed to be said.

Imogen kept pushing. "Jaron, she's your friend, and she's concerned about you."

"I've got nothing to say."

"That's not true."

"I've got nothing to say to her!" An awkward silence fell, until I added, "Amarinda's friends are already inside the chapel."

She courted friendships with the regents who disrespected me most. And she had laughed so much with the captain of my guard at supper last night that I finally went to my room so I wouldn't be in their way. I wanted to trust her, but she had made that impossible.

After more silence, Imogen murmured, "Then talk to me." She smiled shyly, and added, "I think I'm still closer to you than anyone else."

She was, which was a tragedy. Because now that she'd put it into words, I realized someone else understood it too. Roden said he knew exactly whose death would hurt me most.

Imogen. If the pirates wanted to hurt me, they'd take Imogen.

I couldn't imagine a day of my life without her there in some way. But if I failed to keep the pirates out of Carthya, then Roden would lead them straight to her. The thought of what might happen then was unbearable. A hole opened up inside me as I realized how dangerous it was for her to stay here. Allowing her to remain connected to me in any way was a potential death sentence.

As much as I hated the thought of it, I knew what must be done. Imogen had to leave the court. Worse still, she had to want to be as far from me as possible, so that nobody could ever suspect there was any benefit in harming her.

My stomach twisted, as if the lies I was about to tell were knives pulled from my gut. I slowly shook my head and said,

"You're wrong, Imogen. We're not friends and never were. I only used your help to get back to the throne."

She froze for a moment, unsure of whether she'd heard me correctly. "I don't understand —"

"And you're using me to stay here at the castle. Where you don't belong."

"That's not true!" Imogen stepped away with a look of shock as if I'd slapped her. Once she recovered, she said, "When you were Sage —"

"I'm Jaron, not Sage." My lip curled as I added the worst thing I could think to say. "Did you really believe I could ever truly care about someone like you?"

Imogen's struggle to contain her emotions was clear. That tore at me, but I did not, *could not*, flinch. She bowed to excuse herself and said, "I'll leave at dawn."

"You'll leave at once. A carriage will be prepared to take you home."

Shaking her head, she said, "If there's something you need to tell me —"

I turned away from her, so as not to betray my own feelings. "I don't want you here. Gather your things and go."

"I have nothing here," Imogen said. "I will leave just as I came."

"As you wish."

She left without looking back at me and with her head held high. Watching her hide the pain I'd just caused was worse than if she'd let it show. I had never been so cruel to anyone, and I hated myself for it. She would hate me as well, and I'd never be able to explain that sending her away with such indifference, even hostility, would save her life.

A new sort of pain flared inside me, something different than I'd ever felt before. If there was ever someone I could one day give my heart to, I had just sent her from my life forever.

· FOUR ·

I wasn't alone for long. Only minutes after Imogen left, King Vargan walked out of the chapel doors, holding his back as if in pain. He didn't see me in the darkness behind him, so I had a moment to watch him. Vargan was tall and well built but slowly wilting. He had dark eyes and a graying face of deep lines. His hair was still long and thick but the color of coals on a dead fire.

As I watched him gaze over the courtyard with a hungry eye, my hands curled into fists. Here he stood, having played some role in the attempt on my life only an hour ago, and yet I was powerless to stop him. The pirates wanted my life, Vargan wanted my country, and my regents wanted to paint rainbows over reality and claim all was well.

Luckily, I was dry enough now that my appearance looked sloppy, but not soaking. I rotated my cloak to hide my bandaged arm, pushed my hair off my face, then stepped forward.

Vargan heard me coming and twisted around, startled, then grabbed his back again. "King Jaron, I didn't realize you were out here. I had expected to see you inside."

"It looked pretty crowded. I thought maybe nobody had saved me a seat."

He smiled at the joke and said, "You could've had mine. Those chapel pews torture my spine. Forgive me for leaving your family's funeral."

"I'm not sure it is my family's funeral. Other than their names, I don't recognize the people they're speaking about in there."

Vargan laughed. "Such disrespect for the dead! I'd expect that of an Avenian, but I thought Carthyans were better than that." His expression grew more serious and he added, "I'm told you passed yourself off as an Avenian over the past four years while you were missing."

"I was never missing," I said. "I always knew exactly where I was. But it is true that a lot of people believed I was Avenian."

"Why?"

"I can do the accent."

"Ah." He put a finger to his face while he studied me. "You're such a young king. I barely remember being your age."

"Then clearly we're talking about how old you are, not how young I am."

His amused grin faded as he said, "You look more like your mother, I think."

I had my father's solid build, but I was far more my mother's son. I had her thick brown hair that tended to curl at the ends and her leaf green eyes. More than appearances, however, I had her mischievous nature and sense of adventure.

Thinking about her made me uncomfortable, so instead I asked, "Are our countries friends, King Vargan?"

He shrugged. "It depends on what you mean by that."

"I'm asking how concerned I should be about protecting my borders from an Avenian invasion."

His forced laughter came out awkward and condescending. I didn't even smile, and his laughter quickly died out. Then he said, "I'm sure you have much bigger problems tonight than worrying about my armies."

"Oh? What problems are those?" Vargan probably didn't know the attack on me had happened earlier than planned. Therefore, I used the same innocent tone that had always worked on my father when I gave excuses for missing my lessons. Although the stakes now were far higher than a reprimand to my backside.

Vargan's mouth twitched, but the smiling was over. "If you're as clever as they say, how can you fail to see the danger in front of you?"

"You're in front of me. Should I be more concerned about you, or my old friends, the pirates?" I paused to let that sink in, then added, "Or is there no difference?"

Without a flicker in his voice, he said, "The pirates live within my borders, but govern themselves, even have their own king. On occasion we may work together, but only when it's for our mutual purposes."

Obviously in my case, it suited their purposes very well.

"Will you pass them a message for me?" I said. "Tell them

I've heard rumors of war on my country, and that if such a thing is attempted I'll destroy them." Vargan stared blankly at me as I continued, "I won't start the battle, but if it comes, I will finish it. Tell them that."

Vargan chuckled, but it didn't hide his irritation. "That sounds like a threat against me, young king."

"It couldn't have been, unless you're threatening me." I arched an eyebrow. "Correct?"

With that, his face relaxed. "There's some courage in you, and I admire that. In my own youth I was just the same. I like you, Jaron, so I'll forgive your arrogance . . . for now."

That was good news, though I didn't much like him. He had fish breath.

Vargan leaned closer to me. "In fact, I'll make you an offer. Let's begin with an easy agreement. Before his death, your father and I were negotiating for a small area of land on our borders, near Libeth. The Carthyan land has a spring that my farmers need for their crops. Carthya has other springs nearby, so you won't miss it."

"My father wouldn't have missed it, but I would," I said, with no actual idea of which spring he meant. "It happens to be my favorite water source in all of Carthya, and I won't part with it."

Vargan frowned. "This is a time for cooperation. Work with me, as your father did, and keep Carthya at peace."

"What's the point of gaining peace if it costs us our freedom? I won't trade the one for the other."

He took a step forward. "Listen to me, Jaron. I'm trying to warn you."

"And I'm warning you. Do not bring war to my country. Either from your own forces or from pirates working in your stead!"

This time when I mentioned the pirates, I saw a flash in his eyes, something he wasn't able to control.

He knew. I was sure of it.

"Your Majesty?" Gregor Breslan, captain of the Carthyan guard, emerged from the chapel and approached with caution. "Where have you been? Is everything all right?"

Gregor looked exactly as a captain of the guard should. He was tall and muscular, with dark hair and a stern face that communicated his serious nature. He also had a close-cut beard that I'd heard he grew to cover battle scars from years ago. Gregor was highly competent and intelligent enough, but also a bit of a wart. We pretended to tolerate each other's failings, and frankly, he was trying harder at it than I was. I completely blamed him for being so grating. But to be fair, it wasn't his fault now for coming at exactly the wrong moment.

Still facing the Avenian king, I said, "It seems our privacy is at an end. I hope your back feels better, unless a sore back keeps you from invading me."

Vargan laughed. "Give me no reason to invade, young king. Because if you do, a little back pain won't stop me."

We shook hands, then I gestured to Gregor and said, "Walk with me."

He fell in step at my side as we crossed the expansive court-yard. "But the funeral —"

"Is nothing but good theater for nobles unable to love anything but their own reflections."

"It's not my business to tell the king how he should behave at his own father's funeral, but —"

"You're quite right, Gregor. It isn't your business."

Beside me, I could feel his temper boil, but in a carefully controlled voice he said, "What did Vargan mean about giving him no reason to invade?"

"He made me an offer. In exchange for a promise of peace, he wants some of our land."

"A heavy request. But it always worked for your father."

"It does not work for me. We will defend the borders of this country!"

"With what army? Your Majesty has sent nearly every man that could be spared down to Falstan Lake, for no other appar-ent reason but to take earth from one area and leave it in another. It's a waste of manpower and an unnecessary decision."

Actually, it was a tactical decision for a fallback plan if war did come to Carthya. I had wanted to share the plan with Gregor and my regents, but Kerwyn had cautioned me against it. The regents already questioned my competence as king. Kerwyn felt this would only reinforce their doubts.

"Bring the men back to Drylliad," Gregor said. "I need them here."

"Why? To shine their shoes and march in formation? What good is that to anyone?"

"Respectfully, sire, if we're asking questions, then I might wonder why you're wearing a vigil's cloak, and why you're hiding your arm."

I stopped walking and faced him, but huffed extra loudly to be sure he heard me. Then, with some reluctance, I unfolded the cloak so he could see my bandaged arm. Most of my sleeve below the bandage was colored by blood that had soaked into the wet fabric.

At the sight of it, the muscles on Gregor's face tightened. Still staring, he said, "You were attacked."

Another brilliant deduction from the captain of my guard. Even through Imogen's bandage, the wound's exposure to air sharpened the sting, so I covered it again.

"Two pirates got inside the castle walls," I explained. "Vargan must have helped them somehow."

"Do you know this for a fact?"

"Yes."

"And you have proof?"

"Well . . . no."

Only thinly concealing his disgust, he said, "Your Majesty, what if this whole idea of war is just in your head? Maybe Vargan isn't behind tonight's attack, but you see it that way because you've already decided he might invade."

"He is *going to* invade!" Gregor shifted his eyes from me, but

I continued anyway. "They want our land, our resources. They will take all that we have and destroy all that we are."

"We've had years of peace, sire. Your return home shouldn't change anything."

"Of course it changes things. Four years ago, my father let everyone believe I died in a pirate attack. Now that I've returned, these countries will consider my father's lies to them a grave insult. There are consequences for my coming to the throne, and we have to deal with them."

Gregor had pursed his lips while I spoke, but now he answered, "If you were older, you could order the soldiers to war right now, and I would lead them. But until you're of age, you must accept that there are some actions you cannot take without the support of the regents. And if you will forgive me for speaking so boldly, the decision to give you the throne last month, rather than considering a steward, was granted too quickly and only in the enthusiasm of the moment. They should have welcomed you home as a prince and then given you time to adjust before putting the whole weight of the kingdom on you."

"But they did," I said. "And with your help, I can defend this country."

His eyes narrowed. "You do not yet have the hearts of your people, or your regents. Nobody will follow you into a war based on your *instinct*. You need proof. Were these assassins captured?"

"They were messengers, not assassins." At least, not yet.

"What was the message?"

"I already told you. That war is coming." I held out my injured arm. "And this is your proof."

But Gregor saw it differently. "The pirates must be open to negotiation. Otherwise, they'd have just killed you when they had the chance."

"It seems their king wants to handle that part personally." I didn't dare to think of what that might involve, but it probably wouldn't end up being my best day ever.

Walking again, I angled toward a rear entrance of the castle, used mostly for the transport of prisoners, their visiting families, and dungeon vigils.

"Where are we going?" Gregor asked.

"I want to speak with Bevin Conner."

Gregor's eyes widened. "Right now? In your condition?"

"He's seen me in worse shape."

"What could you possibly want with him?"

"Does the king need his servant's permission now?" I asked.

"Of course not. It's just —"

"What?"

"Jaron, you destroyed everything that man wanted." Gregor's tone had softened now. "You know what he'll do if you see him."

I set my jaw forward. "After what I've been through tonight, do you really think he can hurt me any worse?"

"Oh yes," Gregor said solemnly. "He can and he will. Tell me what you want from him. I'll get it while you rest."

The idea that I might find any rest tonight was becoming

increasingly absurd. I asked Gregor, "Do you know why the pirates tried to kill me four years ago?"

"Conner confessed it all, sire. He hired them, hoping to force your father into a war to protect our borders."

"Clearly, the pirates haven't forgotten their agreement."

Gregor clicked his tongue. "Then tonight wasn't about war. They intend to kill you."

I picked up the pace and muttered, "Everything started with Conner. And if there's any hope of ending this, I need his help now."

FIVE

Since I'd had him arrested on the night I was crowned, I hadn't seen Conner face-to-face, and I wasn't looking forward to this reunion. Neither was he, apparently. For no matter how much I dreaded having to look at him again, at least I disguised my anxiety. Conner wasn't even trying. He looked absolutely terrified when he saw me enter.

As it was, I had felt no sympathy when he was convicted for his crimes. After the trial he had been granted his request to be held separately from the other castle prisoners. Now, he remained in isolation in a locked tower room where I was told he spent most of his time looking out over the land through a small and filthy window.

Conner had a chain around his ankle and was thinner than when I last saw him, although I'd made sure he was fed and allowed the basics of hygiene. Yet his beard was ragged, and in the dim light of flickering torches, I was sure I could see gray hairs. I'd never noticed them when we were at Farthenwood.

Conner gave me a slight bow. "King Jaron. I'd ask if you

are well, but frankly, I've seen you look better. And drier, for that matter."

"I'm perfectly well, thanks for asking."

"To what do I owe the honor of your visit?"

"It smells like a sewer in here so I'll be brief." Looking directly at him, I said, "Was King Vargan ever part of the plot to kill me four years ago?"

The fear melted away, leaving a wide sneer on his face. "No. The pirates didn't want Avenia involved. They don't like working with Vargan unless they have to, and they figured Avenia wouldn't want a part of my plan anyway."

Avenia was certainly involved now. According to Vargan, it suited their mutual purposes.

"Tell me again about the night you killed my family."

With a weary sigh he said, "There's nothing more than what I've confessed to a thousand times."

"I've been reading about the dervanis oil. Did you know it takes over a hundred flowers to produce just one drop of the poison? That's why it's so rare, and so hard to acquire. I don't think you got it here on your own."

Gregor put a hand on his sword. "Jaron —"

I brushed him aside. "Where did you get it?"

Conner laughed, his arrogance on full display. "If you don't ask the right questions, then coming here is only wasting my time and yours."

"Do not insult the king!" Gregor said.

This time he drew his sword, but I motioned for him to put

it away. Conner hadn't intended to be insulting. He wanted a different question from me. But I didn't know what.

Distracted, I used my boot to tap an empty plate on the floor with a napkin folded over it. "Where did this come from?"

Conner smiled. "The betrothed princess said you missed a meal with her this evening. So she brought me your portion."

Amarinda had been here? I tried to look as if that didn't bother me, but he knew it did. She'd have no reason to come here, unless . . . Suddenly, I didn't want to be here anymore.

Gregor stepped forward. "She didn't think you'd mind."

"Don't defend her actions!" I ordered. Of all her friendships, this one was unacceptable.

Silently, Gregor dipped his head and retreated against the wall, though his hand never left his sword.

I turned back to Conner, who was now standing tall with his arms folded, a quiet challenge to my authority. It hadn't even been a month ago when I'd faced him with a similar look of defiance.

He said, "It's about time you came to thank me."

"*Thank* you?" He was lucky my thanks didn't come in the form of a noose.

"You are king now, just as I promised," he said. "Maybe you hate the things I did that got you here, but the fact is you would not be king without me."

Something exploded inside of me. It was all I could do to hold my temper. When I finally spoke, my words reeked of bitterness. "After what you've done, you really expect my gratitude?"

"All of Carthya should be grateful to me!" Conner arched his head. "Your father was weak. Eventually, the countries that surround us would have swallowed Carthya whole. Darius was a risk as well. He was too close to your father to see him for who he was."

"They were my family!"

"Your family rejected you. Not just once but twice. They made you a nobody, then gave you to the world. But I have given the world back to you. I made you king."

Still angry, I cocked my head. "Now I have everything. Is that what you think?"

"With one exception." Conner nodded at the empty plate Amarinda had brought.

I stared again at the dish on the floor. Did she really think I wouldn't mind her coming here? Of anyone in this castle, she was supposed to be on my side. Conner was absolutely correct in his insinuation that Amarinda and I were not friends. Nor did I have any idea of how to fix things with her, if that was even possible.

Conner lowered his voice and continued, "I've paid for my crimes against you. Let me go free and I will serve you now."

I grinned, feeling my edge again. "You might reconsider those terms. I just got a visit from the pirates. They want you."

Conner gave me exactly the look of fear I'd expected. His eyes widened and something roughly the size of a boulder seemed to be lodged in his throat. "Don't let them have me, Jaron. You know what they'd do."

"Whatever it is, I'm sure it'd hurt," I said coldly. "Maybe I will release you after all."

I started to leave, then in a panic, Conner called, "Jaron!" Without waiting for my attention, he added, "I betrayed your family, that's true, but I never betrayed Carthya. I still consider myself a patriot."

I turned back to him. "How can that be? Do you have any idea what you started when you hired the pirates?"

Conner pressed his lips together, then nodded at my bandaged arm. "Oh. They want you, too." The long lines of his face softened. "So it's both our lives at stake."

"All of Carthya is at stake," I said. "You opened floodgates I might not be able to shut again." Now I turned and stepped closer to him, so close that I could see the dilation of his pupils as he returned my stare. "I need the name of the pirate you hired to kill me. Tell me now, or you will go to them tonight."

Defeated, Conner whispered, "His name was Devlin. He bragged that your death would give him a place of honor with the pirates. The fact that you're alive will be humiliating to him."

"And to you, too, I suppose."

Conner wasn't fazed. "The truth is that nobody cares about your life but me! I'm the only one here who's worked with the pirates. You need me."

I shook my head. "Carthya needs you the way we need the plague."

His tone turned nasty. "And you think you're more wanted by your people? Do you really believe anyone wants to fight for a boy who has caused them nothing but trouble? Did anyone want you back? No, Jaron, you are alone here."

His words stung as if he'd slapped me. Conner must have sensed the emotion building inside me and chose to strike again.

"I remember your father's announcement four years ago, that he couldn't go to war because there was no proof of what had happened to you. It was a lie, of course, and no king wants to lie to his people. Wouldn't things have been easier if you had died? Don't you think in a way that your father wished you had?"

My knife was already in my hand. I lunged at him, my hands shaking with so much anger that the knife scratched his throat. "You destroyed everything!" I yelled.

Conner arched his head to gather a breath. "And I'm the only one who can save you now. The regents won't help you. Think of how convenient it'd be for them if the pirates got to you."

Unfortunately, he was right about that. From their perspective, my death would solve a lot of problems.

"Your people won't help either," he continued. "Listen to them. They're laughing at you."

Fixed on his eyes, I said, "Do you laugh at me?"

He was quiet for a moment and finally the tension drained from him. "No, Jaron," he said darkly. "I curse you with every breath I exhale. But I do not laugh."

Gregor had remained behind us, and it occurred to me that he wouldn't object if I used my knife now. He'd never approved of my decision to imprison Conner rather than execute him. But then, he hadn't agreed with most of my decisions so far. I released Conner, who fell to his knees, his hand massaging his throat.

I drew in some air until I'd calmed down, then said to him, "Where did you get the dervanis oil?"

"From the pirate Devlin," Conner mumbled. "But knowing that won't help you now. Only I can fix this. Let me help you save Carthya. Forgive me, my king, here and now."

I clicked my tongue, then said, "I'll forgive you once I get my family back. Good-bye, Conner." He was still yelling my name as the dungeon door closed. Gregor silently followed me down the steps of the tower. I continued forward while he reinstated the vigil.

My hands were shaking as I entered the main passageway. Conner had unnerved me in a way I could never have expected. Even in chains, he knew my vulnerabilities.

Once Gregor had caught up with me, he asked if I was all right, but I gave him no answer. Then he said, "Conner denied any connection between Vargan and the pirates. Perhaps you are wrong."

"I'm not. Tell me what I'm missing. Conner said I wasn't asking the right questions."

"He's a manipulator, toying with your weaknesses. He's not to be trusted."

I stopped walking so that I could look at him. "Do you trust me, Gregor?"

"Should I?" He shifted his weight while he reconsidered his

boldness. In a humbler tone, he continued, "After everything tonight, you must be exhausted. Get some rest, and know that I'm here to protect you."

"As you protected me tonight?" I took a breath, then added, "Tell me this. If the pirates attack us, does Carthya have any chance of winning?"

His eyes widened. "You're not suggesting —"

"I need to know."

"Our numbers are greater," he said. "But it would be like fighting a bear. Carthya may come out of it alive, but with terrible wounds. And once wounded, we'd be easy prey if Avenia chose to invade."

Just as I had thought. "We'd survive only long enough to be destroyed," I mumbled. Then I added, "What if we attacked the pirates first?"

Gregor shook his head. "The pirates are hidden inside Avenia. To get at them we'd have to attack all of Avenia. With both enemies against us, Carthya would be destroyed in a matter of weeks. Whatever aggression the pirates showed against you tonight, war cannot be an option."

I hated the thought of war. Yet even more, I despised the fact that we were so unprepared to defend ourselves. Ever fearful of war, my father had treated his soldiers as parade decorations rather than as warriors. My mother had always understood the threats against us, but obviously even she couldn't overcome his fear of battle. Worse than anything was the realization that had my father lived, he and I would never have come to a mutual understanding. We would always have found some way to disappoint each other.

I thanked Gregor, then told him I'd see my own way to my rooms and meet him again in the morning.

I walked away only until I found a quiet corner where I could back against the cool wall and breathe. Conner may have been right about one thing: I had never been more alone, and my situation never more desperate. Every minute of the night had pushed me another step closer to my death, and my options were narrowing. It was becoming clear what had to be done, but I was certain there was no hope that I could do it. One way or another, I would have to face the pirates.

SIX

Mott and Tobias were waiting at the doors to my chambers when I arrived there, and bowed when they saw me. I didn't mind too much when staff at the castle bowed, but it was still uncomfortable for me when they did it.

Tobias was the last of the orphans Conner had taken. Mott was Conner's former servant, and both he and Tobias had caused me no end of misery while at Farthenwood. Considering the odds against us there, it was an amazing thing now to call them both my friends. Over the past month, I had sent them throughout Carthya to find Roden. Now I realized what a foolish errand that had been.

Tobias was taller than I, had darker hair, and until my recent loss of appetite, he had been thinner too. Mott stood at least a head taller than Tobias. He was almost entirely bald, dark-skinned, and made of little else but muscle and disapproving frowns.

Mott's eyes went immediately to my bandaged arm, and his brows pressed together in concern. "You're wounded," he said.

"Never mind that," I said. "When did you get back?"

"Just now." Mott's gaze remained fixed on my arm. "The funeral for your family was ending as we arrived. Obviously, that's not where you were."

"They didn't need me there. Everyone was mourning their own loss of power far too much to bother with grieving." I turned to Tobias and noted the dark circles beneath his eyes. "You look exhausted. Haven't you slept?"

"Not really."

"Get some rest," I said. "Mott can fill me in for now and we'll talk more tomorrow." I prodded him forward. "Go, Tobias."

He bowed again. "Thank you, Your Majesty."

"I'm Jaron. You know me too well for anything else."

"Thank you . . . Jaron." Tobias excused himself and hurried off.

Mott frowned at me. "You shouldn't scold him when he was only using your proper title."

"If it is my proper title, then you shouldn't scold me at all," I said sharply.

"They warned me you were in a terrible mood, but I underestimated it."

"A mood to match this day," I said.

Both his tone and his face softened. "What's happened?"

The servant who held my door open adopted the notable traits of a statue when my eyes passed over him, though he was clearly absorbing every syllable we uttered. I paused in the entrance and said to Mott, "Let's talk where there are fewer ears to gather gossip."

Mott followed me into the chamber. My nightshirt and robe were laid out in case I was ready for them. A part of me wished to crawl between the plush quilts of my bed and try to sleep off this horrid night. The other part wondered how I'd ever sleep again.

No sooner had the doors shut before Mott tore away the rest of my cut sleeve, then reached for the bandage on my arm. "Who did this?"

"It seems I have even fewer friends than I thought."

Mott harrumphed while he finished untying the bandage and studied the cut. "This needs some alcohol."

"It's not that bad."

"It's bad enough. Fortunately, this isn't your sword arm."

"They're both my sword arms." I naturally preferred my left hand, but my father had forced me to train with my right. As a child, that had frustrated me, but the ability to fight with either hand had become a valuable skill as I grew older. "How is that relevant?"

"Because I've heard that the king spends every minute he can spare in the courtyard practicing with a sword. Why is that?"

"The girls enjoy watching me." Mott scoffed, so I added, "It's simple. I've been out of practice for the last four years. That's all."

"Except that nothing is ever simple with you."

"Ow!" I yanked my arm away as he touched a sensitive area of the wound. "Whatever you're doing, stop it!"

"I'm cleaning it. Next time you're cut, try not to get dirt in it."

"Next time I'll get help from someone who doesn't treat a wound like he's scrubbing a chimney."

Clearly annoyed, Mott said, "You should thank me for tolerating you. I had hoped that becoming a royal would cure your foul manners."

"That's interesting. My father had hoped that stripping me of royalty would do the same thing." Then, more gently, I said, "Now tell me the news from your trip."

He shrugged. "We traced Roden as far as Avenia soon after you were crowned. We think he's back in Carthya now, but can't be sure of that."

I could be sure. Nodding at my arm, I said, "Roden just gave me that."

"He was here?" Mott furrowed his thick eyebrows together. "Are you all right?"

"I already told you, the cut isn't so bad."

He shook his head. "That's not what I asked. Jaron, are *you* all right?"

Such an easy question for an answer that turned my stomach to knots and choked off my air. Quietly I said, "It feels like a lifetime since this day began. And every time I think nothing more can go wrong, it does."

"You got through Farthenwood. You'll get past this too."

I grunted at that, then said, "As horrible as it was, Farthenwood was a test of endurance. I always knew that I'd beat

Conner, if only I could outlast him." I looked at Mott. "But I can't see the end of what must be done now. Or, I don't want to."

Silence fell while Mott continued to work on my arm. As he began wrapping it with a bandage, he asked, "Why did you send us off to find Roden? Why not just let him go?"

"Because I thought . . . we'd once been friends. It was Cregan who turned us against each other. I believed that."

"And now?"

"It seems I was wrong. Everything we went through . . . none of it mattered. All I saw in his eyes tonight was hatred."

As Mott finished tying off the new bandage, he said, "I'm worried about you."

"Good. I didn't want to be the only one." I drew in a slow breath, then added, "If my only choice is between the unacceptable or the impossible, which should I do?"

"Which choice means you will live?" Mott asked.

We were interrupted by a knock at the door, and I was grateful for the distraction. He wouldn't have liked my answer. Mott went to the door, then turned to me. "Lord Kerwyn asks to see you."

I nodded, and when Kerwyn entered the room, Mott made an excuse about finding more alcohol and left. I thought he looked a little exasperated when he glanced back, but people often did when they talked with me so it was hardly worth noting.

Kerwyn bowed before he approached, then said, "Jaron, your arm."

"I know."

"Gregor told me you were attacked. Praise the saints that it's no worse."

"It'll get worse before this is over." And I couldn't think of any reason the saints would have an interest in me.

The creases in Kerwyn's face deepened. I wondered how many of his wrinkles had been caused by me. More than my share, I suspected.

I said, "Will you call a meeting with the regents tomorrow morning? Gregor won't support my position, so I'll talk with them directly."

Kerwyn frowned. "Actually, that's one of the reasons I came. Gregor has just assembled the regents together. They're meeting right now."

"Without the king?" I muttered a string of curses, inventing a few new ones in the process. Then I stood and began unwrapping my damp tabard so that I could change clothes. The ache in my arm brought a grimace to my face, and Kerwyn stood to assist me.

"The regents will have to act now," Kerwyn said. "While on the throne you're a target."

"As long as I'm Jaron I'll be a target." Then, in a stronger voice, I added, "Help me get dressed, Kerwyn. I have to be at that meeting."

· SEVEN ·

Minutes later I charged through the doors of the throne room. All eighteen of my regents were there, with Gregor in the seat once occupied by the snake Lord Veldergrath. I still hadn't selected regents to replace either him or Conner, and probably wouldn't for a while. At least not until those who wanted to be chosen stopped preening themselves every time I walked by. Whatever conversation there had been extinguished like a flame in water. In a somewhat disheveled fashion, everyone lowered themselves into bows or curtsies, no doubt also tainting their noble breaths muttering the devil's vocabulary.

"Whoever forgot to invite me to this meeting should be beheaded," I said as I slumped into the king's chair. "So, which of you is that?"

Most of the regents became suddenly fascinated with the folds of their clothes. Either that, or they were avoiding looking at me. The silence didn't bother me in the least. Lord Hentower was seated closest on my right. I stared coldly at him and rather enjoyed watching his growing discomfort.

Gregor chose to break the tension. "Your Highness, this was a hasty gathering, and no offense was meant. If we had known you wanted to attend —"

"I never *want* to attend," I corrected him. "Yet here I am. So what are we discussing?"

Again, the regents took an interest in their clothing, or their hands, or the tiles on the floor. In anything, really, but answering me.

"Lady Orlaine," I said, "can I assume we're all here to discuss the mating rituals of the spotted owl?"

She faltered for a few words before finding her tongue, then sputtered, "There was an assassination attempt tonight, sire."

"Yes, I know. I was there." I focused on Gregor. At least he had the courage to look back at me. "How did pirates get inside my castle walls?"

"That question is being investigated as we speak," he said.

"But not by you." I glanced around. "Unless you suspect one of my regents."

"No, of course not." Gregor cleared his throat. "We'll find the people who did this."

"It was done by the pirates. And King Vargan helped sneak them inside."

Gasps followed the accusation, then Lady Orlaine asked, "Can you prove this?"

"Proving things is his job," I said, pointing at Gregor. "He may not have told you, but earlier tonight I spoke with Vargan. He warned me that we were going to be attacked."

"Why would he do that?" Gregor asked.

"You know why. To intimidate me into handing over our land first."

A fact that didn't seem to bother Gregor nearly as much as it should have. "Are you sure he said 'attack'?" he asked. "Perhaps he meant it in another context."

"Ah, one of the cheery definitions of the word, then?" I asked. "Such as an attack of affection, or an attack of goodwill toward Carthya? I know what I heard, Gregor."

"What you *think* you heard," Master Westlebrook, a younger regent at the far side of the table, corrected. "We cannot make any accusation based on such thin reasoning."

Gregor leaned forward, his hands clasped on the table. "Jaron, our greatest concern, of course, is your safety. I've explained to your regents the threat that was made against you, and we believe we have a plan."

"Which is?" This should be good.

Lord Termouthe picked up there. "First, we've agreed to give them Bevin Conner. We must make some concessions if we hope to have peace between us."

From across the table, Gregor continued, "And of course, sire, your life must be preserved. We decided that you cannot be turned over to the pirates."

I grinned. "A decision that probably came only after a long debate."

I had expected some smiles at that joke, but there wasn't

even one. I cocked my head at that, wondering if there *had* been a debate.

"The regents believe that until the immediate threat passes, you must go into hiding," Gregor said. "However long it takes, we will keep you safe."

"Until when?" I was nearly at the end of my patience now. "Another four years? Or shall it be forty this time?"

Without answering, he continued, "Finally, we have to remove the motive for the pirates wanting you." Gregor took a deep breath before this part. "I've proposed to the regents that they install a steward until you're of age. If you're not on the throne, then the pirates gain nothing by killing you." He looked at me to respond, then with my silence added, "You may not like that idea, but it will save your life, Your Majesty."

At the mention of a steward, my heart had stopped cold in my chest. I didn't know where to aim the anger that had so suddenly filled me. At Kerwyn, for failing to warn me this was coming? Or Gregor, for pretending to be the most loyal of servants even as he plotted to pull me off the throne? Or myself, for giving the regents reasons to trust Gregor more than me? I settled on Gregor, because I was already annoyed with him anyway.

Then Lord Termouthe said, "Jaron, will you support this plan?"

I rapped my fingers on the armrest. "No."

"Which part do you object to?" Gregor asked.

"The part where you began speaking." I stood and began

walking the room. "To start, we must protect Conner until I understand everything about my family's murder. He's our only link to the truth. The dervanis oil —"

"Conner told you that was irrelevant," Gregor said in a raised voice. "Why this obsession with chasing shadows when the real question is how to keep the pirates out of Carthya?"

"It's the same question!" I shouted back. "Can't you see that it's all connected? Something is wrong with his story!" Already, my talk with Conner had begun nagging at me. Something had happened there that I should have noticed, perhaps a message coded in his words, or in the tone of his voice. And yet the clues remained hidden.

"Nothing is wrong with his story. You've become so unstable, obviously the only thing wrong is with you!" Gregor paused and checked himself, then lowered his voice. "Forgive my outburst, Your Majesty. I didn't mean that."

But he had meant it. And from one glance at my regents, I could tell he wasn't alone in thinking it. Only Kerwyn, standing silently in the corner, seemed to be on my side.

I swallowed my emotions, then calmly said, "You misunderstand the reasons why the pirates want my life. Whether I'm hiding or not, whether I'm king or not, they intend to finish the job Conner hired them to do four years ago. They don't want a treaty or a trade agreement. Nothing will satisfy them but my death. This is a threat that cannot be negotiated away."

"Negotiations always worked for your father," Mistress Orlaine said.

"My father was wrong!" Which was something I'd never spoken aloud, never really even dared to think. I straightened up and said, "When the other side only wants our destruction, what is left to negotiate? I'm asking you to follow me. Because if we don't defend ourselves now, then after the pirates come, Avenia's armies won't be far behind."

"Which is why we believe the solution is to remove the pirates' motivation for coming in the first place." Now Gregor stood, facing me directly. "Jaron, the regents will not support any act of war as a solution to this problem."

I stared at them, aghast. "As of tonight, the pirates are already at war with us. Ignoring that reality doesn't mean we're at peace." A few heads nodded back at me, but not enough.

"We'll find a way to avoid war . . . without you." Gregor's voice was icy now.

My mind went to what Conner had said in the dungeon. Without me alive, Carthya probably could avoid war, a convenient option for everyone. Except me, of course.

I set my jaw forward. "Has there been a vote?"

He shook his head, then said, "Maybe we can't force you to hide, but we can install a steward until you're of age and ready to become king again. Don't make this a fight, Jaron. You're alone here."

Also as Conner had said. "And will you be the steward?" I asked.

Gregor cleared his throat again. "In times of war I'm the logical choice. Besides, Amarinda will be queen of this country one day. She fully supports my leadership and I'm certain would give that endorsement to the regents."

"She's not queen yet," I said.

Kerwyn stepped between us and addressed Gregor. "There are two vacancies amongst the regents right now. One is from the regent who would have killed Jaron if he'd found him at Farthenwood. The second is from the regent who did kill Jaron's family. The king is young. But I still trust him above anyone in this room."

"Hopefully one day we'll learn to trust him, too." Gregor turned back to me. "It's just until you come of age, Jaron. And for your own good."

I started to retort but Kerwyn put a hand on my arm, urging me not to continue the argument. He was right to stop me. I couldn't win this battle.

They had left me with only one choice now, and my palms were already sweating at the thought of it. I felt as if I were standing deep inside my own grave, with the climb out beyond anything I could reach. And yet I must climb. My first step would begin right here with my regents.

Already anticipating the answer, I forced my hands to unclench and looked at Gregor. "When am I leaving, then?"

"At dawn. We'll complete an investigation of what happened tonight, and then move forward with diplomatic efforts to solve this problem."

I shook my head. "You must delay any vote for a steward

until that investigation is complete. The pirates gave me ten days. You give me nine."

Gregor hesitated, but Kerwyn said, "That's acceptable. No investigation could be adequate any sooner than that."

"And what about the princess?" I asked. "Her safety?"

"You were targeted tonight, not her. I'm certain that she's safe here." Then Gregor added, "You are right to support this plan, Your Majesty."

I took that in with a slow nod. "Do you think I want to run?"

He only said, "You'll return soon. And you'll see, in the end, everything will be for the best."

· EIGHT ·

I left the throne room alone, too wound up for sleep and too exhausted for everything this night still required of me.

The last thing I needed was to come face-to-face with Amarinda, who had clearly been waiting in the passageway for the meeting to end. I offered her a curt nod of respect, then said, "Which of the regents are you waiting for? Or is Gregor the one you want most?"

Amarinda's almond-colored eyes narrowed as her gaze descended on me. She was uncommonly pretty and had a way of unnerving me whenever I looked directly at her. So I rarely did.

"I came to speak with you." Her tone was livid. "I heard what you did to Imogen. How dare you? She did nothing to deserve that!"

I turned on her with my own anger. "And tell me, what did Conner do to deserve such a fine meal, hand-delivered by you?"

"You were supposed to have eaten it tonight, at supper with me!" I couldn't argue with her there. For the past week, I'd found something better to do at nearly every mealtime. Then her temper cooled. "I had hoped you'd be there, so we could talk."

Something in her voice made me regret having so casually dismissed the time with her. "All right. Perhaps we should talk now."

I held out my arm for her and we began walking down the corridor. Several seconds passed when I couldn't think of anything to say, and she seemed equally uncomfortable. Finally, she said, "You want what's best for Carthya and so do I. Why are we so far apart?"

Because she had brought food and comfort to a man who had tried to kill me. And confided in another man who was at that moment working to take my throne.

I replaced her question with one of my own. "How was the funeral? I only heard a small part of it."

She pressed her lips together, then said, "It was lovely. Though I must say that even if you're angry about what your family did to you, it was terribly disrespectful not to attend."

"I'm not angry with them, and I didn't want to miss it."

"Then what could possibly have taken priority? Unless you were lying somewhere half-dead, you should have been there!"

I stopped and stared at her. She tilted her head as she realized what that meant. "Oh no. Forgive me for not knowing. What are we going to do?"

She said *we*, and that stopped me for a moment. Despite her loyalties to Gregor, was it possible she wanted a stronger partnership for us?

"Before anything else, will you help Imogen?" I asked. "See that she has whatever she needs to live in comfort . . . elsewhere."

"Please let her stay. Whatever she did to offend you, she's still my friend, and she has nowhere else to go."

"She cannot stay here," I mumbled. "That decision is final."

"But why —" Then she caught herself, as if understanding the things I could not explain. "All right. I'll help her."

"Send word when that's done, and we'll finish talking." If nothing else, I owed her total honesty about my plans.

It was rude not to offer her an escort to Imogen's room, but I didn't want to go anywhere near that part of the castle tonight. So with our exchanged bows, she left in one direction and I in the other. Only seconds later, I heard Gregor's voice near the princess. "My lady, may I see you to where you're going?"

Amarinda cooed in delight, then accepted his offer. And with that, any goodwill between her and me vanished. If she did not seek me out later tonight, I would not find her.

Before returning to my room I stopped in the library to find some books for the trip. The castle library wasn't my favorite place. This was because in the center of the main wall was a large portrait of my family, painted a year ago. In it, my parents sat beside each other with my brother standing behind them. After I found the books I wanted, I stared at the painting for a moment, wondering if any of them had thought about me while they posed. As often as I tried, I could not sort out my feelings about what my father had done. Did he cost me the life I should have had, or did he save my life?

It was too much, and I left the room without looking back.

I returned to my chambers as quickly as I could, where Mott was anxiously waiting for news. His eyes went to the items in my hand. I attempted to cover the title of the top book but it was too late. "Pirate books?" he said. "What are those for?"

"No, Mott."

"I remember you telling Conner that you're not a great reader, unless the subject interests you."

I pushed past him. "We leave at dawn. Tobias too. Make sure he knows."

"Where —" Mott stopped when I turned to him, then said, "Jaron, are you ill? You don't look good."

I slowly shook my head as I backed into my room. "No questions. Just be ready by morning."

· NINE ·

Morning brought a cool drizzle that made everything look gray and dreary, as if even the sun was ashamed of this plan. Gregor had assembled a large number of vigils and several servants to accompany me away. The expressions on their faces ranged from pity at my leaving in such a cowardly way to poorly disguised contempt at my incompetence. Other than two vigils who would act as my drivers, I couldn't dismiss them fast enough.

Gregor spat out a protest, but I said, "How will I hide with half the kingdom as my escort? Mott is all I need, and Tobias can help with things until he becomes too annoying." I looked around. "Amarinda isn't here?"

"I believe the princess was awake quite late helping Imogen prepare to leave."

I wondered how Gregor could know this about Amarinda, while I did not. No doubt he was courting her endorsement of him as steward. Or maybe he was courting her for other reasons too. I really didn't know.

Kerwyn pulled me aside as the last of the supplies were being loaded. "Please, Jaron, don't go."

Despite his pleas, I could only shake my head. "There's no other choice now."

"I thought a little sleep would change your mind."

Placing my hand on Kerwyn's shoulder, I said, "I had the same concern, so I kept myself awake."

Kerwyn's eyes moistened. "I've always loved you, Jaron, you know that. When you were lost four years ago, I lost a part of myself. And now we've had you back for only a few short weeks. You must promise to return."

My attempt at a smile failed. "I promise this, that if I don't return it's because I wasn't strong enough to be king. In which case, Carthya should have a steward."

That did nothing to comfort him, and left me feeling hollow too, for that matter. He bowed low and said he would watch every day for news from me. I wished he wouldn't have said that. I wouldn't be sending any news, good or bad.

After I got into the carriage with Mott and Tobias, I directed the driver to take us to Farthenwood.

"Farthenwood?" Mott asked in surprise. "But Gregor had another place in mind."

"Gregor doesn't command me," I snapped.

With a quick glance at Mott, Tobias said, "We have to talk."

"Go ahead," I said, slouching into my seat. "But do it quietly so I can sleep."

"Talk *with you*," Tobias clarified. But my eyes were already closed.

Once they thought I was asleep, I heard Tobias whisper to Mott, "He looks terrible."

"I asked his door vigil this morning. They're sure he was awake all night, and he might have snuck out of his room for who knows how long."

I had. It had taken me all night to work through the books from the library. My hope was that Amarinda would send for me so that we could talk, but she never did. Once I gave up on her, I'd found Kerwyn and shared with him the details of my leaving, a plan that had been received with even less enthusiasm than I'd expected.

"You're walking into the jaws of the beast that would devour you!" he had cried.

"I'm being devoured now!" was my response. "Kerwyn, this is the only chance I have. The only chance any of us has."

Eventually, Kerwyn had given me his reluctant blessing. It wasn't much to bring with me on this trip, but it was all I had.

Seated across from me now, Tobias whispered to Mott, "How's his arm?"

"Not bad. It'll need a few days, but it will heal."

"And it was Roden who stabbed him? I knew Roden wanted the throne, but I never guessed he'd try something like this."

"Don't give Roden too much credit," I murmured. "He cut me, not stabbed me." Then I peeked at them and grinned. Neither Mott nor Tobias returned the smile.

So I closed my eyes again, and this time I allowed myself to sleep. It must have been a deep sleep, for when I awoke, the carriage was still and the sun was high in the sky. Mott and I were alone.

"We're at Farthenwood?" I asked.

"Yes."

I yawned and pushed several stray hairs out of my face. "Where's Tobias?"

"He went in to make arrangements for our stay. There was no advance word of our coming so nobody was prepared to receive you."

"Dismiss anyone who's still here. Tell them we'll be gone in a few days and they can return. And I want you to find something in the hills for the vigils to protect, like a rock or a thornbush. I don't want to see them around here."

"Fine. But they're nowhere around right now. We're alone." He licked his lips and added, "We must talk about Roden's attack last night."

I stared out the carriage window but saw nothing. "All right, talk."

He leaned forward and clasped his hands. "Last night you told me your choice would come down to either the unacceptable or the impossible. So which did you choose?"

With little to offer him, I only shrugged. "Well, as I said, the unacceptable is . . . not acceptable."

"Then the impossible clearly means you're planning something with the pirates."

"Don't ask me about that right now."

"Then you ask me!" Never before had I seen such an intense look of concern in Mott's eyes. "Jaron, all you have to do is ask, and I would follow you into the devil's lair." After a beat he added, "Or even to the pirates."

"I know that." My words were barely a whisper.

"I can hear the fear in your voice. Let me help."

I was afraid, and I really did want to talk about it. But I also couldn't allow Mott to change my mind. If I gave him enough time to talk, he'd eventually succeed.

So I only said, "If you want to help, get rid of the vigils for me."

Mott sighed, then reached for the handle and left the carriage. After he'd gone I left the carriage as well and wandered toward the back of Conner's estate. It was strange to be here again with Farthenwood so unchanged, and yet my entire life once more turned upside down.

The memories of my time here remained fresh and raw. This was where I'd received two scars on my back as reminders of the price of returning to the throne. One was given to me by Tobias, and the deeper one came from Mott. They were now the two people I needed most in this world.

"We were looking for you." Tobias was already bowing when I turned around.

"Stop that," I said.

He rose up and smiled awkwardly as he ambled over to me. We stood beside each other, facing the back of Farthenwood.

Directly in front of us was Conner's room. Maybe they'd suggest I use it, since it was the nicest one. I wouldn't be here tonight, but even if I were, under no circumstances would I sleep there.

"I heard Gregor wants to replace you with a steward," Tobias said.

"That's his plan."

He kicked at the ground. "You never wanted to be king, so maybe it's a good thing."

"Is it? Should I celebrate that?" He apologized, and as we headed back to the house, I said, "Maybe I should appoint you as my steward."

Tobias chuckled. "Definitely not! But I'd love to be a physician one day. Or maybe a teacher. I'd be a good one, I think."

"Yes, you would."

"The problem is, there're no children at the castle to teach. Maybe one day you and Amarinda —"

"I wouldn't count on that," I said flatly.

"She still hates you?"

"I don't know what she thinks about me. I don't know what she thinks about anything, really."

"Have you talked to her?"

I rolled my eyes. "Don't you start too."

"Sorry." Then he added, "Jaron, why are we here? Does it have anything to do with those pirate books from last night?"

Barely able to contemplate it all, I only nodded and said, "Yes, Tobias. It has everything to do with them."

· TEN ·

Once inside Farthenwood, I made every attempt to avoid Mott and Tobias. I had nothing to offer for real conversation and too many thoughts filled my mind to leave room for idle chatter.

With nothing better to do, I took to wandering the halls, and inevitably found myself on the lower floor of Farthenwood, standing inside Conner's dungeon. It wasn't clear to me why I felt compelled to come here. Maybe it was just to be able to stand here as a free person, to know that I could choose to leave any time I wanted.

"I didn't think you'd come down here."

I turned to watch Mott walk down the stairs. He came to stand beside me and folded his arms.

"I didn't think so either," I said.

"You brought me to your side in this room, you know. Everything I had believed about Conner changed here."

"How could you ever have worked for him, Mott?"

"It's all I knew. And I swear that I never knew the worst of his crimes."

"He never spoke of his plans?"

Mott thought for a moment, then said, "A week before he killed your family, Conner mentioned that your father had grown suspicious of the regents and had begun requiring searches upon their every entry into the castle. I never thought about it then, but in hindsight, I'm sure that complicated his plans. If I had known, I would've stopped him."

I nodded, and kicked at the ground with the toe of my boot.

He was quiet a moment longer, then added, "Jaron, can you forgive me for what happened here?"

"You whipped Sage, not Jaron." He shook his head, not understanding, so I said, "Do you want forgiveness now because I'm Jaron, because I'm king? Would you ask for it if I were only Sage?"

Now Mott understood. He turned away from me and it looked as if he was unbuttoning his shirt. "Do you remember when Tobias cut your back? You told me the wound was from a cut on a window."

It had been an outright lie from me, which I still regretted having to do. But it was the only way to force Tobias to back down from trying to become the prince.

"All you got was the loss of a day's meals, and Tobias got no punishment at all," Mott continued. "When Conner found out I'd tried to keep that from him, he gave me this." Mott lowered his shirt enough to reveal a whipping scar on his back, not as deep as the one he'd given me but certainly enough to have caused significant pain, and I ached to see it. As soon as he'd shown me he raised his shirt again. Still facing away from me, he said, "I took that for Sage, not Jaron." He left before I had a chance to say a word, as if there were any words I could have spoken then.

I found him again at suppertime in Conner's small dining room. Tobias was with the cook, arranging final details of the meal, so Mott and I were alone. He rose when I entered and we stood at angles, too uncomfortable to face each other directly.

After a brief silence, I said, "The only reason I'm alive today is because of what I've done wrong in my life. My crimes may have saved me, but I never meant for them to harm you."

Sadness filled Mott's eyes when he looked at me. "Jaron —"

"You will never again ask my forgiveness for what happened in the dungeon." It hurt to speak the next part. "And you will let me ask forgiveness from you."

"That's not necessary."

"Maybe not yet." I glanced briefly at him. "But it will be."

"I know you've got some heavy concerns," Mott said. "But we are friends. You can tell me everything."

I shook my head. "No, Mott. Not everything, *because* you're my friend."

At that, Tobias entered with a tray laden with three bowls of stew. If he sensed the awkwardness in the room, he didn't acknowledge it. "There's no bread because the cook didn't have time for it," Tobias explained, serving me the largest of the bowls.

"This is enough," I said. "Sit down, both of you. Let's eat as friends tonight, and nothing less."

Even so, the time passed in an uncomfortable silence, until Tobias asked, "Was it a surprise to see Roden last night?"

"The kind of surprise that makes your heart stop for a beat," I said. "When I saw him again, I had wanted it to be on my terms, not his."

Tobias nodded. "You should have killed him the night you were crowned, when you two fought in the tunnels. Why did you let him go?"

After taking another bite, I said, "Until last night, I didn't think it was in him to harm me. I suppose that's changed now."

"The only thing Roden wants is to matter, to be important," Tobias said. "If he has to hurt you to get that, he will. Maybe Gregor is right and you should be in hiding."

I glared back at him. "You think I'd ever be so cowardly?"

"Enough of this!" Frustrated with me, Mott threw his spoon down. "If you insist on us not bowing to your royalty, then I'll treat you like the obstinate boy you are. Why are we here? I demand an answer."

"Or else what?" I grinned and folded my arms. "I can beat you in a sword fight, and we all know what'll happen if you lock me in my room."

"Nothing so complicated as that." Mott also folded his arms. "I'll simply decide not to like you anymore."

My smile widened. "That's a serious threat."

"It gets worse. I'll call you only by your title and quietly roll my eyes when you give me orders, and I won't make it fun for you to insult me ever again."

"Well, we can't have that." I couldn't help but laugh and even Mott broke into a smile. My eyes darted from him over to Tobias. "If we must discuss the truth, then I need something to drink. I noticed a half-finished bottle of cider in the buttery. Not much but it'll do. Retrieve it, will you?"

Tobias leapt to his feet and scurried from the room.

I turned back to Mott. "What if you don't like what I have to say?"

"I rarely like what you have to say. So I'll expect the worst."

"I promise not to disappoint you there."

Mott shifted in his chair, but I barely moved while we waited for Tobias to return. He came in a few minutes later with the cider and three goblets. I held out my hand for them and poured the drinks myself.

"You should have the most," Mott said when I handed him his goblet.

I shook my head, insisting he take the cup that was being offered to him. "I already know my news. Trust me, you'll want enough to drown your anger."

He frowned but toasted a cheer in my honor. They drank to my health and long life. The part about health never concerned me, but I hoped the devils heard the part about my long life and were inclined to grant it.

I remained silent until Mott cleared his throat, prompting me to begin. I looked at him and said, "If I don't turn myself over to the pirates in nine days, they'll attack Carthya.

They'll fight until either I'm dead, or all of them are."

"War," Tobias mumbled.

"The regents have made it clear that they won't support a war." I took a slow breath. "They believe the best way to avoid war is to let the pirates have me. That's why we're here, and not where the regents wanted me to hide."

"Just because they want a steward doesn't mean they want you dead," Mott said.

"Maybe not. But what if you're right and a steward is chosen? Do either of you really believe that puts me out of danger? I'll be sent to the schoolroom, to watch those fools pretend that all is well while our armies crumble."

"Then find a way to prevent them from naming a steward," Tobias said.

"Until I'm of age, I can't stop that vote." I shrugged. "I've already lost it anyway."

Mott's eyebrows were pressed close together and his hand was wrapped so tightly around his goblet I thought he might crush it. "And you have a solution to all this?" he asked.

I sat forward with the intention of speaking directly to them, but in the end my courage failed and I lowered my eyes to talk. After a moment's hesitation, I said, "I'm going to the pirates, alone. You two will return to the castle without me."

There was a long silence while the news soaked in. Mott spoke first, surprisingly calm. "I don't believe you'd give yourself up so easily."

"I'm not surrendering. I'm joining them."

"What?" Mott's eyes widened. "Jaron, no. Please tell me you're not that foolish."

Foolishness was a trait I could never deny with much credibility, but my temper warmed anyway. Pounding a fist on the table, I said, "I'm out of options. Every solution leads either to my death or to the destruction of my country. This is all I have left."

"So your plan is to walk into their camp? How does that accomplish anything but helping them kill you faster?"

"What if I could turn the pirates' loyalty? Get them on my side. Then if Avenia attacked —"

That was as far as I got before Tobias snorted his contempt for the idea and Mott began staring at me as if I had blisters on my brain.

"Exactly how do you plan to turn these enemies into allies?" he asked.

"I don't know! But it's better than the alternative."

"Which is?"

I huffed. "The pirate Conner hired four years ago to kill me is a man named Devlin. He also provided the poison that Conner used to murder my family, and he'll be the one behind the attack on me last night as well. If I can't turn his loyalty, then I'll have to remove the threat." Feeling the racing of my heart, I added, "I'll have to kill him."

Those words hung in the air for a moment before Mott said, "And you'll do this alone?"

I nodded.

Mott shoved his chair behind him and stood, then began to pace angrily. "Nobody comes back from the pirates," he muttered. "Ever."

"I did, four years ago."

Mott stopped right in front of me. "No, you escaped the ship before the pirates were anywhere near it. Luck saved you that day, nothing more."

Tobias tried taking the rational route. "What if they recognize you?"

"Roden and the man who came with him will be at sea. The other pirates would know my name, but not my face."

"You can't do this," Mott said, shaking his head. "I won't allow it."

That made me even angrier. "I'm not asking for your permission, Mott, or your approval! You asked me to tell you the truth about my plans and I have."

"Your plans will get you killed!"

"Doing nothing will get me killed! Staying at the castle and pretending everything is fine — that will get me killed!"

Mott's face was fiery red, and I think if I were anyone else I'd have found myself thrown against the wall to force me to my senses. But that was not an option for him, so after taking a deep breath, he sat back in his chair and clasped his hands.

"You've made your decision, then?" he asked.

"I have."

"Then here's mine." Mott stared directly at me and spoke

slowly so I wouldn't miss a word. "I will not allow you to go, not alone."

My hands folded into fists. "As king, that is my order."

"Forgive me, but the king's order is the most reckless thing he's ever said, which we both know is quite an accomplishment. If you want to stop me from dragging you back to Drylliad, then you'll have to kill me here."

"I can't do that," I said. "Who'll make sure Tobias gets back safely? He can hardly cross a road without endangering himself."

"I can too," Tobias said.

Mott barely reacted and kept his focus on me. "Jaron, listen to reason. You are my king, but you can't expect me to accept such a foolish plan."

There was heat in my glare at him. "Perhaps you also want a steward for me, then, a nursemaid for the crown."

"Maybe you need one." Mott sighed loudly as if that would make me change my mind. Even though it would have been unfair to leave without warning them, I almost wished I'd have done it so we could've enjoyed this evening instead.

Getting nothing further from me, Mott put his hand on my arm. I looked up at him as he said, "If you must leave, then you will have to figure out how to bring me along, because I will not leave you alone. Whatever reckless plan is in that foolish, royal head of yours, it will have to accommodate me."

I pulled away and swiped my other arm through the air, knocking over the bottle of cider on the table. Mott jumped back to avoid the splatter as it ran onto the floor.

I cursed, then stood and ran my fingers through my hair. "Give me until morning, Mott. I have a foolish, royal headache and I'm too tired to think about changing plans tonight."

Mott nodded and wished me a good night before I had time to change my mind. Which was completely unnecessary because I had no intention of changing any part of the plan. It was true that my head throbbed and even more true that I was tired. But whether I waited all night or all month, one thing would remain the same: I was going on alone.

· ELEVEN ·

Tobias was deeply asleep and didn't hear me enter his room late that night. I hadn't poured him much of the cider, but he still got some of the sleeping powder I'd found in Conner's office.

When I shook his arm, his eyes opened and he awoke with a start. I put a finger to my lips to warn him to be silent. Yet his voice was still too loud as he whispered, "Jaron? What's going on?"

"I'm going to talk and you will listen. Agreed?"

He nodded stiffly. I sat in the chair near his desk while he rolled out of bed. I could almost hear his heart pounding from here. Or was it mine?

Despite our agreement, Tobias spoke first. "You're still leaving? You told Mott you'd change your plans."

"No, I told Mott I was too tired to think about changing plans," I corrected him. "Big difference."

"But Mott was right before. Nobody comes back from the pirates. Maybe you'll kill Devlin, but how will you escape all the others?"

I grimaced with a pang of worry at that question. The

truth was, I had no answer for him. All I knew was that my odds of succeeding were no better in Carthya. At least this way, I faced the pirates on my own terms.

"Just wait a few days and think this over," he said.

"I don't have a few days. If I can't fix everything before the regents' vote on the steward, I will be powerless to fix it afterward."

"There's not enough time."

"Then stop wasting it. Now hush, I need you to do something for me."

"What is it?"

I removed the king's ring from my finger and set it on the desk. I hadn't taken it off since the night I was crowned and was surprised by the difference in weight of my hand. "I don't want the regents to think I'm hiding — that only makes their vote against me that much easier. You and Mott must return to Drylliad in the morning." I nodded toward a stack of my clothes on a chest in the room. "You will return as me. We look enough alike that with the ring and in the shadows of my carriage, you won't have any trouble getting through the front gate. Be sure to arrive at night so that you can get to my quarters under the cover of darkness. Mott will help you avoid seeing anyone. Have him make up a story, that the king is ill or that the king is embarrassed and doesn't want to see anybody. Tell anyone who asks that the king prefers to hide from the pirates in the comfort of his room."

"Jaron, no," Tobias whispered, shaking his head.

I continued as if he hadn't spoken. "They might ask you a question at the gate. It's a request for a password and the way for the vigil to verify that you're Jaron. I changed the password myself this morning. The question will be what does the king want for dinner. The answer is that you know what the king wants and it has nothing to do with dinner."

Tobias smiled, despite himself. "What does the king want, then?"

"He wants you to hush and pay attention. There's a letter in the pocket of my clothes for Amarinda. Give it to her and answer any questions she may have, if you can. She'll be angry, but I think she'll help you maintain your cover."

"Angry?" Tobias said. "She'll be furious, and that's if she believes us. What if she accuses us of trying to take over the kingdom?"

"The letter will explain things," I said. "Amarinda is fully capable of making any necessary decisions, so all you need to do is remain in my apartments. I've spent so much time alone since I became king, nobody will question that."

"Is that why —"

I sighed. "Don't attempt to understand me, Tobias. I can't even do that. Now, what do you suppose happened to our old clothes from when we were here?"

I already knew the answer to that. The nicer ones had been stolen away by the servants who had worked here. But my old clothes from when I was brought here as Sage were still in the drawer of my old wardrobe. Nobody wanted them.

I peeled off my royal clothing and tossed it onto the trunk, then put on Sage's clothes: the worn trousers that had been too long on me when I first got them and were bordering on too small now; the shirt that one of Conner's servants had mended, and even so, was riddled with several small tears; and my old boots that still fit fine, due to the fact that I'd only recently stolen them before Conner had taken me from the orphanage. They had a hole in the right toe, but that only bothered me during rainstorms.

It was as if everything about Sage returned to me once I stood again in his clothing. The instinct to trick when I could and lie when I must. The feeling that no matter how hard I tried, I would never be anything better than a sewer rat.

"I can't do this," Tobias said as I finished dressing.

"If you fail, then I will fail. Tobias, you must do this. Mott will want to follow me, but you can't allow that. If he does, he'll expose me, and then I really will be in danger."

Slowly he nodded. "After you leave, if I don't go running to Mott and tell him what's happened, he'll kill me. Literally."

"There's a solution to that, but you won't like it." I smiled, then reached for the sheet on Tobias's bed. I ripped the fabric down its length and told him to put his arms behind his back. "I've got to make this tight. Mott will be suspicious if I don't."

"It's all right," Tobias said, holding out his arms. "Odd that I should be thanking you for this."

I tied him to the bed, then gagged him, although I left that a little loose so his breathing wouldn't be uncomfortable.

"Do not fail," I said to Tobias when the knots were finished. "We will see each other again."

Moments later I slipped quietly out of Farthenwood, and from the stables chose Mystic, one of the faster horses. Other than a white star on his forehead, Mystic was as black as tar and more loyal to his rider than any courser I'd ever before ridden. He was also well groomed, so anyone who saw him would assume I'd stolen the horse, which in a way, I had. When he was saddled, I climbed astride and in minutes had left Farthenwood behind.

At least for the rest of this night, I was free.

· TWELVE ·

Riding alone through the Carthyan countryside was like emerging from a deep pool of water. Each breath brought me more alive, as I absorbed every moment of freedom I could. The cool wind caressed my face and greeted me with every change in the landscape on my journey. Even at night, Carthya was a beautiful place. Our trees grew firm and tall, while the winding rivers and streams kept our fields green and our farms fertile. It was no mystery why the countries on our borders looked to us with such greedy eyes.

Still, for all the happiness I felt, this was not a pleasure ride. Although I had a full moon to guide me, I also had to watch for irregularities on the road. I couldn't afford an injury to Mystic, not here. And there was always the danger of thieves hiding in camps near wooded areas. Nobody would expect a traveler this late at night, which gave me an advantage. Then again, I wouldn't know when to expect them, either. I wasn't afraid, but I definitely was cautious. The last thing I needed was a distraction.

So I pushed Mystic as hard as he'd bear. Only four hours remained before dawn would creep over the horizon. I needed the cover of night to pass across the border into Avenia. My chances of making it in time were good. Mystic was both a fast and sturdy horse, and we traveled light. I only carried a sword strapped to my side, a knife at my waist, and a knapsack with some spare provisions and several handfuls of garlins I had taken with me from the castle treasury.

The stars gradually rotated in the sky as my distance from Farthenwood increased. I wondered how long Mott would sleep. Probably late into the morning. He'd feel the effects of the sleeping powder and instantly know he'd been tricked. Since I became king, no one had dared curse me to my face, but he'd undoubtedly use every word in the devil's vocabulary tomorrow when he checked my room and found it empty. Then he'd find Tobias. I hoped Tobias would be able to persuade Mott to do what I'd asked. No, it was more than just hope. I *needed* Mott to obey me.

I was less than an hour from the border when I first heard the signs of trouble. The frenzied voices of men yelling and a woman screaming. Horses in random movement. The unsteady flicker of a torch in the distance. I withdrew my sword and turned Mystic in their direction.

The screaming stopped abruptly, and all the voices quieted for a moment, then a man cried, "There's one more!"

I was close enough by then to have a good idea of what was going on. There were several men, all with Avenian accents, and they were armed. One man saw me coming and left the group to charge for me. I easily blocked his sword with my own, then sliced deeply into his arm. With a scream he shrank into the shadows.

The other men seemed unsure of what to do, maybe from the surprise at being caught, or perhaps because I had bested the first man so quickly. However, there was no hesitation from me. I galloped forward and caught another man in the back with my blade.

That prompted a confusion of orders from the other horsemen, though they all seemed to agree that I could not be allowed to escape. It was their foolish miscalculation to think escape was anywhere in my plans. They rounded on me, which should have forced me back into the dense brush. Instead, I rode forward, aiming for the man holding the torch since he only had one hand to fight with. He had a jagged scar running down the side of his face and somehow became even uglier as I rode closer. He got in one good swipe at me, but I ignored the sting across my stomach and turned Mystic back at him. I hammered my sword down hard onto his, and both it and the torch fell into the dirt. I thrust at him again, not sure exactly where it landed, but the wound went deep. Another man rode up beside me and clashed his horse into Mystic, but Mystic was a far more powerful animal and the man's horse stumbled. I swerved around and made a slice at his leg, and with a yelp he backed away from me, following his companions as they fled into the darkness.

A branch cracked behind me and I turned, sword ready. Silence filled the air again, but I wasn't alone. I dismounted and led Mystic by the reins toward the bush. Then, in a sudden move, I dropped the reins, reached through the leaves, and yanked whoever was back there up to my blade.

"Please don't hurt me!"

I stepped back, surprised. It was just a child, a young girl who couldn't have been older than six or seven. She stood nearly to my chest with light blond hair that fell halfway down her back. She wore a plain cotton nightdress and had bare feet; she probably had been rushed from her bed in an attempt to escape.

I immediately lowered my sword and crouched down to her. "It's all right; you're safe now. But what are you doing out here?" It was too dark to know for certain, but she didn't appear to be injured. "Are you all right?"

She took my hand and led me a little farther away to the base of a tall elm tree. A woman who must have been the girl's mother was lying on the ground there. Her breathing was so shallow and forced I knew she had to be injured. She must have been the woman whose screams brought me this way.

I knelt beside her and felt near her abdomen for any sign of a wound. When she sensed my presence, she opened her eyes and touched my arm. "Don't bother," she whispered. "It's too much." Her accent was Carthyan. She was one of my own people.

"Who did this?" I asked.

She closed her eyes for some time and I thought perhaps she wouldn't answer. Then she opened them and mumbled, "You can't be from this area and not know what happens here."

"I'm not."

She nodded. "Avenian thieves. They cross our borders at

night to steal our cattle or frighten us from our homes."

I shook my head. "Why doesn't anyone in Drylliad know this? The king —"

"Eckbert's dead. Haven't you heard? Besides, he knew for months that this was happening." She arched her back and gasped. I put my hand beneath her to help support her weight and felt the warmth of her blood. There was so much. Too much to survive. Her breathing was becoming more labored. "My husband . . . they killed him. Nila . . . take her to her grandfather's . . . Libeth."

Nila placed her small hand on my shoulder. Libeth was north of here and would set me back several hours. Besides that, I had planned to avoid all towns. There was too great a chance of someone recognizing me, or of leaving a trail in case Mott decided to follow me.

Nila's mother rose again and used my arm to hold herself up. "Please," she whispered.

"I'll get her there, I promise." Even if it meant going backward for me. As if my words gave her release, she finally relaxed, closed her eyes, and was gone.

Nila knelt beside me and touched her mother's shoulder. "Is she dead?"

I nodded as a new anger surged inside me. Had my father known this was happening? Had Gregor, or Kerwyn? Why had no one told me about this?

"There's a lilac bush near where I left my horse," I told Nila. "Pick as many as you can for your mother."

Without expression, Nila stood and walked back to Mystic while I dug with my hands and knife into the soft springtime earth for a grave. It took well over an hour to bury Nila's mother, and after the flowers were laid on her grave, I put Nila behind me on Mystic and we headed for Libeth.

People were already awake and working in their fields when we reached the outskirts of the town. Libeth was a sleepy place that was protected from Avenia by marshlands that neither country particularly cared to claim. I'd never been anywhere near here before, but I liked the town.

Nila didn't know where her grandfather lived, only that he had a big farm and that people paid him from their crops. I had audibly groaned when she told me. It meant he was probably a noble. One of the useless snobs I detested.

I wondered if he had been in attendance at my family's funeral. If so, perhaps he was still in Drylliad. I wasn't sure whether to hope for that or not. Because if he'd already returned to Libeth from the funeral, he was sure to recognize me. But if he was still in Drylliad, what was I supposed to do with Nila?

A couple of hours earlier, Nila had finally begun acting sleepy, so I put her in front of me where I could prop her with my arms. Now as we entered the small town square, she sat up and rubbed her eyes. "I remember this place," she mumbled.

"Do you know where your grandfather lives?"

"No."

We stopped near a stall where a woman had a variety of meats on display. I glanced at a roast and couldn't help but think of the time I had tried to steal one and nearly gotten myself killed by the butcher. It hadn't been my best idea ever. Unfortunately, it hadn't been my worst either.

"I am looking for this girl's grandfather," I said to the woman in the stall. "I think he's a —"

"Nila?" The woman ran from behind her stall and held out her hands for the girl, who fell into her arms. "What are you doing here?" Then her eyes narrowed as she looked at me, covered in dirt and dried blood. "What happened?"

"Do you know her grandfather?" I asked.

The woman nodded and pointed to a home that was high up on a hill at the far end of town. "Master Rulon Harlowe is her grandfather."

I slid off Mystic and held out my hand as an invitation for her to ride with Nila. "Will you take me there?"

Someone I hadn't noticed took the woman's place in the stall. Then with my help she lifted Nila back into the saddle and climbed up behind her.

I tried to get information from the woman as we walked, but she shushed me and gave her attention to Nila. So I listened as Nila described what had happened to her family. From what Nila said and the woman's questions, I gathered that several younger families from Libeth had gone into the countryside to try to build their own farms, away from any nobles who might tax their lands. As their farms began to prosper, Avenians had started raiding. At first it was for simple thievery, of crops or cattle. When the farmers began fighting back, the raids turned violent. Things had quieted over the winter but with the melting snow the raids returned. Nila had seen her father shot by arrows while her mother raced her away. Her mother had been cut with a sword shortly before I arrived last night. It seemed that Nila had seen far too much death for someone her age.

"Do you know if King Eckbert knew about these troubles?" I asked.

The woman scoffed. "What did the king ever do for us? Master Harlowe was denied a meeting with him, but spoke to one of his regents."

"Who?"

"Does it matter? The master was told that we needed to keep the peace with Avenia, and the farmers would just have to leave and move farther inland."

I shook my head, hoping that what was happening here had never reached my father's ears. Because if he knew and did nothing — no, I couldn't think of that. The more I learned of my father's reign, the less I felt that I had ever known him.

· THIRTEEN ·

Harlowe's estate was nothing compared to Farthen-wood, but it was grand compared to the cottages we had passed on our way. It was a square-cut home of maybe fifteen or twenty rooms, and felt sturdy and commanding. Broad steps led to a wide porch and dark-stained double doors. I stared at them, torn between desperately wanting to ask Harlowe whether my father had known about the Avenian thieves, and knowing there was a greater need to continue on to Avenia. I opted for the latter.

The woman with Nila refused my offer to help her down, so after she dismounted I held out my arms for Nila to fall into. But the woman pushed past me. "I can manage with the child," she said. I backed up and she added, "No offense to you because of what you did, but you're clearly not someone —"

"Joss will carry my granddaughter," a man behind me said. Harlowe obviously. He was as tall as Mott and probably in his early fifties, though with the strong build of a much younger man. He had a thick crop of hair that was more gray than black and eyes with long laugh lines at the corners. With him was the servant Joss, who stepped forward and took Nila off the horse. Harlowe tenderly brushed a hand across her dirty forehead, and for the first time I saw tears fall on Nila's cheeks. Then, with a nod from his master, Joss took her inside.

"Now about you," he said, turning my way.

My eyes shifted, but the woman who had brought me here spoke first. "Master Harlowe, as you can plainly see, this boy —"

"Looks exhausted." He put a firm hand on my shoulder. "Can you tell me where Nila's parents are?"

I searched for an answer, but by my hesitation, he knew. Large tears flooded his eyes. "I see. There's no way I can ever thank you for bringing Nila. You . . . you . . ." He tried to say something more but choked on the words. Finally, he said, "Come with me."

Instinctively, my knees locked against the pressure of his hand.

"It's all right," he said gently. "Please come. I know you're hungry."

Until he said so, I hadn't realized that he was right. Suddenly, nothing sounded more desirable than a solid meal. So we entered his home, tastefully decorated but not overly ornate. We entered a hallway on the left and passed a small room that looked like his office. He led me from there to a modest dining room where a servant was already waiting with a platter of fresh-baked bread and a bottle of milk.

"We don't eat fancy here, but you're so thin I doubt you eat much at all," Harlowe said.

"Not lately." But the bread smelled good, and for the first time since I'd been made king, I was hungry.

"Forgive me for leaving you alone, but I must check on Nila," Harlowe said. "I'll be back before you're finished."

True to his word, Harlowe returned to the dining room as I was downing my third cup of milk. He smiled, obviously pleased that I had enjoyed the food, and then sat across the table from me. I slouched when he looked me over. Now was not the time to be impressive.

He studied me a moment before speaking. "Nila's father — Mathis — was my son. Stubborn boy, always had to do things his own way, no matter how foolish. I loved him and begged him not to leave Libeth." He pulled a gold pocket watch from his vest, bearing the marks of age and use, but no doubt invaluable to him. "When Mathis left two years ago, he gave this to me. He told me that where he was going, he'd know the time of day by the sun overhead."

I had stopped eating while he spoke. There was so much sadness on his face, but in it was a resolution to carry forward. He looked the way I had felt when I found out about my family's deaths. I said, "I'm sorry I couldn't prevent your son's death. I didn't know what was happening here."

He tilted his head, unsure of my full meaning, then said, "Forgive me for prying, but you're obviously a stranger to these parts. What were you doing out there so late at night?"

"Just passing through."

"Are you Avenian?"

"No."

"Are you a thief?" I hesitated, then he shook his head. "You're not. Those clothes you wear suggest it, but your nails are too clean, your hair is trimmed, and if I may say, you don't smell like a thief. You've bathed recently."

The last thing I wanted was to make the conversation about me. "Is Nila all right?"

"She's mourning, but with time and care I believe she'll pull through." His eyes moistened and he added, "You saved her life." I started to shake my head but he said, "No, you did. She told me the whole story. You fought all those men off on your own."

"They weren't much for opponents," I said, forcing an expression calmer than I felt. How was it possible to feel so at home and so uncomfortable at the same time? I set my napkin on the table and stood. "Thank you for the meal, but I really must go."

"That's fresh blood on your shirt." Harlowe rose from his chair and called for a servant to enter. Then without even asking, he walked to me and lifted my shirt, revealing a long cut across my stomach. "You got this in that fight?"

I backed up and pulled the shirt down, which did little good since the shirt was also cut. "It's only a scratch."

"Scratches don't bleed like that."

The servant entered and Harlowe directed him to get a

bandage and some alcohol. I groaned. Wherever they were, the devils must be laughing. In repayment for my good deed, I was yet again to be treated to far greater pain than any wound could cause.

"Take him to the guest bedroom and bandage him up. He may rest there as long as he wishes, and then we'll provide him with some more appropriate clothes."

I objected, but it was pointless. Harlowe's servant pulled me out of the room, and as exhausted as I was, there wasn't enough in me to resist.

I insisted on removing my own shirt before the servant cleaned the wound, then lay on the bed so he couldn't see the scars on my back. My preference would have been to keep the shirt on, but it was stained with my blood and the blood of Nila's mother, so until it could be washed it was completely unusable.

In a vain attempt to distract myself, I tried to make conversation while the servant gently washed the cut with warm water.

"What kind of master is Rulon Harlowe?" I asked.

"The best. He's kind and generous and sincere. Libeth couldn't exist without him."

"Does he have a wife?"

"She died a year ago . . . sir." He nearly choked at having to address me with a respectable title.

"And does he have any children other than his son?"

"No. He lost another child many years ago due to a great tragedy. And forgive the observation, but you look a little like his son Mathis. He was older than you and there are differences of course, but anyone who knew Mathis would be able to see the resemblance."

Maybe that was why Harlowe treated me so kindly. Perhaps I reminded him of what he'd lost. I started to ask more about that but the servant had moved on to patting the cut with an alcohol-soaked sponge. I howled and arched my back, then told him if he didn't stop I'd hurt him. He removed the sponge and stared at it a moment, unsure of whether to finish tending the wound as he'd been ordered to do, or opt for self-preservation.

"Put the sponge down and wrap me up," I said. "Enough alcohol soaked into this wound on my arm; it'll find its way to this new injury just fine."

The servant reached for a bandage. "Do you mind if I ask what happened there?"

"Yeah, I do."

He finished up quickly, then offered me another sponge and a pan of warm water to wash myself. "I'll let you have some privacy now," he said, and left the room.

I sponged off until I was as clean as I cared to be, then wrapped myself in a robe the servant had left behind. I couldn't explore Harlowe's home in only a robe, so I lay on the bed to wait for the servant to return with some clothes. It had been my plan to stay awake, but when my eyes opened again, a thick blanket was spread across me. A clock on the bedside table indicated it was early afternoon, much longer than I'd ever wanted to sleep.

I tossed the blanket aside and quickly dressed in a set of clothes laid on the bed. A full-sleeved linen shirt went beneath a long, copper-colored vest trimmed in silver-plated buttons. The woolen pants were a little big on my waist, but then most pants were lately, and the leather boots fit perfectly. When I opened the door, another servant waiting for me said, "You're awake, then? Master Harlowe has an afternoon meal ready for you, if you'll join him."

"Where are the clothes I had before?" I asked.

"They've been burnt, sir," he said.

I groaned. The clothes I now wore were new, clean, and reeked of money. I couldn't go into Avenia wearing them, and I should've been there already. Only a week remained until the regents met with Gregor.

"Apologize to Master Harlowe for me, but I must leave," I said.

"Your horse is being groomed," the servant said. "After the fight you got in, we thought you'd want him carefully checked for any injuries. He should be ready at about the time you finish your meal."

I relented. "Take me to your master, then."

Harlowe's table was spread with food by the time I arrived. Considering how much was there, I was surprised to see only three plates set for dinner. Nila was already sitting in her seat. She had also cleaned up, and though she was solemn, she looked better than before. Harlowe stood to greet me when I entered the dining room, then directed me to my seat.

Servants waiting in the room began offering food until it was impossible for me to accept any more. It all looked and smelled delicious, but there was simply no room left on my plate. When every dish on the table had been offered to us, Harlowe dismissed the servants and we were left alone. I decided to get through the meal as quickly as possible, and so set to work on my food.

"You never did tell us your name," Harlowe said.

I spoke with a mouth full of warm bread. "No, sir, I didn't."

He smiled knowingly. "What matters with a name anyway? Perhaps you wish to hear a little about me first." I glanced up and Harlowe said, "My family has lived in Libeth for generations. We take care of the people in this village, and they take care of us."

"Are you a noble?"

He shrugged. "I suppose, but it's only a title. Titles don't matter here."

"They matter in Drylliad. I thought all the nobles were there for King Eckbert's funeral."

"And what is that but a parade of egos?" His smile fell. "I keep myself as far from the king's politics as possible. Besides, we have our own troubles here."

"With the Avenians?"

"Many of them are very dangerous. I hope that wherever your travels lead, you will not meet them, son."

Our eyes locked on that last word, though I quickly had to turn away. Nobody had called me "son" in years. My father might have at one time, but it was meaningless to me then. Now, the word had far more value.

I filled the awkward silence that followed by eating more of the supper. It was simpler than the food at either Drylliad or Farthenwood, and I liked it. Now that I had an appetite again, I felt ravenous.

Seated across from me, Nila barely touched her food, which wasn't surprising considering the trauma she had endured. She had changed into a pastel yellow dress and had her hair tied back into braids. It was an odd contrast for how miserable she must be feeling inside. Although mourners in most surrounding countries wore dark colors, Carthyans rarely did. It was felt the life of the deceased could be better remembered through wearing colors that honored them. While I watched Nila, I became aware of Harlowe's eyes on me. I let more of my hair spill over my face and made every effort not to betray my identity, by either my words or my manners.

"Will you stay the night?" Harlowe asked.

"I can't." Although for reasons I didn't fully understand, I wished that I could. I suspected if I did, he'd convince me to stay yet another night, and then to finish out the week, and pretty soon the spare room would be offered as mine. Harlowe struck me as a man with that kind of persuasive ability. Or maybe I didn't want to admit that the thought of staying was so tempting.

"Of course you can stay," he insisted. "That cut on your stomach needs to heal, and I'm told there's another bandage around your arm too." He hesitated, then gently said, "What's happened to you? You're just a boy, too young to bear such wounds."

And for the first time in weeks, I felt my age. Other boys my age were choosing apprenticeships for their careers and teasing pretty girls on their way to the market. They could still be found enjoying a game of Queen's Cross in the streets or working an extra job to earn money for their first horse. Suddenly, I felt heartsick for a life I'd never known.

Harlowe frowned. "Son, where are your parents? Have you no family?"

I stood so quickly my chair nearly tipped over. "Will you call someone to get my horse? I need to leave. Now."

"Did I say something wrong?" Harlowe stood as well. "Please, at least finish your meal. I owe you that, for what you did for Nila."

"I'm glad I could help, but I really can't stay a minute longer."

Harlowe tenderly brushed a hand over Nila's hair, then called a servant into the room. When he entered, Harlowe directed him to fetch my horse and to have a satchel packed with food for me.

"You've already given me enough," I protested.

"It's nothing compared to what you have given me," Harlowe said.

When Nila stood, I crouched down to put myself at eye level with her. Like me, she was an orphan now, though I dared not explain that to her, not with her grandfather listening. All I could do was whisper, "This pain you feel inside, it will get better in time."

Wordlessly, she patted my cheek with her small hand, then kissed my other cheek. I had to turn away for a moment while I straightened up, not trusting myself with the emotions surging through me.

Harlowe said, "I'd like to repay you. What can I do?"

My eyes darted to Nila, then back to Harlowe. "Will you keep me secret? If anyone comes to Libeth looking for me, no matter what they say, I need you to deny that I've been here."

"And what would they say when they came looking?"

That I was a fool. That I was on the verge of losing everything. That I was going to get myself killed.

I shrugged. "If they come, you'll know they're speaking about me, whatever they say."

Harlowe escorted me out of the dining room and toward the doors of his home. "We'll keep you secret, but we will never forget you. You saved my granddaughter, and for that, you will always be a part of our lives."

I stared at him for a moment, still fighting the urge to stay a little longer. Then a servant handed me the satchel of food, which was so heavy I had to sling it over my shoulder to carry it. Harlowe and Nila walked me out in front of his home, where Mystic was saddled and waiting.

"Son —" Harlowe put a hand on my shoulder. I turned and without knowing why, closed him into a hug, like a frightened child might give a beloved father. He hesitated only a moment before I felt his hands on my back.

My father wasn't an openly affectionate man. I knew he loved me, but he was never one to speak the words, and if I'd ever tried a gesture like this, he would've become stiff as a board, uncertain of what to do. Thinking of him, I stepped back from Harlowe, embarrassed, but he didn't seem to be. He only said, "Good luck in your travels. If you have a home, return there safely. And if you don't, you'll always have one here."

Not trusting myself to speak, I only nodded. Then I tied the satchel over Mystic's back, climbed on, and nodded again at Harlowe before I prodded Mystic forward and hurried away.

· FOURTEEN ·

I had one job to do before leaving Libeth, which I accomplished in what appeared to be a poorer area of the town. I found a boy about my size walking down the road with a bundle of sticks in his arms. I called to him, then dismounted and untied the satchel of food as he came over to me.

"I have an offer for you," I began. "Are you hungry?"

"Yes, sir."

I opened the satchel to show him the food inside. His face lit up, then he reined in his enthusiasm, suddenly suspicious. "What do you want?"

"I have this problem," I said. "Perhaps I've grown recently because my clothes are too small and they're uncomfortable for riding. I'd prefer the clothes you're wearing."

His face twisted in confusion. "Sir, my clothes are little better than rags. Yours are —"

"Too small. Didn't I make that clear? If you will trade with me, I'll give you all the food in this satchel." I didn't really want to part with the food, but it was obvious this boy needed it far more than I did.

The boy stared at me for a moment, still confused. Finally, I hoisted the satchel back over my shoulder. "Never mind. I'll find someone else."

"No, sir, please." Spurred into action, the boy stripped off his shirt and held it out to me. "Take it."

I grinned, lowered the satchel, and unbuttoned my shirt. Minutes later, I was back on Mystic, without food but in the proper clothing again. And I could hear the boy whistling a bright tune as he skipped down the street with the clothes of a noble and a heavy satchel of food. His bundle of sticks, long forgotten, remained in a pile at the side of the road.

A few short hours later, I crossed the border into Avenia. Considering all the effort it had taken me to get this far, it was a rather unremarkable moment. I'd come north of the swamplands and stayed away from any roads or trails, so the border was marked only by a nearby stake in the ground.

The closest town of any size was Dichell, a pigpen for humans and one of the rougher places in Avenia. But it was where I needed to begin.

I left Mystic in a dense thicket of woods outside Dichell. There was a risk that he'd be stolen from me here, but he'd definitely be stolen if I brought him into the town. I made sure he was near some grass and had a small spring for water. Then I traveled the rest of the way on foot.

Due to the street gangs that patrolled the darkness, nights

in Dichell were fairly dangerous. But in the daytime the miscreants shrank into the shadows as the more honorable citizens took over. However, safety was never a guarantee at any time of day or night. Evening was approaching, but I was armed with both a knife and a sword. Hopefully, it would keep any trouble far from me. Besides, my destination was the church, which had always been left alone.

The church had played a significant role in my life four years ago. After I'd escaped the ship in Isel, it was here that the kind priest first suspected who I was. Eventually, my father came to see me and this is where we had agreed that I'd be stripped of my royal identity and become Sage the orphan. If I had returned to the castle with him, I'd probably be in the grave now with the rest of my family.

But when I approached, I was appalled at how much the church had fallen into disrepair. The rock steps I had scrubbed for meals and shelter were cracked and pitted and thorny weeds grew between them. Windows of the church were broken out, and even the heavy wooden front door was off a hinge, so it didn't close entirely.

Maybe the church hadn't been left alone after all. I wondered about the priest who had taken me in before, and what he must think about this. I was eager to speak with him. Hopefully he'd remember me and would offer his help again. It would take some creativity on my part to convince him, but in the end, he'd tell me how to find the pirates.

"Who are you?" a boy asked. He was sitting on the steps,

playing with a rat, which he placed on his shoulder as he stood to greet me. Like most Avenian children he was little more than skin and bones, but he had a bright smile and dark blond hair, closer to the color mine had been when I'd dyed it as Sage. He looked to be ten or eleven, and wore clothes that hung crookedly on his thin frame. I wasn't sure whether he'd stolen them or if they had been handed down from an older sibling. Regardless, they weren't made for his body. The only exception was his shoes, which were in good repair and the exact size they should be.

I replied in an Avenian accent. "Is the priest of this church still here?"

"No." He squinted at me. "Never seen you before. You from out of town?"

"I've never seen you before either," I said. "So maybe you're the one from out of town."

That amused him. "My name is Fink. Well, that's not really my name, but it's what everyone calls me."

"What's your name, then?"

"Dunno. Everyone just calls me Fink."

"Don't you have anywhere else to go?"

"Not really. Why d'you want the priest?"

"A doctrinal question. What punishment does the Book of Faith recommend for a kid who's being too nosy?"

Fink missed the point and only said, "You can't ask him that because he's dead. Got himself killed about four years ago."

Dead? The news hit me like a blow to the chest. My world

blurred, and I had to stare forward in silence until I could speak. "Are you sure?"

"I saw it myself." Fink pointed to a grassy area in front of the church. "Right there, a pirate cut him down."

I didn't dare ask, but the word escaped me in a breath. "Why?"

He shrugged. "How would I know? I was just a kid then."

No explanation was necessary. Four years ago, the priest who had given me shelter sent word to my brother that the prince was here. The messenger undoubtedly told others of the rumor. The priest was eventually convinced I was only an orphan boy, but if the pirates thought there was any possibility I was Jaron, they would have come here. I'd already left, but the priest paid the penalty intended for me.

"You all right?" Fink asked.

I wasn't. It was hard to breathe. Feelings of sadness and anger flooded me, choking me. "Who was the pirate?" I asked. "The one who killed him."

Fink shook his head. "I'm not telling you that."

I grabbed Fink's collar and shoved him against the church wall. "What's his name?"

Fink looked nervous, but Avenian boys are used to getting roughed up so he kept calm. "Why should I tell you?" he asked.

I reached into the satchel tied around my waist and withdrew a garlin, probably a month's worth of money for him. "You'll tell me because you're hungry."

He held out his hand. I put the coin on his palm, but

pinched it firmly between my fingers. Fink glanced both directions before he leaned forward and whispered, "Devlin did it. But you won't find him in these parts because he's the pirate king now. You probably don't want to find him at all, unless you want the same end as the priest."

Devlin was their king? That explained why Avenia was willing to help with the assassination attempt. Because it wasn't just about revenge on me for escaping the pirates four years ago. Together they were seeking the total destruction of my country.

I released the garlin, and as Fink's fist tightened around it, I pulled him close to me again and muttered, "Now go away, or I'll tell everyone where I heard that name."

This time, Fink got the message. Without a second glance at me, he ran. I waited until he had gone, then left in the other direction.

I held my composure only until I found an alley where I could duck behind an old wagon that had been mutilated for spare parts, probably during the recent winter.

In the privacy of the alley, I pulled out my knife and stared at the blade, angry at Devlin for having killed an innocent man. No, angry at myself. Because I was the reason Devlin killed him. And because the priest died without even knowing I really was the boy he had initially thought me to be.

I first cut the bandage off my arm. The wound from Roden was tender but sealed. It was too soon to remove the bandage wrapped around my waist, but I tore it off anyway. I could not look cared for. A grim smile crept onto my face as I pictured what Mott would say if he saw me. Then it vanished. If Mott saw me now, he'd have nothing good to say.

Down on my knees, I grabbed a fistful of hair and sliced through it with the blade. There was enough hair in my grip that the blade cut unevenly, which is how I wanted it. The last person to cut it had been Errol, my manservant while I was at Farthenwood. He'd faint now if he saw what had just happened to the strands he had worked so carefully to trim.

The first cut had been in anger and felt to me like a rebellion, a rejection of the person everyone thought I should be. With the second cut I turned the anger inward, furious with myself that I didn't think the way others did, and that my solutions to any single problem always created several new ones. With the third cut I found myself fighting back tears until it was pointless to pretend that any amount of resistance would matter. Devlin had killed a man whose only crime was to shelter a hungry and frightened boy. For reasons I didn't understand, I wanted to know if anyone other than me had cried for the priest. Did he have a family? Anyone who would blame me for the part I had played in his death?

I had told Mott that I needed to kill Devlin, which was already an unbearable weight. But if Devlin was the pirate king, then the way out of this was so much harder, so much worse. I'd never get their loyalty, and if he controlled the pirates, Devlin would never give up wanting my life. The only way to make Carthya safe from them, and the only way I could survive this, was to destroy them all.

Mott was right. That was impossible. But it was my only choice now.

I drew in a long, steady breath to calm myself, then made a final cut of my hair, this one with resolve. I had to keep moving forward, and if the devils were willing, I could go home again.

· FIFTEEN ·

W hat's the matter with you?"

With a jump I turned, knife out, and saw Fink staring at me, his finger casually hooked around the rope that acted as his belt. The rat still sat on his shoulder, watching me cautiously. Rats weren't my favorite companions. I'd experienced enough rodents in the orphanage to develop a healthy hatred of them.

Embarrassed, I wiped my eyes and stood, then replaced my knife in its sheath and continued walking down the alley away from him. He followed.

"So you're telling me the name of that pirate is Devlin?" I said loudly. "You, *Fink*, are telling me the pirate's name?"

"Stop it!" Fink said, running up to me. "Everyone can hear you."

"Really, Fink? So everyone can hear that you told me the name of that pirate? Stay away from me or I'll keep talking like this."

He stopped walking. "Oh, I see. You don't want me around."

"Nope."

"But —"

I glanced back. "But what?"

He licked his lips, which were already cracked and dry. "I know you've got other coins, and I'm really hungry. I know you're new here, and so if you need anything, I'll help you find it."

I walked back to him. Although I wasn't particularly tall, I still seemed to tower over him. "What do you think I need?"

Glancing down at the ground, he mumbled, "Why'd you want the name of that pirate?"

"I'm making a collection of pirate poetry. Thought he'd be charming to write about."

Fink made a face and started to turn away from me. I jangled the satchel of coins at my hip, getting his attention again.

"I asked you a question," I said. "What do I need?"

"Well," Fink said. "I think you need a place to stay tonight."

"I can pay for anyplace I want."

"No, I mean a place where someone like you belongs." Fink's eyes remained locked on the satchel.

"I belong with the pirates," I said. "Where can I find them?"

Fink held out his hand. "They'll kill me if I tell you. So information like that is pretty expensive."

I untied the satchel and held it out for him, waiting for an answer.

While eyeing the coins, Fink lifted the fat rat off his shoulder and began stroking his back. A part of me felt bad for

tempting him to talk to me, because I appreciated how dangerous it might be. But without the priest's help, I didn't have any
other way to find Devlin.

Then I heard a faint thud behind me, movement. Fink's
expression didn't betray a thing, which meant he wasn't surprised at whoever was coming our way. The kid had set me up.
Of course he would. Nobody survived alone in Avenia.

I turned around to see the half-dozen boys who had joined
us. Fink was the youngest and smallest. Several of the boys were
older and bigger than me, all of them unfriendly. Each was
carrying a homemade weapon of some type: a club, or a whip, or
a knife carved of bone. A few bounced large rocks in their
hands. Even the ignorant could use a rock.

One hand went to the handle of my sword, but I didn't
take it out. In that instant, a memory tugged at me, something
vital to the mystery about my family's murders, but I couldn't
think about it here. A fight was brewing, which was the last
thing I wanted. I'd get some of them and some of them would
get me, and to be honest, it was that second part which concerned me more.

I tossed the satchel to the ground, at Fink's feet. "Take it,
then. There's plenty more coins where they came from."

He raised an eyebrow. "You haven't been on the streets
long."

"Why do you say that?"

"You're never supposed to say that you've got more coins.
That only attracts worse trouble later."

I grinned. "Trouble from who? A kid like you could never steal everything I've got access to."

Fink's eyes widened while he contemplated that, then he nodded toward the belt at my waist. "If that's true, then you can afford another sword and knife."

"You said there's somewhere I belong. Wherever that is, I'll need my weapons."

"If you stole the coins, then you stole these weapons too, so they're no more yours than ours. Give 'em up and you'll walk out of here. Try to fight us and you won't."

"Fighting would mess up my new haircut," I said. "Tell me where you think I belong."

"Give me your weapons."

He replaced the rat on his shoulder and cocked his head at a mountain of a boy behind me. To keep him away, I tossed my knife and sword on the ground by Fink's feet.

"There's a tavern on the far edge of town from here," Fink said. "Maybe you belong there. Ask for room eleven."

Fink crouched to get the weapons and as soon as he looked down I kicked him in the head. He cried out and fell backward. He already had my sword but I retrieved my knife and ran. The other boys started to chase me but it was only a halfhearted effort. They knew as well as I did that there were plenty of hiding places in Dichell, carved out either by the street gangs waiting to ambush a traveler, or by a traveler hoping to save his life in the shadows. The problem was that I couldn't hide. I had pirates to find.

I ducked into a bakery on the street where a rather pretty girl was just closing up her shop. I chatted politely with her and took a couple of sweet rolls to tuck beneath my shirt. She might have noticed, but she let me walk out anyway.

Much as I dreaded the idea of going to the tavern Fink had suggested, I knew that's where I needed to be. And seeing it later that evening was worse than I'd anticipated. No degree of darkness could mask the fact that there were barns more hospitable to humans than this place. It was partially hidden by overgrown weeds and grasses and littered with whatever wreckage a customer didn't feel like carrying with him. It had a few windows on the main and upper floors, but they were too covered in grime to let in much light. Most likely, there was nothing inside worth seeing anyway, so perhaps that was for the best.

I debated with myself for a long time before walking in. It wasn't a good idea, but I seemed to be experiencing a shortage of better alternatives. When I set eyes on the owner, I decided he looked enough like a pig that it made sense why his tavern reminded me of a barn. Like most other taverns, this place was too dark and seemed unnaturally crowded with tables and chairs. A couple of scabby men sat behind cobwebs near the edge of one wall, but their interest seemed to be in nursing their drinks rather than caring who I might be. The corners of the room were filthy and I knew by the chewed chair legs that the tavern owner had rats.

"What do you want?" the owner asked.

My heart raced. Once I spoke, there'd be no turning back,

not until my fight was finished, or I was dead. He cocked his head, impatient with my silence, and I said, "I want a room. Number eleven."

If there were eleven rooms in this muck trap, they'd have to be the size of coffins. Obviously, I was giving him a code word.

He rubbed a hand over his jaw and surveyed me. "Show me your money."

I smirked at him. "Can I pay you later?" If I was here in the morning, I could probably steal enough from his till to cover my debt.

He frowned. "What's your name?"

"You don't need it."

The bartender took offense at that. "I'm doin' you a favor, boy. You could be more friendly about things." He passed a drink across the counter to me. "Here."

The drink was dark brown and frothy and smelled like a stable floor. I pushed it back to him. "Not for me."

"Just a sip. I'm sure you're thirsty. Besides, it's a new batch and I want to know if it's any good."

"I can tell you from here that it's not." And if this place was what I suspected, the drink also contained the same powder I'd used to put Mott to sleep, or worse. I turned around. "Where's the room?"

He nodded to a flight of stairs. "First door on the right. Sleep as long as you want and maybe you'll work for me later on."

No, I wouldn't.

Room eleven was unmarked as such, and the furnishings inside were simple, with nothing but a mattress stuffed with pine needles and moss. It was flat on the floor and had a thin blanket for a covering. I didn't care. I sank onto the mattress, ignored the ends of the needles that pricked through the fabric, and fell asleep immediately.

Some time later, something creaked in the hallway and my eyes flipped open. The room was very dark, but I remembered seeing a candle in the corner. I started to roll toward it, then froze, certain I heard footsteps on the stairs.

My initial thought was that the tavern owner was finally going to bed, which signaled the time for me to have a good look around before deciding whether to stay, as Fink had suggested. But as I listened, it clearly wasn't the owner, who was a large man and would have heavier, less cautious footsteps.

And more than one was out there. I lay still on the floor. My hand was inches away from my knife, but I didn't reach for it.

In the hallway, I heard the hiss of the tavern owner, saying, "Yeah, that room. But be quiet. He didn't take the drink."

Everything fell silent. Waiting there, knowing what was coming, was torturous. But it had to happen.

The door creaked open, letting in only a sliver of light from the hallway. I could feel them around me, like snakes slithering into a room. One was near my head, and I wasn't sure how many were behind me, maybe four or five.

I'm not sure what the signal was, but they moved on me in

unison. I grunted as one stuffed a gag in my mouth. As soon as it was tied, a canvas bag went over my head, then a drawstring pulled tight at the end of it. Another bound my wrists behind me, and it took two of them to clamp down my legs to tie them. Someone took the knife at my waist and placed it at my neck.

"Give me a reason to use this and I will," a man growled, his face near mine.

I nodded, very slowly, then a large man picked me up and threw me over his shoulder to haul me out of the tavern.

Wherever Fink thought I belonged, that was where we were going.

· SIXTEEN ·

They laid me across the back of a horse and we rode out of Dichell. Once the roads became more pitted and uneven, I knew we'd left the city limits. And I doubted we were on a main trail because I felt tree branches occasionally brush against either side of me.

Other than that, I had no idea where we were going.

There was little conversation, and when someone spoke, it was almost always the man who had threatened me inside the tavern, so it was impossible to tell how many men were in our group. At least a half dozen, I guessed, but maybe a couple more. It didn't really matter.

The knots around my wrists wouldn't have been too difficult to untie, but this time, escape wasn't in my plans. All I could hope was that they gave me a chance to speak before they killed me. Although as I thought about it, it was usually only after I began speaking that most people felt like murdering me.

I did manage to work the gag out of my mouth. I wasn't going to yell and there wouldn't have been much point in attempting it anyway, but the gag made it hard to breathe, especially because I was being carried facedown on the horse so my lungs were already compressed.

There were campfires wherever we stopped some time later. I heard the fires pop when they hit moist wood and I could dimly see their light from behind the canvas bag. Whoever rode with me did the disservice of pushing me off the horse with his hand. I landed on my feet, but since they were tied up I crumpled straight to the ground.

"What've we got here?" someone asked.

"That boy who was asking about Devlin."

"Fink said this boy was upset when he heard what Devlin did to the priest."

The fact that Fink had spoken to these men was not a surprise. I knew he was connected to higher powers somehow, likely as a runner for supplies or to gather information in town. That had always been obvious since the only thing Fink wore that fit him were his shoes. They would have been provided to him by these men to ensure he could carry out their tasks.

I had to admire him for having already talked to them. Fink worked fast.

They propped me against a tree, fastened a chain to the rope around my wrists, tethering me to the trunk, then pulled the canvas bag off my head.

It was a simple thieves' camp, with tents randomly sprung up wherever they fit between trees, and no visible discrimination in the darkness between cooking, sleeping, and latrine areas. Still, by the look of things, this camp had been here for some time.

A man crouched down beside me for a better look. He was in his early forties with broad shoulders and a slightly hunched back. His thin hair was cut short and probably used to be redder. Still, his eyes were intelligent and his face was marked with premature lines. He wasn't likely to have great tolerance for me.

"Didn't like that gag?" he asked, untying it.

"It tasted bad," I said, still using the Avenian accent. "Are you sure you used a clean cloth?"

He chuckled, then slapped me. Not too hard, though, and I appreciated that. "That's for being mouthy. I'm Erick Loman. I'm in charge around here. What's your name?"

I hesitated, then with a loud huff said, "Sage."

"That's it?"

"You think someone like me is gonna have more than one name?"

Erick smiled. "I'm surprised anyone even bothered to give you a name at all."

My expression mirrored his. "They didn't. I gave myself this name."

And that was the end of the smiling. With introductions out of the way, Erick got down to the business of having abducted me.

"Why were you asking Fink about the priest?"

"I have some sins to confess," I said. "For ruining the life of the last man to kidnap me."

His second slap was less kind. "Fink said you're trying to find Devlin."

"I'm trying to find the pirates. I have a job and need their help."

"I've worked with them for years, boy. Pirates don't help anyone but themselves."

"This job will help them plenty."

He frowned, then refastened the gag around my mouth. "Spit this out again and I'll carve out your tongue. Got it?" He didn't wait for an answer before the canvas bag went back over my head.

They left me that way and soon everything went quiet. Once I was certain they were asleep, I undid the knots that tied my hands, then removed the gag and the canvas bag. After untying the rope around my feet, I lay down to sleep as well, using the bag as a thin layer of padding between my head and my arm.

I awoke with a boot to my ribs, which was better than I'd expected. When I opened my eyes, Erick towered over me, his arms folded. Fink stood in the shadows behind him. He had a dark bruise on his forehead from where I'd kicked him. A better person might've regretted kicking a kid. I didn't.

"You've got a rat behind you," I muttered to Erick.

Fink shook his head. "No, my pet's in her cage."

"I wasn't talking about your pet."

"Call me whatever names you want," Fink said. "They said as long as I watch out for you, I can stay too."

If he expected a congratulations from me, he was going to be disappointed. This was no place for someone his age. Nor mine, I supposed.

"Why didn't you run?" Erick asked. "It appears our knots were no good for you."

"Undoing all those knots made me tired. Besides, you and I have business to discuss." I eyed Fink. "Without him."

"If it wasn't for me, they would have killed you already," Fink said.

"If it wasn't for you, I wouldn't be here in the first place," I retorted.

Erick grabbed my shirt and yanked me to my feet, then led me forward with Fink at my heels. Every time he got too close I stopped walking, forcing him to run into me, then I turned around and grinned back at him. It irritated him, but I was bigger so I didn't think he'd try anything back. Of course, the last time we met I had kicked him in the face, so maybe he would.

They led me into a makeshift tent on the edge of camp. From the looks of it, this was a supply tent, though there wasn't much here to offer. In the center was a small table. Lying on it were my knife, sword, and the satchel of coins I'd given to Fink.

Erick motioned to the items. "Explain these."

I flashed a wry smile. "If you don't know what these are, then you're in the wrong business."

He wasn't amused. He picked up the satchel by a seam and

dumped the coins on the table. "These are Carthyan and in new condition. How do you come to possess so many of them?"

"I took them." Which was easy to do because as king, they were mine.

"So you're a thief."

Casually, I shoved my hands into my pockets. "Looks that way."

"Are you any good?"

My answer only required a nod at the coins.

"Where'd they come from?"

"Why do you want to know?" As if that weren't obvious.

"You told Fink you could get more."

I eyed Fink. "He should've realized that secret divided better between only the two of us."

Erick was quickly losing his patience. "So are there more?"

Folding my arms, I said, "You can't expect me to answer that. If there are, I'd rather save that news for the pirates."

Erick grinned slyly. "Ah. You think with some treasure you could earn yourself a seat at their table?"

I didn't need a seat. Just a sword and a lot of luck.

Erick continued, "It won't work because they don't know you. They would take the coins and then give you a quick beheading."

"I'm very opposed to any beheadings involving my own neck," I said. "So tell me how to make it work. Maybe you know the pirates."

"I know a few." Erick scratched his jaw. "If you told me

where this treasure is, I could tell the pirates."

"Which still results in my headless problem," I said. "I have access to the coins, but I can't get them alone. And no offense, but I wouldn't trust your amateur bunch of thieves with stealing a single coin from a wishing pond, much less the treasure I have access to. It has to be the pirates and it has to be me who tells them."

Erick pulled out a knife and shoved me against a post of the tent. "There's no treasure. I think you're making it up."

Which was rather insulting, because if I'd intended to make up a story, I could have done far better than this. However, my focus remained on the knife at my throat. "You don't want to do this."

His lip curled. "Yes, I do."

I considered that. "Fair enough. But it'd be a mistake. The coins are real and there're thousands of them. They're in a secret cave in Carthya. The royals keep only a small portion of their wealth in the castle. If it's ever overrun, they don't want their enemies to have all the treasury."

"How do you know this?"

I raised an eyebrow. "You don't? It's common practice for all royals, not just Carthyans."

"I thought that was a myth," Fink said.

"I've been there," I said. "I've stood inside the walls."

That had happened only once, when I was still quite young. I had a memory of having gone there with my father and Darius. My father had caught me using the coins as skipping rocks across a wide pond at the far end of the cave. My backside still remembered his anger for that.

Erick finally released me, then rubbed a hand along his unshaven jaw. "Where's the cave?"

"You think it's that easy to find?" I chuckled. "I could draw you a map and you'd still miss it. You'll have to keep me alive if you want to see it."

"How much is in there?" Fink asked.

"More than you'll see in a lifetime. There's enough for every pirate to split a healthy share, and I figure it's more than enough to earn me a seat at their table."

"And perhaps me as well." Erick shook his head. "You can't go to the pirates alone, but if I brought you along, they'd hear you out. I could bargain with them, that in exchange for the treasure, I'd earn a place with them too."

"Could you include keeping me alive as part of that bargain?" I asked.

Erick grinned. "That's not my top priority." I started to protest but he added, "You're not leaving here on your own. But if you're one of my thieves, with me as your partner, then you might have a chance. Besides, there's no other way you can find their camp."

With a stubborn frown, I said, "You'll get all the glory for my coins."

"We'll both have it. You said yourself you couldn't get them on your own and the devils know I won't let you go without my share. So don't look at it as losing the glory. You're gaining a partner."

In fact, I looked at it as neither of those. But I made the appropriate expressions of thinking his proposal over, then nodded. "All right, I'm in. But we don't have a lot of time."

"Why not?"

Because time was not on my side. It was now only five days until the regents met. However, I figured that detail would only complicate our tenuous relationship, so I said, "There're others who know about the cave. We have to get there first, or not at all."

"Then we'll go to the pirates soon. But first, you must prove yourself."

Suddenly anxious, I cocked my head. "I already have. I brought you those coins."

"Yeah, but I never saw you take them. Did you think I'd recommend you to the pirates unless I saw you for myself?"

Not necessarily, but I'd certainly hoped for it. "What do you suggest, then?"

"Every now and then a few of my boys cross the border into Carthya and cause a little trouble. The last group returned a couple of days ago, but, unfortunately, there were some injuries."

If it was the men I had run into near Libeth, then I hoped there were some career-ending injuries.

"I haven't gone with them in some time," he continued.

"You come with me and I'll watch you in action, see if you really belong with us."

"What if I don't fit in?" I asked.

"Then you won't come back."

I smirked. "I know about those raids. They're pathetic."

He didn't like the insult, but he was still listening. "And why is that?"

"There's rarely enough wealth to make it worth the effort. You stir up plenty of trouble but don't bring home much of value. Isn't that what matters?"

He stroked his chin again. "You have a better plan?"

My mind raced. I had to have a better plan. Because if I didn't help them, they would kill me. And under no circumstances would I attack my own people.

Almost immediately, an idea came to me. It wasn't very good, but it was better than Erick's. "There's a noble who lives in Libeth," I said. "His place isn't well guarded and he's rich."

"We don't go into nobles' homes." Erick firmly shook his head. "Too much danger, and we're in foreign territory so we'd get no support from Avenia if we were caught."

"Send me in alone, and I'll come out with anything I want."

Erick continued shaking his head. "It's too risky."

"But it's my risk," I said. "If we're going to prove ourselves to the pirates, border raids are meaningless. Let me show the pirates we deserve a place with them."

Erick glanced over at Fink, who nodded eagerly. "All right,"

Erick said. "But if you try to trick us, we'll burn the place down with you and anyone else inside."

I smiled in agreement, but my stomach churned. It was no trick. In a few hours I would return to a man who had shown me nothing but kindness, and there I would steal from him everything I could.

SEVENTEEN

We planned to leave for Libeth late that afternoon. In the meantime, I was allowed free rein of the camp, though everyone there kept a close eye on me. It was a good thing I wasn't trying to escape because it would've been impossible anyway.

When it was finally time to leave, I half expected Erick would order me hooded, but he didn't. Maybe he had decided to trust me and accept me into the group.

I rode with Erick on his horse until I gave him directions to find Mystic, who amazingly was still tied up where I'd left him. Erick never asked about Mystic, obviously assuming he'd also been stolen. I almost wished he had asked. At least, it would have been fun to tell the story I'd prepared about how I obtained this horse.

Because of the swampland behind Libeth, we had to take almost the same path as I had taken in coming to Avenia yesterday morning. It was nearly midnight when we entered the town, which was silent except for the occasional shuffle of farm animals in the fields or restless crickets at the roadside.

"Where's the house?" Erick asked.

I pointed up the hill. From here, it looked entirely dark, which was a relief. If there'd been evidence of anyone awake, I would have made an excuse to cancel the plan. "For a job like this we need quiet," I said to Erick. "I'll go in alone and everyone can wait for me."

"You and I will go in," Erick said. "This is a test to see how you operate, remember?"

I remembered that all too well.

Erick handed me my knife. "I assume you want this."

I took it and strapped it to my waist. "What about my sword?"

"It's still in the tent, still safe. Let's see how everything goes tonight."

Once at Harlowe's home, Erick directed the men to wait at the edge of the estate. He and I would walk the rest of the way on foot.

"I don't like this sneaking around," Erick said. "I much prefer the use of force."

"The last time your thieves used force, several of them came home injured." I decided not to burden him with the detail of who had caused their injuries. "This is better."

We fell silent as we got close to the house. I wondered how many people were inside. Did Harlowe's servants live here or travel to their own homes at night? Did he have vigils like Conner used to have? Every part of me hated what we were about to do, and hated myself for bringing the thieves here.

Once we reached the home I hesitated, debating the best course of action. Erick's presence made the situation far more complicated. I could climb the exterior walls of the house and enter through an upper story. Erick likely wouldn't follow me, so it was my best chance to be alone. I could find Harlowe and explain to him as much as was necessary to get his help. But if Erick did follow me, that would put him on the same floor as the bedrooms. I knew very little about the layout of Harlowe's home. If I startled someone, there was too much risk it would create a fight, and Erick was well armed.

So I led Erick around the front of the home. We'd go directly into Harlowe's office and hope no servants were still awake.

It was not so many hours ago when I'd been a welcomed guest inside these walls. Could I really have fallen this far so fast? I made a silent vow to repay Harlowe for my crimes as soon as possible. Still, what I was doing felt like the ultimate betrayal. Harlowe would understand someday why I persuaded the thieves not to go to the border settlements. But I wasn't sure I could ever make him see that I needed to take them somewhere, and that this was the only place I felt I had some control.

The window to what I thought was Harlowe's office was high off the ground, so I'd have to shinny up a tree to get in. Hopefully that was enough deterrent for Erick to follow me. I doubted he was a man who did much climbing.

I brushed my hands on my pants to dry them. Erick glanced up at the window, then grabbed my shirt and pressed me against the tree trunk. "You swear to me this isn't a trap?" he hissed.

"It isn't a trap," I assured him. "Trust me, I want to get in and out as much as you do." Probably more.

"If anything looks funny, I'll signal my men and guarantee nobody leaves here alive. Especially not you."

"If you don't want anything to go wrong, then stop making so much noise," I said, pushing back at him. "Now let's do this."

I climbed the tree with no more noise than the occasional rustle of leaves. Then, keeping myself shielded by the wall, I peered into the window. With the little moonlight available, I could see that this was Harlowe's office and it was empty. Even better, the door was closed, and as far as I could tell from looking beneath the door, the halls were dark. If servants were awake, there would still be some lights on the main floor.

"Wait for me here," I told Erick. "I'll be out in five minutes."

I wormed my fingers beneath the window and slowly raised it. It slid silently and easily, an indication that Harlowe often opened it, perhaps for a breeze during the warm spring afternoons. The leap from the branch where I was perched wasn't too bad, and within a few seconds I was standing inside Harlowe's office.

In the low light, the challenge would be to figure out where he kept his valuables. I didn't need much. Coins were best because they'd be the most valued by the thieves, the easiest to replace, and the least sentimental. If Harlowe had coins anywhere in the home, they were most likely here.

I had worked my way around a desk in his office and was fingering across shelves of books when I heard footsteps in the main hall. I froze, hoping it was only a passing servant.

But the footsteps were followed by voices, and the light of a candle flickered from beneath the office door. They were coming closer.

When it became obvious they were approaching the office, I hurried toward the window. The voices were of two men, though with the muffle of the door I couldn't recognize them. I assumed one of them must be Harlowe.

The door opened before I was as far as the window, so I began to duck beneath the desk, but a voice commanded me to stop.

I didn't draw my knife. There was no point in it. And turning around to face the two men who had entered the office was one of the hardest things I'd ever done.

Both men gasped when they recognized me. Harlowe was the one holding the candle. The other man, who had ordered me to stop and who had withdrawn his knife, was none other than Mott.

· EIGHTEEN ·

None of us spoke for what seemed like an hour. Slowly Mott lowered his knife and finally Harlowe whispered, "You're Jaron. But why —"

My heart pounding, I glanced at Mott for help, still unable to speak.

At almost the same time, I heard a sound behind me and Erick climbed through the window. "I saw the light," he said. "I thought you needed help."

"I don't." Now I withdrew my knife.

Mott put a hand on Harlowe's arm. "This isn't who you think it is," he said. "This boy is one of the finest thieves of Avenia. I've seen him before and I know he's capable of everything he says he is. You should give him whatever he wants. He'll always get it anyway."

Erick looked at me. "What are you capable of?"

I ignored Erick and looked at Harlowe. "Whatever coins you have here, I want them. Now."

Harlowe remained frozen, unable to put together the various explanations of who he had thought I was when we first met, whatever Mott must have told him, and what he was now seeing unfold. Finally, Mott pushed him forward, and Harlowe said, "I don't have much here." He reached for a frame on his desk. "But this is made of gold. It's worth a lot."

A sketch of a young child was inside the frame. I wondered if it was Nila's father, or the other child Harlowe's servant had told me about. "I don't want that picture," I said. "But I'll take the frame."

Harlowe removed the sketch and set it carefully on the desk before Erick took the frame and dropped it in a bag he'd brought with him.

Next, Harlowe reached for something inside his vest and handed it to me. "You can take this too. It's also gold." It was the watch that had belonged to Nila's father.

I tossed it back at him. "That's imitator's gold. It's worthless." Unable to avoid Mott's eye, I added, "Surely you know that I can tell the difference between that and real gold."

"Obviously you can't." Erick frowned at me while holding out his hand. "It's real enough for my needs."

"If anyone's taking it, I will." I reached for the watch, but Erick swatted my hand out of the way and flashed the blade of his knife. There was nothing to do but give in.

"This boy doesn't mean anything more to us than imitator's gold," Mott said, staring at me. "Give him some coins and he'll go."

Harlowe padded to his bookshelf. He pulled out a box from an upper shelf, then walked over to me and said, "Hold out your hands." I took the bag from Erick, and Harlowe widened the box, letting dozens of garlins fall inside it.

Behind me, Erick actually gasped with delight. Then his eyes fixed on Mott. "What about him?"

Mott looked at me. "You won't get me, thief." And he ran from the room.

I pointed to Harlowe and told Erick, "You watch him." I stopped as I passed Harlowe. "Don't move. Don't give him a reason to do anything." Then I left the room, chasing after Mott.

Mott was waiting for me as I rounded the corner into the main hall. He grabbed my arm and yanked me against the wall.

"What are you doing here?" Mott hissed.

"You should've heard the alternative." Suddenly, there was so much to tell him. About the Avenian thieves who stole across our borders to attack our women and children. About the nobles in Carthya who covered it up. And about my father, who, worst of all, had ignored the pleas of his own people for help. But there was no time. "Why are you here?"

"Can't you guess?"

"You should be helping Tobias at the castle." A beat passed. "How's he doing?"

"Amarinda and Kerwyn will protect him. But there's talk everywhere of the regents' vote against you. If you don't come back now, there might not be anything to return to."

I stepped back. "And if I don't finish here, there's no point in returning."

"Killing Devlin won't solve this problem."

"Yeah, you're right." I dreaded the words I'd be saying next, and even as I spoke I understood the impossibility of it all. "I have to destroy the pirates. All of them."

Mott's eyes flared. "What? This is madness! Not the plan of a king!"

Angrily, I hissed, "Then join those who vote for a steward and let me be!"

I started to march away, but Mott grabbed my arm. "I don't want a steward in Carthya any more than you do. But your actions only give ammunition to those who think you lack the judgment to be king. You are helping them destroy you."

Turning back to him, I said, "Why can't you see this, Mott? Forget the steward and see the dangers for Carthya. This is our only hope *not* to be destroyed. Our troubles are far bigger than Gregor's political ambitions."

Mott wasn't convinced. "You should've let Gregor in on your plans. Other than Kerwyn, there was nobody your father trusted more. Please, come back while you still can."

"If I do that, how long until the pirates invade Carthya? Is it days, or will they give us a whole week to prepare? I don't *want* to be here, Mott, so give me another option. Give me any way in which Carthya has a chance to survive and I'll do it."

But he couldn't. In a voice thick with sadness he said, "Nobody comes back from the pirates, Jaron."

"I've got to. Who else makes your life this interesting?" And I even offered a smile.

Mott breathed out a curse, then said, "If you need me, I'll

be at the church in Dichell. For your own safety, that's as far as I dare follow you." I started again to leave, but this time he added, "Give me your knife."

"What?"

Mott held out his hand, palm upward. "You've been gone too long. So give me the knife."

It was the second time Mott had injured himself to save my secrets. Watching him slice the blade across his arm hurt almost as much as if it had been my flesh. When I took the knife back from him I hesitated, hearing a small sound behind us.

Nila held a small candle out to see us better. "Oh!" she said, startled. Then as she recognized me and saw the blood on my knife, she took a step back. "Oh no." She turned and ran up the stairs. I didn't dare call after her. I couldn't risk Erick hearing us.

"Go now," Mott said. "I'll try to stop her before she wakes anyone. And, Jaron, you must come back."

"I will." I spoke with more confidence than I felt, but it seemed to comfort him. "And it probably doesn't matter at this point, but I am sorry."

Before Mott could respond, I returned to the office, then rushed at Erick who had Harlowe backed against the wall with his knife. I pushed between them and cried, "What are you doing?"

"He asked your name," Erick said.

I turned to Harlowe. "No, sir, I don't want you to remember my name. Nor to remember *this* night." Then I pulled Erick away. "We've got to go."

Erick's eyes locked on my bloodstained knife, and Harlowe let out a horrified gasp when he realized what I must have done. "So that's what you're capable of," Erick mumbled. "I underestimated you."

"He asked for it," I said, then nodded to Erick. "You go first."

When he ducked out the window I turned back to Harlowe, who said, "Tell me you didn't just —"

"Someday I hope you'll understand." I spoke so softly I was nearly mouthing the words. "Forgive me."

Harlowe only shook his head, feeling horrified and betrayed if he felt anything at all. And I climbed down the tree, knowing that this was a crime for which I might never be forgiven.

· NINETEEN ·

Y ou look upset," Erick said as we rode out of Libeth only a few minutes later. Beside me, the other thieves were quietly celebrating, counting the number of drinks they could buy with their share of Harlowe's money. It was disgusting how they already considered it theirs, and how they congratulated me as if I'd done something good.

"Smile," Erick said. "This is a time to celebrate."

"He saw my face," I mumbled.

"Is that all?" Erick's laugh was crass and made my muscles tense. "You've got nothing to worry about. What's Carthya going to do about us? Nothing! You must know the reputation of their king."

"Eckbert's gone. They have a new king now."

"That's who I'm talking about. Eckbert's son. What was his name again?"

"Jaron."

"That's right. I don't know much about him, but from what I hear, we'll have all the freedom in Carthya that we want."

For some reason, I couldn't help but chuckle. "What's wrong with Jaron?"

"They say he's wild and reckless, always has been. Everyone knows he was missing for a long time, but now he's come back to rule. What could a boy with that history possibly know about ruling an entire country?"

"Probably not much." I knew just enough to understand that I'd already made plenty of mistakes. Riding here with Erick right now was undoubtedly the biggest of them all.

"Exactly." Erick chuckled. "But all we care about is that our own stupid Avenian king can deny knowledge of what we do."

"Does he know?"

"If he does, we're too small for him to care. When he wants something done without getting his own hands dirty, he'll use the pirates."

Which Vargan himself had all but admitted. Avenia wanted my land. The pirates wanted my life. They were a natural team.

Erick didn't seem to notice my distress. Beside me, he chuckled to himself, then said, "Vargan's main target is Carthya. You should know that if he finds out you're a pirate, he might use your knowledge of Carthya to help him destroy it."

Yes, that I knew.

Getting little response from me, Erick rode forward to tell the others more details about what had happened inside Harlowe's home. He even pulled out the pocket watch to show them, then tucked it back inside his shirt without the slightest care for its real value. I couldn't understand why Harlowe had given it up so easily and cursed myself for not keeping control of it.

We were almost back to our camp when my irritation turned to sudden anxiety. As we approached the ridge of a hill, we saw at least a dozen horses standing across the road, much farther down, blocking our passage. With one look at who was astride the horses, I knew I was in serious trouble.

I halted Mystic and said to a pockmarked thief beside me, "Are those King Vargan's men?"

He squinted to see better, then frowned. "Looks that way. I suppose the good king has decided it's time to collect taxes again."

Erick was already riding toward us. "Everyone, back up your horses."

We obeyed until we were protected from the soldiers' sight. Then Erick gathered us closer and pulled from his saddlebag the sack of coins I had stolen from Harlowe. "Everyone take a share and hide it wherever you can," he said. "In your boots or beneath your saddles, or wherever. Hurry!"

"Let's just go another way," I said, barely able to hide the concern in my voice. "Or wait until they're gone."

The thief nearest me laughed. "Sage doesn't know the king's tricks."

I emphatically disagreed. I probably knew his tricks better than anyone here and had far more to lose than a handful of garlins. I absolutely could not go forward and risk any encounter with Vargan's soldiers.

"They've probably already spotted us," Erick said. "If we don't go riding down that hill soon, they'll come after us and make things much worse."

For my part, I couldn't see how things could get any worse.

Sensing my despair, Erick said, "We worked hard last night, and I know it bothers you to lose the coins. I hate this too, but we can't avoid it. Now take some handfuls and let's hope we get through with at least something left to us."

I dreaded the thought of going forward. But equally risky was that if I abandoned Erick now, I'd lose any hope of getting to the pirates. Erick held out his saddlebag again, and when I reached into it, I noticed some rags beneath the coins and asked what they were for.

Erick shrugged. "In case one of my thieves is injured while we're away from camp."

I reached in again and withdrew the rags, then began unrolling them to their full length.

"The tax is the same whether or not you're injured," Erick protested. "Besides, there's dried blood on them from the last time they were used."

"Even better." I began wrapping the bandages around my head, covering one eye and cheek and all of my hair. I made sure the part with the blood landed directly over my eye.

"Take that off," Erick said. "You look ridiculous."

"I look injured, which is completely different." I ripped off an end of the fabric, then stuffed it in my mouth, between my cheek and gums. I hoped it gave me the look of having my cheek swollen. "There, *now* I look ridiculous," I said.

Erick cursed under his breath, then told his men to stay relaxed and perhaps everyone could get through the barrier untouched.

The soldiers sat at attention when they saw us coming and commanded us to halt and dismount. I kept my head down and slid off Mystic, then backed into the group of seven or eight thieves.

"We've got nothing of value," Erick said to the soldiers. "We're just trying to get back to our camp."

The soldier nearest Erick harrumphed, then ordered us to line up and lay any weapons we might be carrying on the ground. I was reluctant to move, but the men around me were already forming into a line. I stood beside Erick, and he motioned that I should set down my knife. I did, but put a toe of my boot over it, at least to keep that bit of control if a fight started. Not that it would help much. There were many more soldiers than us, and all of them better armed. Maybe I'd need these bandages after all.

The soldiers began by searching Erick. They immediately found Harlowe's pocket watch and tossed it onto a cloth on the ground. Then they dug into his saddlebag and found the coins the rest of us had not divided. With that discovery, a soldier struck Erick hard across the jaw, knocking him to the ground.

"You would lie to your king?" the soldier said.

"I lied to *you*." Erick groaned a little and wiped blood from his lip. "You have no right to our property."

"But I do," a voice said.

I quickly turned, then immediately buried my chin to my chest. King Vargan emerged from a carriage that was stopped in the shade of some tall trees. With my head down, I hadn't paid much attention to it before, but now that I looked, it was clearly the same carriage he had taken to my father's funeral.

Vargan stepped forward and surveyed us. The other men went to their knees, but I turned away from him to help Erick off the ground. If Vargan noticed that I hadn't knelt, he let it go. Instead he said, "A glorious day is coming for Avenia. Soon, my friends, we will be more than a great country. We will be an empire."

I gritted my teeth. He intended to achieve his glory on the backs of my people — and with the help of the pirates. Unless I found a way to stop them.

"Throw down your coins now, and there will be no punishment for attempting to hide them from me," Vargan continued. "Then be grateful that you were given this opportunity to contribute to Avenia's greatness."

The men around me quietly grumbled, but their king was in front of them now, and nothing they said would matter in the face of his greed. They withdrew the coins from wherever they had been hidden and dropped them on the cloth. Much as it infuriated me to use Harlowe's wealth to benefit my enemy country, I handed over my coins too. The last thing I needed was to draw Vargan's attention my way.

Vargan surveyed the collection of wealth on the ground, then stepped over it to look us over. Luckily, all the men had their heads down as I did, so other than the bandages, we all looked the same.

"I have more good news." Vargan's tone mocked us. Whatever he was about to say, we all knew it would be anything but good news. "In addition to these taxes, I am also looking for men to join my army. You're nothing but thieves now, mere rodents. But you can come with me today and I will make you into heroes."

I nearly laughed at that. In what way was attacking a peaceful neighboring country heroic? He degraded Erick's men for being thieves even as he planned to steal all of Carthya from me. My fingers itched to pick up my knife and start the fight. It would've meant a certain death sentence for all of us — a definite disadvantage — but a part of me wanted Vargan to know I was here.

Vargan pointed to the man on the other side of Erick. "He will volunteer. Take him."

The thief was a large and muscular man who had only twenty minutes earlier promised a round of ale to everyone in celebration of what I had stolen from Harlowe. He backed away from the soldiers, but they grabbed him and at knifepoint dragged him into the back of a wagon beside the king's carriage. Vargan then pointed out two other men, one who I thought seemed like a close friend of Erick's, and another, quieter man whom I'd barely paid attention to since I came to the thieves. He went without complaint, but Erick's friend shouted, "I won't fight!" He drew a knife from a pocket, but the soldiers were quicker and instantly had six swords on him. Both men were deposited into the back of the wagon, then a barred door was shut, locking them in.

It was no wonder that Avenia's armies were so much larger than mine. If this was Vargan's method of recruiting soldiers, then he could have as large an army as he wanted.

"You will fight," Vargan sneered, then gestured at the rest of us. "You all will." To his currish soldiers, he waved a hand and added, "Take everyone. For what's coming, we'll need every man we can get."

With their swords drawn, soldiers immediately began to direct us toward the wagon, but I held my place. Beside me, Erick wasn't moving either, and his fists were clenched so tightly I knew he was debating whether it was worth trying to resist. A soldier answered that question a moment later when he stopped beside Erick, then whacked him across the back of his knees with the blunt edge of his sword. With a grunt, Erick collapsed to the ground. I was struck next, and the force of it jarred my muscles enough to send me down beside Erick. Soldiers grabbed Erick's arms and began dragging him toward the wagon. Another few went for me, but I had my knife in hand by then. However, Vargan told his soldiers to wait a moment and walked up to me.

"You've been injured."

Without looking up, I shook my head.

"Stand up, boy."

I did, but would not meet his eyes. He studied me for what seemed like hours. I was certain he must recognize me. It was true that when we'd last met it had been dark, and I was far dirtier now. Yet I felt so obvious here, as if the bandages called even greater attention to the fact that I was trying to hide my identity from him.

But it wasn't that. In fact, the bandages may have had just the opposite effect, distracting him from looking at my face at all. He stared at them, trying to figure out why they were there.

"If it's not an injury, then what are these wrappings for?" he asked.

Other than a mediocre attempt at disguise? I smiled at him, which hopefully looked pretty grotesque considering the ball of cloth still stuffed between my cheek and gums. In a hiss of a whisper, I said, "Plague wounds."

Which was all that needed to be said. In whatever way the plague traveled from one person to the next, we all knew the hazards of being near someone so diseased.

Vargan nearly leapt away, and for better effect I groaned and raised a hand toward him. The way he twisted to get away from me would surely increase any back pain he had felt before. At least, I hoped it did.

"There's plague with these men!" Vargan shouted. "Release them all!"

The soldiers dropped Erick as if he burned their hands and emptied the wagon almost faster than I could blink. They rushed their king into his carriage nearly as quickly. Within seconds, he and his military escort had left us behind in the dust of the horses' hooves.

The men let out a cheer as I unpeeled the bandages, but Erick only stared at me as if I'd done something wrong. He finally folded his arms and said, "You owe me an explanation."

That was probably true. But he wasn't getting one. I only said, "If I hadn't done that, we'd all be waking up tomorrow as Avenian soldiers."

"Maybe so. But that's not *why* you did it."

"I did it because someone here had to have a plan." With that, I replaced my knife in its sheath and began walking over to Mystic. I climbed astride and without looking back, continued on the trail to the thieves' camp. The other men followed my lead, and after another minute, I noticed Erick had taken up the rear on the trail, the stolen coins jangling again in his saddlebag. Only when we had left that area of the road did I allow myself to breathe freely again.

It was late morning when we returned to the camp. Fried eggs and biscuits were prepared, and I forced them down only because one of the men I had saved from recruitment — the pockmarked thief — insisted on it. Fink sat beside me, full of questions about our adventures away from camp, and disappointed because I didn't answer any of them. His rat was back on his shoulder, eyeing my breakfast.

"You're family now," he said. "That's what the men are saying."

"I have no family." And if I did, they wouldn't be thieves.

Fink only chuckled at whatever thought was breezing through his brain. "Told the king you had the plague? Ha! When I'm your age I'll be just like you."

"Go away," I growled. "You don't want to be anything like me."

He was unconvinced, and continued to eat his meal by my side. After I'd finished, he pointed to a bedroll near some tents. "Erick said if you're tired, you can sleep there. I'm supposed to keep watch on you."

"I thought I was family."

He shrugged. "Erick just wants to make sure you're not the kind of family who runs when we're not looking."

"I'm not going to run, Fink."

"I know. But I'm supposed to watch you anyway."

True to his word, Fink parked himself on the ground with a direct view of my bedroll. I lay down and closed my eyes but sleep was impossible. After a short while, it must have looked like I was asleep because Erick approached Fink and whispered, "What do you make of him?"

There was a brief hesitation, then Fink said, "He's no ordinary thief, not like any of us."

"I agree. He didn't want Vargan to see his face. Why do you think that is?"

"Dunno. You said he'd be more open with me, because

we're both young. But he doesn't act young. And he doesn't tell me anything."

"He's probably seen a lot in his life, and learned to keep his secrets. But you were right — he is a good thief. Which means he must have some very interesting secrets. Keep an eye on him until I figure out what he really wants. I don't think he cares a devil's inch for the treasure inside that cave."

In fact, I cared plenty about it. Most of the wealth of Carthya was stored there. I'd let the pirates kill me before I told them where it was.

There was a backup plan. Before I left Drylliad, I'd asked Kerwyn to order extra soldiers to guard the cave. If I failed, I wanted to make sure nobody would get at Carthya's wealth. But if everything went well, my plan would be complete long before it came to having to reveal that location.

I finally drifted off to sleep, with a pit in my stomach reminding me that since the night of the funeral, nothing had gone well for me.

· TWENTY ·

The sounds of applause and cheering woke me later that afternoon. I sat up and brushed my hair out of my face. "What's going on?" I asked Fink.

He was standing on a rock and leaning over a tree branch to see something behind my tent. "A Queen's Cross game has started. Want to go watch?"

There was a serious risk of Fink dissolving into a puddle of disappointment if I didn't say yes, so after a long stretch of my arms I rolled to my feet and we walked to the field where several men were playing.

Queen's Cross is played with two teams, each seeking the other's flag, or "Queen," from behind their zone. Players fight for control of a leather ball stuffed with grains of wheat or rice. The ball can be kicked, carried, or thrown toward the other team's zone, but only with the ball can a player enter the zone to steal the Queen and win the game. Queen's Cross games are very physical, often laden with injuries, and always a lot of fun.

As we walked up to the field, I saw Erick throw the ball to someone farther down the field, who was immediately tackled to the ground. He waved at us, then tripped an opposing player trying to clear a path for his teammate. A few of the players had ridden with us to Harlowe's last night, and all of them encouraged me to come onto the field, but I still held back.

"Sage, join us!" Erick called. "We need another player."

"I'm not very good," I replied, which was perfectly true. I had enjoyed Queen's Cross as a child until I realized that the children of nobles who played with us had been instructed to let my brother and me win. Darius had tried to explain that this was the way of life for a prince and that it was the duty of the other boys to allow us the advantage. To demonstrate what I thought of the "advantage," I had climbed with the leather ball to the top of the chapel, then impaled it on a spire where it stood until my father ordered a hapless page to climb up and retrieve it. Queen's Cross was banned from the castle after that. Games were occasionally played while I was at the orphanage, but Mrs. Turbeldy discouraged them because they almost always ended in fistfights.

"Go on and play," Fink said. "You look like you want to."

I'd have had to be blind not to see the desire in his eyes to go onto the field. I called to Erick, "Fink's going to play with us too."

"That'll give us an extra man," Erick said.

"He's barely a boy, much less a man," I answered. "Let him play."

Just to get the game moving again, the other team gestured for Fink to come out with me. "Thanks," Fink said, clearly excited.

The game began as soon as we were close enough to take positions. Fink was knocked over immediately, but he signaled that he was fine and the players ran past him toward our zone. I dove into other players to stop their progress and their teammates tackled me down in return. One of them tugged at my shirt, revealing the injury I'd received in defending Nila three nights ago. We looked at each other, but I didn't recognize him from that night so I rolled away and rejoined the game.

After several minutes more of play, the other team called for a break so everyone could catch their breath. Erick huddled us into a circle and said, "They're getting tired. We should make another play for their Queen."

"We're tired too," a player next to me said. "We can't push through all of them."

"Yes, but they don't know that," I said. Everyone looked at me and in turn, I looked at Fink, then explained my idea.

The next time we got the ball near their zone, instead of only one strong man attempting to push through their team to get to the Queen, all of us made a run to go around their team, far down the field and away from their zone. All of us, but one.

When we were far enough away, Erick kicked the ball back to Fink, who was innocently waiting alone near the zone. He caught the ball and ran with it into the team's zone. The Queen was in his hand before most of our opponents even realized they'd been tricked.

My team members ran toward Fink to celebrate and Erick even put him on his shoulders. Fink's smile was so wide it practically stretched off his face. At one point, Fink looked down at me. He still had both the Queen and the ball in his hands. He saluted me with the Queen but kept the ball close to his chest.

I smiled up at him, though I felt a tinge of sadness. This place was all he knew, and yet for all his potential, Fink already seemed locked into this world where he had absolutely no chance of a future.

· TWENTY-ONE ·

The remainder of the afternoon was spent with Fink recounting to me every detail of his win against our opponents. It didn't matter that I was there and had seen every moment unfold, or that the strategy had been my idea to begin with.

"Did you see their faces when I got the Queen?" he said. "Now they're sorry."

"They're not sorry enough to ignore you now." I tilted my head at a few of the men who were walking by. "And if you don't hush up, they'll come over and show you how not sorry they are."

Fink laughed, but he did quiet down, at least until everyone passed us by.

I was sitting on a crate at the back side of the tent, looking out over the field where we had played. It was difficult to concentrate with Fink's relentless talk, but eventually he became background noise, just a louder version of a chirping bird.

The field was empty now. The grasses had been laid flat by more than one game played there, but in the center of it all, a single wildflower caught my attention. It was bright purple and stood erect where a hundred others around it had been smashed. I wondered if it had somehow escaped harm, or if it had been stepped on before but refused to lie down.

After a while, Erick came to see me. He propped a crate beneath himself, then dismissed Fink, who said he had to find some food for his rat anyway.

"I've been thinking about what you did this morning with King Vargan," he said.

I remained silent, though I had been thinking about it too. I felt lucky that it had worked out as well as it did, but that's all it was: luck. I couldn't hope to do what I needed to with the pirates based only on luck.

"How do you like it here, amongst my thieves?" Erick asked, changing tack.

"They're as fine a collection of liars, brutes, and criminals as I might've hoped to be kidnapped by."

"I think you wanted us to kidnap you from that tavern."

With a slight grin, I said, "Actually, I hoped the pirates would've taken me that night. It would've saved me some time."

"You're a living paradox, Sage." I felt the weight of his gaze as he added, "That bald man in the noble's house immediately knew who you were. He clearly respected your reputation as a thief, or at least, he wasn't happy to see you there."

"He definitely was surprised," I agreed.

"And for reasons you won't share, you are obviously not on friendly terms with the king. Why is that? Did you commit some crime against him?"

"No." Not yet anyway.

"Yet I've never heard of you. How is that possible?"

"I've spent my time in Carthya. I'm only here in Avenia because it's gotten too dangerous for me there."

"Ah. That's why you didn't want that noble to see your face. And why you couldn't leave the bald one there alive."

Not exactly, but Erick seemed content with his own explanation so I let him keep it.

"And if I bring you to the pirates tomorrow, will you go as their friend or enemy?"

"Neither," I said. "There's just nowhere else I can do what I have to do."

"To get that treasure?" Again, I didn't respond and Erick continued, "Listen, I'll do everything I can to get them to accept you, but they're always a dangerous group. More so in your case because there's no history between you and them."

I looked away, amused by the irony of his words. Erick didn't seem to notice. He continued, "It's not too late to change your mind. You think you want to be with the pirates, but I can sense your hesitation. Whatever you really want in your life, you could have it here."

He spoke closer to my heart than he realized. I thought about those things I wanted most, the freedom to be who I wanted, to go where I wanted, and to live a life of my own choosing. It was true. I could have that here, away from the politics and pretense of Drylliad. Away from endless duties and obligations, and even from the fear and anger that had driven me this far. Staying here would be so easy.

"Don't answer now," Erick said.

"I have to." The words took effort to force from my mouth. "Because if I don't, my answer might change and I can't risk that. I'm going with you tomorrow."

"Even if it means you'll never leave there again?"

"Yes, even if."

Erick smiled. "That was a test, Sage. Though for a moment, I thought you might accept my offer."

"For a moment, I thought so too."

Erick clapped me on the back when he stood. "I suppose that's the best I could ask for. Now go and get something to eat."

Instead, I returned to my bedroll. Fink came over and watched me a moment before asking, "You hungry?"

"Definitely," I said. "Get me some supper. I prefer to eat alone."

His face twisted. "I'm not a servant."

"Of course you are. Why do they give you shoes for their errands but not clothing for your freedom?"

He hunched down again. "Well, I'm not *your* servant."

"None of my usual servants are here. You'll have to do."

"You might run away."

"I'm starving," I protested. "If I'm going to run, it'll be after supper. Now go on."

He wasn't happy about it, but he obeyed and returned a few minutes later with a bowl of stew for each of us.

"Did you spit in mine?" I asked.

He looked offended. "No."

"It's what I would've done if you had spoken that way to me."

He smiled sheepishly. "Well, maybe I did a little."

I hid my own smile as I traded our bowls.

Fink was quiet for a moment as we ate, then said, "Do you think the men around here only consider me a servant boy?"

"Yes."

"What if I came with you and Erick tomorrow?"

I shook my head. "If you can't make it with the thieves, you'd never make it as a pirate."

Fink straightened his back. "I'd be a fine pirate. I have talents these thieves don't even know about."

"Yeah? What?"

"I can fake tears. Watch."

By the time I looked up, Fink already had tears streaming down his face. "It's just not fair," Fink cried. Literally, he did. "Maybe I'm young, but I deserve a chance."

"You're pathetic," I said, chuckling.

Instantly, Fink was smiling again. He wiped his tears with the back of his hand, leaving streak marks on his dirty face. "I once got a whole meat pie from a woman by using that trick."

"Try that with the pirates and they'll hang you up until you stop acting like a baby."

"No, seriously, Sage. I don't use it often but when I do, it works."

"Then may your talent for spontaneous tantrums earn you great glory and honor."

Fink knew I'd insulted him but didn't seem to care. Instead, he stirred his spoon around his bowl as he mumbled, "Erick said when you went to Libeth you killed a man. Is that true?"

"Whatever I did, he got a lot worse than he deserved," I said softly. In my mind, I pictured Mott's strained expression as I left. Not being able to follow me had to be torturing him.

"I didn't think you were capable of something like that."

"I'm not." And yet it was inevitable that I'd have to destroy the pirates.

Fink slowly exhaled. "Do you want to go to the pirates?"

I glanced over at him. "I have to go. That's different."

"You seem scared."

"Everyone gets scared at times. It's only the fools who won't admit it."

We were interrupted by Erick coming back over to join us. He crouched near me and said, "Will you join us around the fire, Sage? Everyone wants to hear your story about our adventures in Libeth."

I ignored his question and asked my own. "When do we go to the pirates?"

"I've been thinking about that. If I had time to know you better —"

"If time is what you need, then I'll leave tonight and find another way there," I said with total sincerity. "Time is a luxury I don't have."

He massaged his jaw. "Will you promise to give them the location of the cave? Because if I bring you there and you refuse to tell them, both our heads will roll."

I couldn't promise that, but with total sincerity I said, "I'll do whatever it takes to keep my head from rolling. And I'll try not to do anything that will cause them to detach yours."

Apparently that was enough. Stars seemed to dance in his eyes as he said, "All my life I've wanted a chance with the pirates. But I've never had anything worth offering them. Until now."

"So when do we leave?" I asked.

He thought for a moment, then made his decision. "At first light. I want to ride into camp as they climb from their beds. Devlin will be in his best mood then."

I handed my bowl to Fink and picked up my bedroll, dragging it into a nearby supply tent. "In that case, I want plenty of privacy for a good sleep. Morning will come early."

I lay down but never closed my eyes. I'd slept enough during the day that it wasn't too difficult to stay awake. The hard part was fighting the feeling of urgency to leave, to run while I had the chance.

When it was very quiet, I at last decided that I had to take the risk of going back to the church to meet Mott. He had been right from the beginning: This plan was madness. My earlier conversation with Fink festered inside of me. When it came to the moment, could I really do what was necessary to destroy the pirates? I'd taken a life once at Farthenwood, not intentionally and in defense of Imogen, and even then it had nearly broken me. The closer I got to the pirates, the more I saw the flaws in my plan. I needed Mott's help if I had any hope to succeed.

I propped myself up on one arm. Fink had settled in at the door of the tent as my vigil, but that wasn't my exit. I pulled up a corner flap of the tent and silently rolled beneath it.

What I did not expect was to roll into the body of another thief, who sat up and grabbed me by my collar. "Where do you think you're going?" he snarled.

"I've got to go," I said, fully prepared to launch into my usual explanation of having inherited my mother's pea-size bladder.

But he wasn't interested. He shoved me to the ground and lifted the tent flap. "Get back in there 'til Erick comes for you. Wake me up again and Erick won't have anyone left alive to get."

His terms weren't particularly in my favor so I rolled back under the tent. It was safe to assume any direction I went would have someone there as well, waiting for me.

I cursed and kicked at the tent pole, which startled Fink awake. I told him to go to sleep and stop bothering me, then sat with my back against the pole. It looked as if I would not see Mott tonight after all. I'd be going to the pirates alone.

· TWENTY-TWO ·

I was still seated against the pole when Erick came for me very early the next morning.

"Already awake I see?"

Awake and still furious. I didn't even look at him.

"I heard you tried to sneak out last night."

"Everyone else is permitted to move about as they'd like. Why not me?"

"Because you're not one of us yet."

"Then we're not going to the pirates."

"Why not?"

Now I looked at him. "If you don't trust me, how will you convince them to?"

Erick's face reddened. "Maybe I shouldn't trust you." He motioned with his arm and a man with a long scar on his right cheek entered the tent. I closed my eyes a moment, certain that if I listened carefully enough I'd hear the devils laughing at this new joke on me. He was the man who'd held the torch the night I fought to rescue Nila, and he clearly recognized me. I reluctantly stood to acknowledge him. His shoulder was visibly bandaged, which gave me some pleasure. So that's where I got him.

"Fendon returned to us last night," Erick said. "One of the men we played Queen's Cross with thought something was suspicious about you, so he asked Fendon to come see. Fendon said your horse looked familiar. Thinks you do too."

Fendon swaggered forward. Before I could stop him, he lifted up my shirt and showed the cut to Erick. "Yep, this is the boy I told you about. That's where I stabbed him."

"Stabbed?" I snorted at that. "You couldn't control your sword to do worse than scratch me."

"You forgot to tell me about attacking members of my family," Erick accused.

I quietly put a hand on my knife. "You forgot to ask."

Fendon reared back and hit me in the jaw. I tumbled to the ground but grabbed his shirt on the way and pulled him down with me. He landed on his wounded shoulder and grunted in pain. Then I withdrew my knife, putting it at Fendon's throat. "Maybe you should ask why they killed an innocent woman and nearly killed her young daughter?"

Erick's eyes widened. "They did what?"

"It's been too long since you participated in those Carthyan raids." Then I leaned in closer to Fendon. "And if you participate in any again, I'll find you."

Erick grabbed me by the shoulders and dragged me off the thief, then put a foot on his chest to keep him from coming after me. When Fendon signaled that he had calmed down, Erick told him to sit up. He kept his seat, but his glare was fierce and his fists remained tightly balled.

"We have rules here!" Erick said. "We're thieves, not murderers."

"Isn't that what he did in the noble's house last night, to that man?" Fendon pointed a stubby finger at me.

"If that man had escaped, he'd have called others to capture us," Erick said. "Sage saved all of us — twice — and he netted a fine profit besides. But what you did, that is inexcusable."

"It won't happen again." Fendon's pouting tone suggested he couldn't care less if it happened again. Then he addressed me. "You're one of us now?"

"A pea-brained maggot like you?" I said. "No, never. Erick and I are leaving today."

Fendon's lip curled. "I'll be waiting here when you get back. We have a score to settle."

"Get used to waiting. I'm not coming back." With that, I marched out of the tent.

I kept to myself while we completed our preparations to leave, although Erick made several attempts to ask about my part in the raid. I told him as little as possible, and nothing about Nila. It surprised me to find that he was nearly as bothered about the event as I had been.

"The pirates have a code about women and children," he said. "They don't touch them, not if they're innocents. It should be the thieves' code too."

"Maybe the code will protect me," I said. "Do I still count as a child?"

Erick tilted his head. "You don't count as an innocent."

Fink brought me an extra serving of breakfast soon after. "Not because I'm a servant," he pointed out when he handed me the bowl. "But just because we're friends, right?"

"Did you spit in it?"

"No."

"Then we're friends."

When it was time to leave soon after, Fink made a last-minute appeal to come with us. He didn't bring out the tears, so I suspected he'd already played that card.

"You'll be in the way," Erick said.

"I can help," Fink protested, but Erick shook his head.

"Erick doesn't have time to look after you," I said. "He's going to have enough trouble just watching me the whole time, making sure I don't run off."

Erick sighed, then he noticed my grin. "All right, you can come," he finally said to Fink. "But you're too young to become a pirate, so you'll only be there as my boy. And you will keep an eye on Sage any time I'm not around." Then he walked up to me as he untied his horse. "Don't think you've tricked me into taking him," he muttered. "I chose to bring him. He's useful to have around."

I chuckled lightly and mounted Mystic. "Here you go," Erick said, handing me a sword. "You earned this."

It was cheaply made and not weighted properly. Even if I

were only a thief, I still wouldn't have accepted it. I gave it back to him. "This isn't mine."

"But it's good enough for you."

I snorted. "Hardly."

He tried again. "Take this sword."

"I want the one I came here with."

"Why that one?"

"The stones in the handle match my eyes."

"Take this one or none at all." When it was clear I wouldn't accept the sword, Erick frowned at me, then kicked his horse forward, the rejected sword in his white-knuckled grip.

I prodded Mystic ahead as well, only I turned him toward the tent where they still kept my sword. Charging forward, I used my knife to slice through the tent fabric, flashed the blade at the startled thief inside, then grabbed my sword off the table. When I rode out again, Erick was waiting for me.

"You're incorrigible," he said.

"More than you know." I attached the sword and its scabbard around my waist, then said, "Shall we go?"

Erick continued to look at me. "I think I may grow to hate you before this is over."

"But you don't already and that's got to be some sort of record."

To my surprise, Erick laughed. Within minutes we had left the thieves' camp behind and were on our way to the pirates. Erick could barely contain his excitement.

"Tell me about the pirates," I said. "What I should expect."

"Who knows what they'll think of you. You're young, but they'll accept boys your age if they think you're useful. Devlin got in four years ago after making a deal to kill the younger prince of Carthya. He later killed the priest who was suspected of hiding that boy. Not long after, he became the pirates' king." He looked my way before adding, "Fink already told you about the priest, and I can see it upsets you now."

"I knew him once." Of course that was only half the reason that my fists were clenched and my heart was pounding.

"Is that going to be a problem?" Erick asked. "Because if it is —"

"No. *That* will not be a problem." I cocked my head. "How did Devlin become king?"

Erick brushed his hand through the air. "Any pirate can challenge the king to a sword fight. If he kills the king in the fight, then that pirate is immediately recognized as the new king."

"Has Devlin been challenged before?"

"Sure, but he's never lost. He's a fierce warrior and requires strict obedience to the pirate code."

I knew a little about the code, or at least, what the code had been many years ago when the book from the castle library was written. Most of the code related to the mandatory punishments for various wrongdoings. It struck me as odd that a group who made their living off criminal activity would have such strict discipline. But at the heart of the code was the order of loyalty: first to the pirate king, second to their comrades, and third to their home country of Avenia and its crown. If this was true, then it meant they would only follow King Vargan if it suited them. They could attack Carthya with or without Avenia's blessing.

Erick had continued speaking while my mind wandered. I began listening again as he said, "Besides, if the pirates are like my thieves, as long as you're fair, they're just as happy no matter who's in charge."

"What'll happen to the thieves, now that you've left?"

"Someone else will take over. I'm almost sorry you didn't accept my offer to stay, Sage. You seem to have the makings of a leader in you."

Laughter burst from my mouth. "I can provide a very long list of people who'd disagree with you." I imagined what Gregor would think if he knew I was here and not cowering in my bed at the castle. That led me to wonder for the hundredth time whether Amarinda really would keep from him the secret of who truly was there. But I had to push those worries away and concentrate on what lay ahead. "So what's the pirate camp like?"

"They call it Tarblade Bay, or just Tarblade, and it's a rather clever place. There're no marked roads to it, obviously, so the only way you'd know it's there is to pass close by it. And if you do, you're bound to be captured. Once a person discovers the camp, they never leave."

"Obviously," I said.

"Obviously," Erick echoed.

"How many pirates live there?"

"Hard to say. It could easily sleep a hundred, but there are always plenty out on the water, so I'm not sure how many there would be if they were all together. We'll likely see at least fifty there now, possibly more."

I glanced at Erick. "They say that no one returns from the pirates. But you have."

"I was there as a friend, and only left because they allowed it. It's outsiders who don't return, and if they make us pirates, we'll only leave by their permission."

That certainly complicated things. I said, "Tell me more about Tarblade Bay."

Erick nodded. "It exists on three elevations, all of it visible from the sea, but by the time a ship is close enough to see it, the pirates have spotted them. By land, only the highest level is visible, and all it appears to be is a cleared field surrounded by tall, thick trees. That's where they meet as a group. Down a little hill are the kitchen and various tents. But again, a traveler could pass right beside it and not know any of it was there, unless they heard noises."

"Obviously."

Erick was less amused this time. "Do you want to know this or not?" I shrugged and he continued. "There's a steep path that leads from the living areas down to the beach below. It's a cliff wall along most of that beach otherwise. Backed against the cliff wall are places for everyone to sleep, except for the senior pirates up on top."

"That's where we'll sleep, then," I said, "by the beach."

"You'll love it," Erick said. "Each wave hitting the shore is another note in a lullaby."

With that we fell into silence. Although I had to admit an excitement to sit beside the sea again, I was nervous about meeting the pirates. Everything I cared about hinged on my success, and at this point, failure seemed far more likely. It was several hours later when Erick halted our group and pointed ahead. From our position there was very little evidence of anyone living here, yet Erick proudly announced, "Welcome to Tarblade."

· TWENTY-THREE ·

As we rode farther into Tarblade Bay, our reception was as frosty as I'd expected. Pirates dressed mostly in black peered around corners of huts or from beneath their low-brimmed hats. A few of them withdrew whatever weapon they carried and slunk toward Erick, Fink, and me. A quick glance at my companions told me they felt just as anxious as I did. There were far too many ways for this moment to go wrong.

Erick held out his sword, blade down, then signaled for me to do the same. Fink had snagged the sword I'd refused, but it looked large for him and he struggled to manage it with only one hand.

The expressions on the pirates' faces ranged from unfriendly to murderous, with more of them in the latter category than I'd have liked. They looked rougher than most other men I'd ever encountered and were more sordid than any description I'd read about them. I wondered if Devlin was amongst them and how I'd respond when we met. I could hardly think his name without a surge of anger inside me.

As the pirates got closer, one of them recognized Erick. Perhaps this man had been stretched too often as a child, because everything about him seemed long: his height, his face, his nose. His cobalt blue eyes were too close together, but at least they'd escaped the stretching, and his thin dark hair fell like twine and came almost to his shoulders. When he saw us, his face widened into a grin. "Erick, my friend! How long has it been?"

"Too long, Agor. Too long." Erick replaced his sword, then dismounted. Gesturing, he said, "This is Fink, an errand boy of mine" — I noticed Fink blink at that — "and this is a new member of my family, Sage."

I tried to look like whatever Agor would expect to see as he studied me.

"Are you Avenian?" Agor asked. "What's your history?"

"He's Avenian," Erick answered for me. "But his reputation was made in Carthya."

Agor raised an eyebrow and with a chuckle I added, "Trust me, I am very well known in Carthya."

Agor considered that, then said to Erick, "Why have you come?"

"To talk to Devlin. I have a proposal for him."

"Devlin won't return until this afternoon. You can tell me your proposal."

Erick hesitated. He didn't want Agor to get the credit for our news, but he couldn't refuse a direct request either. Finally, with a smile, he made the only choice he could. "Of course, my friend. But I'd rather we spoke in private."

"You make me curious." Agor motioned that they should walk down the hill, to where the huts were located. Fink and I slid off our horses with the intention of joining the meeting, but Agor held up a hand. "Not you two. I don't know you yet."

"But it's my idea he wants to tell you about," I protested.

"It's only talk," Erick said calmly. "You and Fink wait here for me."

"Not here." Agor gestured to a couple of men behind us. "Lock them up."

I went for my knife but Erick got to me quickly and put a steadying hand on my arm. "It's just until I talk to them. Let them have your weapons."

"If we decide you're all right, you'll get these back," Agor said as I reluctantly handed my knife and sword to the men.

"What if you decide I'm not?"

Agor grinned, revealing gaps between several of his teeth. "Then you won't need these weapons where you're going."

"Come this way," a black-haired pirate said, using my own sword to guide Fink and me deeper into Tarblade.

The prison wasn't far from the hut where Agor and Erick went to meet, but it was mostly dug into the ground, with only a small iron-barred window near the roof for air and light. The room itself was tiny and lined with stale earth or rusty bars. Beyond that a chair had been placed, where the black-haired pirate was to be our vigil.

"How long do you think we'll be in here?" Fink asked.

"Dunno." I pulled at the bars blocking the window, but they were firm.

"Pull all you want. You wouldn't be the first to try escaping." The man stood as if someone had caught his attention and went up the steps. I couldn't hear the conversation at first, until he said something about us being fine as we were.

Then a female voice said, "Agor wants them treated like guests. I've got some water here to refresh them."

At the first word, my heart had stopped cold in my chest, for it was a voice that I knew as well as my own. But only seconds later, before I could even begin to grasp what it might mean, Imogen walked down the stairs.

She avoided my eyes, but clearly wasn't surprised to see me. True, several people knew the pirates and I had unfinished business, but it was also supposed to be true that a person couldn't just find the pirates. They had to let the pirates find them. How was she here?

"Will you keep an eye on these two while I'm at the outhouse?" our vigil asked. "They shouldn't be any trouble."

"Of course." As the man ran up the stairs, Imogen turned to us. "Agor doesn't want you mistreated. So how are you?"

The question was so simple I almost couldn't comprehend it. All I could do was stare at her with my mouth hung open. Imogen's servant braid had returned, as had her far more humble clothes, a muslin chemise with a brown overdress that laced up the front. Back at the castle she'd said she would leave as she came, but I'd had no idea then how literally she'd meant it.

"We're fine," Fink said.

I caught Imogen's eye, but only for a moment before she looked away. Had she volunteered to bring us the food so that I would know she was here, or had she come reluctantly, and only on orders?

"The pirates rarely get visitors," she said. "So we were all surprised when you rode in."

Fink pointed to me. "He has something for them."

"Ah. And what could a ragged boy like him have that's worth offering Avenian pirates?"

Fink looked at me, unsure of whether he should answer her. I was too consumed with questions about Imogen to care if he did or not. She had been in my court only five days ago. To be here now, she must have come directly to Tarblade, and yet I couldn't believe she had any prior connection to the pirates. There were very few people in this world whom I trusted completely. Imogen was one of them.

She smiled at Fink. "Is your friend a mute, or is he just pretending that he can't speak? What's his name?"

"Oh, he can speak plenty, though most of it's not very nice. His name is Sage."

Imogen's cheery expression deflated when she looked at me. "Really? Something so familiar?" A frown formed as she dropped the pretense of being a stranger to me. "That can't be your name."

Fink looked from Imogen over to me, and back to her

again. Clearly confused, he asked, "Do you know each other?"

Recovering, Imogen shook her head, dismissing our friendship as coldly as I had rejected her back at the castle. "I once knew someone who looks like him. But no, I don't know this boy at all."

"I demand to know what's happening," I finally said, sounding as angry and confused as I felt.

"Your friend has a harsh tone to his voice," Imogen said to Fink. "Does he always talk that way?"

"Yes," he said. "I warned you."

"Then tell him he's in no position to demand anything from me," she said.

Fink looked over as if to tell me that, then saw my hands already in fists and wisely decided against it. Obviously, she was still upset for how I'd sent her away. But if this was her idea of revenge, it made no sense. Why was she here?

Fink said, "I didn't think they let girls become pirates."

"I'm only hired help," Imogen said. "We work in the kitchen mostly and serve the food." Then she looked back at me. "But I hope my time here is very short."

It would be. I'd make sure of that.

"Can you explain why your friend keeps staring at me?" she asked Fink. "Does he know how rude that is? How *obvious* it is?"

Fink giggled. "Maybe he likes you."

"Maybe I think this is no place for you," I said.

"As if a boy like you would ever care about me." She dipped a ladle into a bucket of water and held it out for Fink, who eagerly drank. Then she put the ladle back in the bucket and moved to leave.

"None for me?" I asked.

She frowned. "Not until I can see some humility in you. From now on, you'll speak politely to me, like a true friend, or not speak at all." And as our vigil returned to his post, she whisked herself upstairs.

There was a brief silence before Fink said, "Wow, she really hates you."

I ignored him and instead used a small stool in the room to prop myself up high enough to see out the window again.

"What do you see?" Fink asked.

"Stop talking and let me think!"

"This is why people don't like you," Fink said. "You're lucky I'm more patient."

There she was, crossing away from the prison. She paused as if she could feel me watching her, then stopped and turned around. She marched to the bars and held the water bucket by the handle and base, then without warning splashed it all in my face.

"Stop staring at me, filthy thief," she said.

I fell backward off the stool, with the top half of my body soaked. Both Fink and the vigil launched into fits of laughter.

"Never seen the flower girl so upset," the vigil said.

I wiped my hair off my face. "Flower girl?"

"She's only been here a day or two, but so far she has spent every free moment collecting flowers in the woods and replanting them around the camp. Says they beautify the place, but I think just having her here does that. Don't you?"

Rather than answer, I considered reaching through the bars to choke him. She was nearly half his age.

"Devlin wouldn't let her plant them at first, but then he decided why not?"

I knew why not. Because she had no business being here.

"That's the most I've heard her say yet," the vigil continued. "Something about you really offends her."

"Yep, she definitely hates you," Fink agreed.

I shook my head to get rid of the dripping water, but a small flash of metal nearby caught my attention. Imogen hadn't only thrown water at me. She had hidden something in the bucket, a hairpin. I palmed it and let it fall into my boot. It probably wouldn't be too much longer before the pirates released me, but if they didn't, Imogen had given me a way through the locked doors.

Maybe she didn't hate me so much after all.

· TWENTY-FOUR ·

We remained in the cell for several hours. I was going mad in the confined space and began pacing in circles like a caged animal. What could be taking so long?

At least I had a confirmation that Imogen was on my side. I wasn't sure how she knew I'd be coming here, but I was furious she had inserted herself into my plans. Her presence here made everything more complicated.

"Calm down," Fink said through a wide yawn. "Erick will take care of us."

"I never trust anyone to take care of me," I muttered.

"Well, you should. That's why you came to us in the first place, right? You couldn't do this alone."

"Sit down," the vigil said. "You're making me nervous."

I was in no mood to take orders from someone like him. "Why don't you go find Agor and tell him I'm no good to the pirates locked up down here?"

"Tell me that yourself," Agor said, walking down the stairs.

I stared at him a moment. "It'd only be repetitive now."

"Erick and I had a long talk about you. He says you're a thief."

"I'm a lot of things."

His eyes passed over me. "Can you fight? It was a fine sword you had."

"It's an excellent sword," I agreed. "And I'm a very good thief."

"Ah." Agor took the keys from the vigil and unlocked my cell door. He shook his head for Fink to remain where he was but held the door open for me to leave.

"Walk with me," Agor said.

I fell in beside him once we stepped outside. The sleepy morning had blossomed into a bustle of activity. It was hard to know how many pirates lived here, but Gregor had been right in one thing: If the pirates and Avenian armies combined, my Carthyan soldiers wouldn't stand a chance.

As we walked, Agor pointed out the various areas of Tarblade Bay. Everything was exactly as Erick had described it, with the meeting area farther up the hill, living area surrounding me, and sleeping areas on the beach below me. So other than a few details, I already knew the layout.

"Where are we going?" I asked.

"Erick insists you know where Carthya stores its treasure. But if you have access to all this gold, why come to Tarblade? You know you'll lose all of it to us."

I smiled. "It got me here, didn't it?"

"Do you think you can handle the life of a pirate?"

"I'd suggest you ask whether the pirates can handle me."

Agor cocked an eyebrow, but still looked doubtful. "You claim to be a good thief. I want to see that for myself." He pointed to the jail. "Go back there. Let's see if you can steal the keys from the vigil and get your friend out without anyone stopping you."

I shook my head. "Fink has this habit of getting on my nerves. I'm afraid I have no motivation to get him out."

"Ah. And what is your motivation?"

"Hunger. Let me steal some food from the kitchen."

"Too easy."

"Maybe, but I'm going to steal the food anyway so it should count for something."

Agor smiled. "There's a meat cleaver in the kitchen. It's well looked after since some of our other knives have gone missing recently. Take whatever food you want, but bring me that knife."

I nodded and started to run off. Agor called behind me, "Be quick about it. I'm timing you."

I slipped into the kitchen through a side window. The interior was sturdily built and amply stocked. The main room contained everything necessary to cook and prepare meals for an entire crew of pirates. Considering how well the exterior was concealed from view, it was actually quite impressive.

As I had hoped, Imogen was working there, kneading a large pile of dough. But she wasn't alone. A dark-haired girl was washing dishes and another fair-haired one was tending a stew over an open fire. Imogen heard me enter and turned, momentarily, then went back to the dough. The dark-haired girl's face lit up when I entered but the other girl barely paid me any attention at all.

"Agor asked me to gather some food for him," I said to no one in particular.

Imogen stared at the other two girls, then threw up her hands. Whether she was actually irritated or pretending, I wasn't sure. "Oh, all right, I'll get it for you," she said. "Come with me."

I followed her down some stairs into a small room stocked with fruits and vegetables. As soon as she shut the door, I turned her toward me and hissed, "Tell me why you're here."

"I might ask you the same thing. Jaron, are you insane? They will find out who you are."

"If they do, then you'll be found out too. How did you even get here? Do you know what it took for me to get here?"

"It's easier for a girl. I went to Isel and inquired about doing kitchen work. I asked around until someone said the pirates were always looking."

"They're always looking because no respectable girl would ever come here."

"I'm perfectly respectable and don't you dare suggest otherwise!" Imogen bit into her words with the same fierce anger as I felt. "Besides, they don't touch us. Not as long as I do my work and stay out of their business."

"But you're not staying out of their business, and you're not safe here. Why do you think I sent you away from Drylliad?"

"That's obvious." She folded her arms. "It's because you're arrogant, and can't trust anyone but yourself, and because you're a fool."

A smile crept onto my face. "Well, I wouldn't have worded it exactly like that."

She was less amused. "I came because you can't be alone here. You need help, even if you don't understand that yet."

"If that's true, then I don't want that help from you. You should have trusted my decision!"

Imogen's face reddened. "You dare speak to me about trust? I appreciate your looking out for my safety back at the castle, but the way you did it is inexcusable. Why couldn't you have trusted me with the truth?"

Unfortunately, there was a very good reason for that. I lowered my eyes and said, "It's because I needed you to believe me too. I needed you to go and never look back."

She fell silent and her lashes fluttered while she considered how to answer. Finally, she said, "I did believe you, until Amarinda and I began discussing the assassination attempt. Knowing you as well as I do, the rest of your plan became obvious then, as did your reasons for sending me away so cruelly."

"Forgive me." She probably couldn't, and I wouldn't blame her for that. "Everyone was supposed to think I was going into hiding."

"But anyone who knows you would never believe it." She paused and read the question in my expression. "You never run,

Jaron. Not from Conner, not from a sword fight, and certainly not from your own castle. You wouldn't run, so we knew you must be using it as an excuse to come here."

That stoked my anger. "If you knew all that, then you knew I was trying to get you away from the danger. And yet here you are in the center of it! Aren't you afraid?"

"Of course I am. But not for me." She knitted her eyebrows together. "Amarinda thinks you're going to try stopping the pirates on your own. Exactly how do you plan to do that?"

I stuck out my jaw but refused to answer, mostly because the details of that plan were still a little vague. Instead I said, "As your king, I order you to leave this place."

"I'm already under orders. I'm not to leave here without you."

"Amarinda's orders?" That was infuriating.

"She asked me to do whatever I could to help you be safe. She said you wouldn't listen to anyone else, but maybe I could get you to leave before it's too late." Imogen arched her neck. "If you force me to choose which order to obey, it'll be hers. Because she's right. You shouldn't be here."

No words could describe the anger I felt. I'd known Amarinda and Imogen had become friends, but this felt nearly as disloyal as Gregor asking for a steward.

Imogen reached out, but I turned away from her. Then it occurred to me that too much time had passed since I left Agor. "If you're here to help me, then I need the meat cleaver from the kitchen. And if anyone asks, you've got to say that I stole it."

Imogen rolled her eyes, then opened the door to leave.

I grabbed her arm as she started to walk out and said, "This isn't over between us."

"No," she said with equal ferocity. "It's not."

I returned to Agor a few minutes later and handed him the cleaver. In my other hand was a warm roll. He grinned. "Did you have any trouble?"

"The cleaver was easy. Getting past one of your girls was a little more work."

"Leave them alone, or it'll be the last thing you do here. Follow me." Agor led me into a small, dark hut. I paused in the doorway, seeing several other pirates already crowded into the room. Erick was there too, but he barely looked at me. That wasn't a good sign.

"Sit." Agor pulled out a chair in front of a small table.

I sat. My hand brushed against my belt where I hoped my knife or sword would have magically appeared, but of course they weren't there. I wished I'd kept the cleaver, but Agor had it and held it in a way that made me uncomfortable. Had Erick failed to convince them to accept me?

Agor pointed to a man sitting directly opposite me. He was of average height but built like a boulder. Numerous scars defined his years as a pirate and gave him authority over the other men. His brown hair was streaked in gold tones and wasn't half as well trimmed as his beard. But it was his eyes I focused on. They were slits of blackness that made him appear completely devoid of any soul.

"Sage," Agor said. "This is Devlin, our king."

I stared at him while blood rushed through my veins. Remembering everything he'd done, venomous emotions rose inside me, and it was all I could do to keep an even expression on my face. The only way to save Carthya was to bring down the pirates, starting with Devlin. And in that moment, I was certain that I was capable of it.

Devlin offered me his hand to shake. I stretched mine out tentatively. Devlin took it, then slammed my arm down on the table. Instantly, Agor got behind me with one arm locked around my neck and his other hand holding the cleaver to my throat. I arched my head away from the blade, but that only gave him a reason to tighten his grip.

"Your name is Sage?" Devlin asked.

"Will there be a lot of questions?" I countered. "If so, you might give me space to breathe."

Devlin nodded at Agor, who loosened his hold, but the cleaver was still closer to me than I liked.

"You have strong forearms, Sage."

"I inherited them from my grandmother. She was a bulky woman."

He smiled at the joke, then said, "That's good to know. Because otherwise I'd think you spent a lot of time with that heavy sword you brought here."

"That's only for when I need to stab someone."

This time, Devlin didn't smile. He said, "I heard you were upset by my killing that priest years ago."

"That's true." My eyes shifted from Devlin to Erick, who

motioned with his hands that I should explain myself. "But not nearly as upset as I'd be if you killed me right now."

That seemed to entertain Devlin. "Did you know that priest?"

"Yes."

"How?"

"He took me in for a while."

"He also betrayed my trust." Devlin looked around the room to be sure everyone was watching him. They were. "That's why he had to die. Does that bother you?"

The blade was sharp against my skin. It was hard to concentrate on what Devlin was saying, but I mumbled, "Yes."

A map of Carthya was spread across the table. I shifted to see it better, then winced as the blade nicked me. Maybe Agor hadn't been paying close enough attention. Or maybe he wanted me to remember what was at stake.

"Show me where the cave is," Devlin said.

I looked away from the map. "No."

Devlin looked up at Agor. "Kill him."

Agor raised the blade. I tried to squirm free, but with Agor's hold on my neck and Devlin's grip on my hand, it wasn't that simple. With my free hand, I grabbed Agor's arm, and quickly added, "You need me to find that cave. And I'll get us there better if my head's still attached."

Devlin shook his head ever so slightly at Agor, then refreshed his grip on me and said, "Erick thinks that given the chance, you might try to kill me in revenge for what I did to that priest."

My heart was still racing, but I kept my eyes locked on him as I answered, "Yeah, I might." It was hard not to think about the priest when I looked at him.

Devlin reached over and patted my cheek. "Good answer, young thief. Had you answered any other way I'd have killed you just now for lying." I pulled away from his touch, and he withdrew his hand. Then he said, "It'll take us a few days to prepare to steal the Carthyan treasure. We'll get our hands on it before Avenia takes it for themselves."

"I didn't know Avenia wanted it," I said.

"Avenia intends to bleed Carthya out of existence. And I need enough pirates to get my piece of the country first. So welcome to my crew."

I cocked an eyebrow, suspicious. "It's that simple?"

The others around me laughed, including Devlin. "Becoming a pirate is simple. The trick is whether you can remain one. For now, all you must do is swear to me."

I eyed Devlin. "Swear to what exactly? Swear to serve you or bow to you? I won't do either."

"Sage!" Erick's scolding wasn't a surprise, except that I had expected it to come much sooner. He shook his head in warning at me.

Devlin only raised a corner of his mouth. "You have the heart of a pirate, that's clear. When the time comes, I want your promise to reveal the location of that cave. And you must swear loyalty to the pirate code. From now on, you will serve out your life as a pirate, which means you will never leave Tarblade without the permission of the pirate king. Swear that you will always obey the pirate king's orders. If you fail to do so, you will face the cruelest method of death."

I closed my eyes to work through everything he was asking of me. Refusing to swear loyalty would undoubtedly mean I'd face death now. But I had come here to destroy the pirates. Could I accept those terms?

"Give me your answer, Sage," Devlin said.

"Be quiet and let me think." A moment later, I opened my eyes and nodded. "I swear."

Devlin gestured at someone behind me, but based on the charred smell that had entered the hut I already knew what was coming next. Agor lowered the knife but his arm remained around my neck. Devlin's grip on my hand tightened, and two pirates grabbed my arms, pressing them onto the table. Sweat creased my brow. It was a good thing they held me so firmly because it was possible I would've tried to escape otherwise.

A fat pirate who reeked of smoke stood between Devlin and me. In his hands was a branding iron, red at the tip.

"Keep still," he said. I started to object, but Agor shoved a piece of wood between my teeth and held it there as the man pressed the hot end onto my forearm.

I screamed as it seared my flesh and tried to pull away from it, but their hold was uncompromising. A second later he was finished and someone else immediately covered my arm with a cold rag.

They continued to hold me until I'd recovered enough

strength not to pass out. I lifted the rag and stared at the imprint burned into my skin, an X constructed of a sea serpent angled to the northeast and a snake angled to the northwest. The symbol of a pirate's ability to create terror on land or sea.

"Congratulations," Devlin said, finally releasing my hand. "You belong to the pirates now."

· TWENTY-FIVE ·

Erick was the first to reach me after I'd left the hut. He clapped me on the back and grinned. "You are the most reckless young man I've ever met. A couple of times I was certain he was going to let Agor have you."

"I thought so too." The rag had become too warm to be useful for the pain in my arm, but I kept it pressed there anyway. "I didn't know about the branding iron."

"Better the iron than the cleaver. You swore to me that you'd reveal the location of the cave."

"But on my timing, not theirs."

Erick glared at me, but there was nothing more he could say. We both knew that if I'd told them where the cave was, I wouldn't have left that hut alive.

Agor was next at my side. "No one's ever spoken to Devlin like that before. But the crazy thing is I think he admired it."

"What now?" I asked.

Agor began leading me down a path. "We eat first. Then Devlin will want to test some of your skills."

"Fink's still locked up. Is he going to that hut now?" I'd put up any fight necessary to keep him from getting branded.

Erick shook his head. "Fink's too young. Maybe in a few years."

"We let him out," Agor added. "He'll join us at the meal."

Minutes later we arrived near the kitchen, where several long tables were set up for meals. Fink was already waiting at one and motioned for us to join him. Apparently, he'd already heard what had happened inside the hut because as soon as he saw me he leapt to his feet and grabbed my arm. "Congratulations!"

I yanked it away with a gasp as his fingers inadvertently pressed near the burn. Fink's eyes widened when he saw the branding, maybe with a new appreciation for what it meant to become a pirate.

"Yes, congratulations." I turned to see Imogen standing behind us. She held a large pot with a ladle inside and must have been dishing up stew for the other men. "You got what you wanted, then?"

I barely looked at her. "You know what I want."

"And you know how to get it." Imogen frowned at me and moved on without putting any stew into my bowl.

Fink had a full bowl and grinned at me as he sat back on the bench. "It would help if you used words like *please* and *thank you*."

"Then I'll thank you to please stay out of my business," I said, squeezing my way onto the bench.

The dark-haired girl I'd seen earlier came by a minute later with another pot of stew. "You're new here?" she asked, ladling a large scoop into my bowl. "I'm Serena."

"Stay away from him." Imogen instantly appeared beside Serena.

"I was just saying hello."

"He's the one I told you about, when he came to the kitchen."

Serena raised her eyebrows. "Yes, I know." Imogen's warning only seemed to improve her opinion of me.

I tilted my head, not sure exactly what Imogen had accused me of, but it had obviously worked to divert any suspicion away from us.

"He did that before he had to obey the code, so it's forgivable," Serena said, letting Imogen lead her away. I thought I caught her whisper afterward, "He's handsome. I wouldn't have complained if he'd tried that with me." That made me smile a little.

Beside me, Fink snickered. "What'd you do?"

"I wish I knew." Then to avoid any more questions, I began eating.

The pirates around us talked, ate, and laughed voraciously. Erick and I were included in the conversation like we were old friends, although Erick was far more engaged in talking with them than I cared to be. For once, it was nice to have Fink nearby so that his incessant chatter could fill the void.

I kept an eye on Imogen as she served the pirates their

various requests, although I also made an effort not to appear too obvious about it. Both of us were newcomers and I'd already been too indiscreet when she came to the jail. As it was, she was probably all right as long as everyone believed her displeasure with me was due to some misbehavior on my part.

As soon as lunch was over, Agor escorted me to an area that had been cleared of grass and where the ground had become nearly as hard as stone. Long nails had been pounded into the trees, and hanging from them were a variety of wooden swords.

I backed away from the swords. "I came here as a thief, Agor, not a fighter."

Agor picked out a sword for himself. "A pirate is both. Devlin wants to test your skills."

"Did he test Erick?"

"Yes, as a matter of fact," Erick said, walking up to join us. Several other pirates had come with him. I couldn't see the area where we'd eaten, but I assumed Imogen had remained there to clean up. That was probably a good thing. She wouldn't want to watch this.

"Choose a sword," Agor said.

I walked to the trees and looked the swords over as if it were the first time I'd seen any. It was probably too generous to refer to them as swords. Really they were little more than thick sticks with handles on them.

After a moment, Agor became impatient and grabbed one off the tree nearest to me. He thrust it into my hands. "Here."

Agor raised his sword and I raised mine. My feet were

braced beneath me but it had to be Agor who made the first strike. When he did, he struck hard against my shoulder and threw me off balance.

"What are you waiting for?" he asked. "Fight!"

"My mistake." I rubbed my shoulder, certain a bruise was already forming there. "I didn't know we'd started."

I swung back at him but missed entirely. He feinted left, which was ridiculous since I wasn't being aggressive enough to need to be tricked, then came at me from the right. I blocked most of it, but took a blow to my arm.

Around us, what began as a largely indifferent audience quickly turned into laughter and hollers for me to be taught a lesson. They further encouraged Agor, who seemed to like the idea of using my poor performance to showcase his abilities. He got in three or four hits at me for every one I attempted at him. Occasionally I'd find a mark, but frankly, he hit hard and I was quickly losing enthusiasm for this charade.

Finally, he struck me in the back hard enough to force the air from my lungs. I dropped my sword. "Enough."

"You're not very good," Agor said.

"I never told you I was."

Agor surveyed me a moment. "I guess we expected more. The last boy to join the pirates was about your age and he's amazing."

That would be Roden, who was probably nearing the end of his time at sea. I replaced my sword on the tree, then said, "What now?"

"If you're smart, you'll stick around here and get in some sword practice."

"And what if I'm not?"

Agor shrugged, clearly disappointed. "I admit that I'm relieved you're this bad at swords. The way you threatened Devlin earlier, I thought maybe you meant what you said."

I had meant it. Every word.

Agor stepped closer to me and continued, "You should know that I watch Devlin's back. And someone's watching mine. And so on down the line. But nobody's watching your back here, so if you try to carry out that threat, it'll be the last thing you do aboveground. You understand me?"

I understood perfectly. If I went after Devlin, I would follow him to my grave.

Agor left me there, taking most of the pirates with him. As they strode away, I saw Imogen carrying some flowers toward a tree. She shook her head at me and I turned my back on her. I refused to allow her to think I needed her help. When I looked a moment later she was gone.

Erick and Fink had also stayed behind with me.

"You were terrible out there," Fink said.

"Thanks." It was too bad I'd been rewarded with so many bruises, because otherwise my performance would have made a funny story one day.

"What about my thieves in Carthya that night?" Erick asked. "You fought them."

I grinned. "Clearly, they're worse than I am."

"You must've caught them off guard. Because a person would almost have to try in order to be as bad as you were just now."

Not *almost*. "How'd you do against Agor?" I asked.

Erick shrugged. "He's good with a sword, but he's not great. I held my own."

"You should teach me some of your tricks."

Erick laughed at that. "There's no trick, Sage. You just need more discipline. And a great deal of practice."

"The practice I can do, but nobody's ever been much good at disciplining me."

Erick began to explain himself, then gave up. He pulled out Harlowe's pocket watch to check the time and thrust it back into his pocket.

"You should be more careful with that," I said.

"It's not as valuable as I thought before," Erick said. "Too many scratches and dings on it. Next time I'm in town I'll have them melt it down and sell it for the gold."

Not if I could help it.

We spent the rest of the afternoon exploring the camp. Near the cooking areas, a hearty freshwater stream fell over the cliff down to the beach. Erick pointed out that I was beginning to smell and suggested I consider washing up there. I told him it had taken a lot of work to smell as badly as I did and I wasn't about to ruin it with a bath. I didn't get around to mentioning that the scars on my back would be visible if I bathed, which at the least would invite questions about my past, and at the worst would reveal who I was.

Once down on the beach, I found a comfortable spot facing the sea and stopped exploring. After a while, Erick and even Fink gave up on me and left to find something better to do, but I was content to sit there and stare. It was calming in a way I very much needed, because it was becoming increasingly difficult to fight the feeling that something was going to happen soon. Something I wouldn't be able to control.

· TWENTY-SIX ·

Sometime late that afternoon, I wandered to the upper part of Tarblade Bay, hoping to find Imogen and try again to make her leave. But my attention was diverted by a ship entering the harbor below. It was unlike the pirate-marked schooners already in the harbor, and yet by the comments of others near me, they recognized several of the men on board. Obviously, this ship had been captured.

I made my way to the top of the hillside where I had a better view. Yet from my distance and without a scope, it was difficult to discern crew from pirates. It was true that pirates had an annoying habit of wearing black and that their general grooming was ragged at best, but these were hardly unique traits amongst many Avenians.

Agor walked up beside me and sighed with pleasure. "That ship looks profitable, don't you think?"

"Where's the crew?" I asked.

"Probably dead," Agor said casually. "If not now, they soon will be, right?"

He laughed, then looked frustrated that I didn't share in

his joke. His tone turned nasty as he said, "Devlin only made you a pirate because of his greed. If it was up to me, you'd never have left that jail alive. Despite the stories Erick told us, I doubt you have the courage for this life."

"It doesn't take much courage to attack what's clearly a peaceful ship," I said, nodding at the ship in the harbor.

A cheer rose up amongst the pirates on land as the men on the boat dumped a body onto the beach. He was moving, but he appeared to be the only crewman they'd left alive.

"What'll happen to him?" I asked Agor.

Agor looked at me as if I had moss for brains. "No one leaves Tarblade."

Devlin had seen the ship too and stationed himself near Agor and me while the crewman was dragged up the steep hillside trail. Once he was dropped at Devlin's feet, I finally got a good look at him.

He was probably in his fifties with a shock of gray hair sticking out from a wide-brimmed hat that identified him as one of the ship's officers. He had the remnants of a bloody nose and a swollen black eye. And despite his attempts to look defiant, he was clearly terrified.

"Who's this?" Devlin asked.

"My name is Swifty Tilagon," the man said. "Ship's navigator."

Devlin swatted him across the cheek. "When I want to hear from you, I'll speak to you!"

Agor stepped forward with papers given to him by one of

the men who'd helped capture the ship. "It's only rocks for cargo."

"Not rocks," Tilagon corrected. "I transport metals for a mine in the south. Copper and lead and whatever else we find."

"Transport it where?"

"To Isel, to sell it. Please release me. That cargo represents several months of labor. Hundreds of men are waiting for their pay."

Inwardly, I groaned. Did he have to tell them its value?

Devlin gestured to the pirates. "My men have been waiting for their pay too. I believe we need these metals more than anyone in Isel." Then he nodded at Agor. "Kill this man, then unload his ship."

The man yelped but by then I had pushed my way to the front of the crowd. "You should think bolder, Devlin."

His glare turned on me, daring me to have a suggestion worth challenging him.

I could only hope that I did. "You have the opportunity to steal from this man twice. Send some pirates to Isel with him tomorrow disguised as his crew. They can sell the rocks, take his payment, and then kill him. If you send enough pirates, you'll have fighting power to keep the cargo too."

With his greedy appetite whetted, Devlin grinned. He pointed to a blond, curly-haired pirate who couldn't have been much older than me. "Tie this man up. We'll fetch him again in the morning."

"Why not put him in the jail?"

"I've already got a couple of men in there cooling off for the night. Just tie him to a tree. There's enough of us around he won't be able to do anything."

There was nothing more I could do now. Tilagon spat on my boots when I walked past him to leave. I stopped and he said, "It wasn't enough to kill my men. Now you'll steal from our investors too. Of all these miserable vultures, you are the worst."

"I saved your life," I said.

"Only for another day."

"Then use it well. Even a day is valuable around here."

"I'll use it to beg the devils to curse you."

"Get in line," I said coolly. "Do you think you're the first?"

Then I wandered to the dinner tables with the other pirates. Erick caught up to me on the way. "It was a good idea back there. At least, Devlin was pleased with you."

"I don't care a devil's inch about what Devlin thinks of me."

Erick glanced around to see if anyone had overheard. "You should. Because whether you like him or not, he's king here." I snorted my contempt, but Erick grabbed my arm to turn me back to him. "Who are you to look down on him? You're no one, Sage. And you won't get anywhere with that attitude."

"Good advice," I said, fully agreeing that my attitude wasn't going to endear me to Devlin.

Dinner wasn't much different than lunch had been. It was loud, boisterous, and obnoxious. I watched for Imogen but only caught a glimpse of her carrying dishes back to the kitchen from where the other serving girls left them as they busied themselves with different tasks.

Several hours passed before everyone settled in for the night. The sleeping quarters for pirates began at sea level as a large hut butted up against the cliff. The steep wall provided some protection but the other three sides were left open to the air. There was a second hut stacked above the one where I slept. It was slightly less exposed to the breeze rolling off the sea, and so was used by the pirates of higher authority. A single room was stacked above that, but I didn't know what it was for. Devlin and Agor and other senior pirates had their own private quarters at the top of the cliff.

Sneaking out of the hut was fairly simple. Apparently, pirates slept in much the same manner as they lived during the day, loud and hard. The bigger trick after I left was to get off the beach and back up to the top of the hill. Directly behind us, the earthen cliff was too steep for a safe nighttime climb. Stairs were carved into the more gradual hill a little farther down, but they seemed well guarded, so instead I moved up the shore and did some scrambling across an old rockslide to get up top.

I was surprised that Tarblade wasn't better guarded than what I saw up there. A few vigils were making rounds, but it was as if they knew nobody would be foolish enough to attack them so they expected little danger. Still, I moved cautiously as I made my way toward the captured navigator.

Tilagon was asleep beside the tree, his head tilted so far

forward it was nearly touching his chest. I wondered how he could sleep like that, when even in the most comfortable of beds I often had trouble sleeping at all. At least they'd given him a blanket. Devlin would've wanted him to be healthy enough to travel in the morning, before they killed him.

The knot binding Tilagon's hands was nearly halfway undone before he awoke. I whispered that if he made a sound we were both dead and he quickly closed his mouth. When the ropes were untied, I helped him move his arms back from around the tree. He gasped with the stiffness in them but relaxed again once they rested on his legs.

"You?" he hissed when he recognized me. "You've come to kill me?"

"Don't be absurd. Now hush."

"In that case, I'm sorry for what I said before."

"Listen to me very carefully," I said. "Your ship and its contents are lost to the pirates. You must leave on foot."

Tilagon nodded. He was already massaging his legs with his hands, preparing to run.

I glanced around to be sure we were still alone, then said, "After you leave here you must not be found. Stay off the trails and go anywhere they won't think to look for you. If they catch you, there won't be anything I can do to help."

He put a hand on my arm. "Tell me your name so I can thank you properly."

"Thank me by staying alive. Give me your hat." Tilagon obeyed, then I said, "It's time to leave. Now."

He nodded again, took my hand and gave it a firm squeeze, then leapt to his feet and ran, never looking back.

I used the stiff wool blanket to prop up a piece of wood to look like a body against the tree and put the man's hat on top. Up close it was obviously a trick, but from a distance I hoped a vigil would think the man was still tied up here. Less than ten minutes later I passed Erick's bed as I entered the sleeping quarters. Harlowe's watch was stored under the bed, and I was tempted to take it and hide it.

But I couldn't. Not yet. However, I silently vowed to get it back before this was all over.

The following morning, I was one of the first at breakfast, though it was interrupted by another group of pirates who had gathered nearby and were jeering at whatever was happening in the center of them all. I hurried forward, concerned that Tilagon had been captured again. Fink stood near the outside of the group, though he was too short to have a chance at seeing anything.

"What's going on?" I asked him.

"They just grabbed the boy who tied up that sailor last night. Devlin said he must not have tied him good enough because the man got away while we slept."

I pushed my way forward. Devlin had fashioned a switch out of a tree branch and was beating the curly-haired boy with it. The boy had crouched into a ball to protect himself but still yelped whenever Devlin hit him.

"Stop it!" I darted forward and grabbed Devlin's arm. "You don't know he did anything wrong. Maybe Tilagon was just good at knots."

"If he'd done it right, nobody could escape."

"Lots of people can escape knots."

Devlin shook my hand off him. "Like who?"

It was smarter to back off, but by the glare in Devlin's eyes I figured it was already too late. "I can."

Devlin forgot about the boy still on the ground. A wicked grin crossed his face when he looked at me. "I want to see that. Tie him up."

"What?" I scowled. A couple of pirates grabbed me but I squirmed free. "I haven't done anything wrong." At least, not for a few hours.

"No one's accusing you," Devlin said as the pirates got hold of me again. "You made a claim and I'm testing it."

Despite my struggles, they bound my hands behind me and made several knots before I was pronounced finished. It wasn't a big problem. I'd held my hands wide while they tied me and had already found one end of the rope.

I'd learned how to untie knots soon after entering Mrs. Turbeldy's orphanage, thanks to the pranks of several older boys who liked to tie us younger ones up in an attic and claim we weren't hungry for supper. One evening, I figured out I could undo the knots with some nimble fingers and a lot of patience. Then it was time for some revenge. They awoke the next morning tied to their beds while the rest of us went to breakfast. The pranks stopped, and my skills with knots had only improved since then.

Except that with a tilt of his head, Devlin now had me dragged toward the stables. I dug my boots into the dirt path to slow the men on either side of me, but two others joined them and picked up my legs. They carried me into the corral and dropped me directly in front of the water trough. I shook my head at Devlin. "Don't you dare. I never said —"

"Raise a hand when you want air. If you can."

And he dunked me face-first into the trough. His foot landed on my back, pressing me down. I didn't bother with fighting. It wouldn't do any good and would cost me air. So I arched my back to keep the rope as dry as possible. Every bit of water it absorbed would make the rope thicker and knots tighter.

My fingers worked as fast as they could, deciphering each knot's shape and worming their way between the loops. I was making progress, but far too slowly and it was hard to concentrate. I hadn't gotten a complete breath before Devlin pushed me in, and my lungs already ached.

I found the next knot, but it was higher on my wrists, and I couldn't maneuver my arms at this angle. I couldn't untie this one while I was submerged.

It was beyond my wanting to breathe now. I *needed* to breathe. The end of my life could be measured in seconds if I didn't get free.

Against my will, my lungs finally exploded and I sucked

in a mouthful of water. My body jerked up, instinctively moving toward air. Then the foot was removed and Devlin yanked me out of the water and dropped me against a tree. I continued coughing on water as it choked its way out.

Devlin crouched down to face me. "You'd better learn fast that if you interfere with someone else's punishment, it's going to become yours. Especially when you make such wild claims."

Wordlessly, I reached for his meaty hand. Into his open palm I dropped the rope that had tied me. "Thanks for the warning," I said, still breathless. "But I never make wild claims."

He cursed at me and threw the rope back into my lap, then left me in the corral as the other men followed him out. I pocketed the rope, just in case I needed it in the future. When I felt better, I stood and started toward the beach.

On the way I passed Fink. He started to say something, but with a growl at him I said, "No, I won't show you how I did that. You've got to get away from here."

Fink only nodded. "Yeah, I know."

· TWENTY-SEVEN ·

Carthya was a landlocked country, one of the crueler fates of my life. It was true that we had a favorable climate and some of the best land for natural resources of any of our neighboring countries.

But no sea of our own.

The pirates' beach was full of rocks that became hot to bare feet if the sun got warm enough. But even an overheated beach was better than no beach. I could sit here all day gazing across the gentle waves at the line where the sea meets the sky. Somewhere on the other side were foreign countries I knew little about. Maybe one day I'd take a voyage, explore their lands and learn their ways. In fact, I had tentatively planned on doing something like that after Mrs. Turbeldy kicked me out of the orphanage for the last time. I had known my parents would hate the idea if they ever found out, which had somehow made it more appealing.

For a long time I watched a flock of seagulls circling just over the water, engaged in a mesmerizing dance in flight. I had some bread left from earlier that day and plucked off pieces to throw on the sand, then waited. A few of them landed and fought for the food. I gave them more, drawing them closer to me each time. Then I pinched a piece between my fingers and held it out to one bird who seemed a little braver than most. His head bobbed back and forth between my face and the bread as he debated whether it was worth the risk to take the crumb.

"C'mon," I whispered. "You want it. Take your chance."

He darted forward to grab the bread, but suddenly flew off as a rock landed in the sand near him. The rest of the flock scattered as well.

Behind me, Devlin snarled, "Miserable pests. They're nothing but scavengers."

As if pirates were any higher order of life. But I clenched my jaw and said nothing as I returned to staring at the sea. It was inevitable we'd have to talk.

He walked up beside me and said, "You seem deep in thought."

I shifted on the ground. "I was."

Devlin carried my sword in his hands, which he stuck into the sand in front of me. He dropped the scabbard at my side, then plunked down on the beach, leaning backward and propping himself with his arms.

I stared at the sword a moment, then asked, "Where's my knife?"

"I'm keeping it," he said. "It's mine now."

"Take care of it. It'd better be in good condition when I steal it back."

He chuckled, then said, "Yes, Agor believes you must be a good thief, because your skills as a swordsman are dismal."

I shrugged that off. "*Dismal* is such a judgmental word. I prefer to say that it was a close match and I barely lost."

"No, I don't think it was that at all."

I smiled over at him, expecting another joke about my lack of skills, but his expression was far too serious.

"The reason I accepted you so easily as a pirate is because of the stories Erick told us about you," Devlin continued. "How you stood up to King Vargan, or tricked him anyway. That you attacked a group of his thieves in Carthya, defending an innocent woman and child. You got a cut but several of them came home seriously injured. How did that happen, Sage?"

"Maybe I took them by surprise."

"Yes, maybe. But in that noble's house, there was a man who said it was better to give you whatever you want because you'd end up getting it anyway. Erick said you later killed that man." He waited for me to answer, but this time I only stared at him. "I'm willing to bet you're a very good swordsman. I think you threw the match with Agor so that you would look even less impressive. My only question is why you did it."

I raised my sleeve so that he could see the assembly of bruises from that match. "You think I'd let him do this if I had the power to stop him?"

"Yes, I do." Devlin's lip curled as he evaluated me. "I think you're more than just a thief. And although there is a cave full of

Carthyan treasure somewhere, I think you intend to keep it for yourself. Above all else, I think that you are a compulsive liar."

My laughter was tense, but sincere. "Hardly. In fact, I consider myself a compulsive truth teller. It's only that everyone else seems compelled to misunderstand me."

"And so that sword fight with Agor was a misunderstanding?" Devlin pointed at the sword. "Pick it up. I want to see it in your hand."

After a loud huff, I stood and picked up the sword. I made no effort to pretend that I couldn't hold it properly or that it was too heavy for me. He'd have seen right through something like that.

Devlin also stood, then widened his arms to show that he had no weapon. "I've been thinking about that priest. How did you say you knew him?"

"He took me in once," I said.

"Ah. His name was Fontelaine. Did you know that?"

I shook my head.

"Fontelaine was well known, not only in Dichell but in all of northern Avenia. He took in a great many street boys over the years, more than could be counted, and never asked for or expected any reward."

I wondered, briefly, whether my father had given Fontelaine any payment for taking me in. Probably not. He'd have worried that a payment might have justified the priest's suspicions that I was someone more than a street boy.

"I gave him the finest reward he could have hoped for," Devlin said. "Martyrdom. He got to die for a cause. Do you know why I killed him?"

The grip on my sword tightened. I had any number of reasons to justify using it against this evil man.

Devlin answered his own question. "He thought he had the young prince of Carthya at his church, a boy who somehow escaped from a ship we attacked."

"You must have felt so stupid when he escaped," I said. "How long did it take to realize you'd been tricked by a ten-year-old boy?"

His right eye twitched before he continued. "We thought he went down with the ship, until Fontelaine sent a messenger out to find the prince's brother, who was searching Avenia for any news of the lost prince. Word of this eventually got back to us. By the time I got there the boy was gone. The priest assured me it hadn't been the prince, but the damage was done. He should have told the pirates as soon as that boy arrived, and let us determine his identity."

"If it wasn't the prince, you killed the priest for nothing," I said.

"Fontelaine died as an example of what happens to Avenians who fail to respect the pirates!" Devlin said. "If you knew him, then you can guess how he died. No pleas for his life, no tears, no bargains. Unfortunately, I had to make an example of him, so his death had to be slow and painful."

"And what about the prince, now that he's come back?"

His eyes darkened, and I saw in them a thirst for blood. My blood. "Don't worry about Jaron. We'll get him too, very soon."

Anger filled me and I wasn't taking it well. If I was going to act, this was my moment. And yet something held me back. The sweat on my palms made it difficult to hold the sword, and I switched it to my right hand.

Devlin smiled. "Perhaps you can use that weapon. Then why not strike me? Earlier, you said you might, to avenge what I did to that priest."

Heat bristled across my body as I glared at Devlin. He was baiting me for a fight he clearly wanted. So why couldn't I do it? Wasn't this why I'd come to the pirates, for this exact purpose? Whatever I might do, he deserved it. And yet I felt weaker than ever, as though I was incapable of doing the one thing that might save my country.

Devlin crouched down and picked up a handful of rocks on the beach. He flung one at me, hitting me in the shoulder. "Maybe Agor was right," he said, tossing another rock at my chest. "You're no swordsman. You're a thief only because you've got no ability to be anything better. Untying knots is a nice trick, but it won't put bread in either your mouth or mine."

Then he flung another rock at me, this one much harder, and it stung the cut on my stomach. "Do you think you're better than the rest of us? Better than me? Now fight!" And he threw the rest of the rocks at me. I ducked to miss the one headed for my face, but it got my cheek anyway.

I raised my sword, finally ready to strike. In response, he planted his feet forward, his face tense with rage. I looked into his black eyes and suddenly realized there was nothing beyond that. No humanity, no love, and no soul. Except for his anger, he was completely empty. It was much of the same anger that I had felt for far too long, and it horrified me.

Since the night I was attacked, I had been so angry, so determined that there was no other choice but to destroy the pirates. But if that choice meant I'd become anything like Devlin, I had to find another way to win. It wasn't that I *couldn't* strike him. It's that I *wouldn't*. I refused to become him.

Wordlessly, I lowered my sword and started to leave. But Devlin grabbed my arm, twisted me around, and yanked me close to him. I stumbled in the sand and bumped roughly against him. Then he said, "That cave had better be full of treasure, because if it's not, making you a pirate was the worst mistake of my life. You are utterly worthless. I just gave you every opportunity to use that sword, and you didn't have the courage to try. Not even against an unarmed man."

With that, he threw me down on the beach and started to walk away. "You weren't unarmed," I muttered, standing again.

"Huh?" He turned and saw in my hand a small knife that had been tucked inside his pants at his waist. I'd pulled it out when I bumped against him. Devlin's face reddened.

"You hoped I'd try something with my sword so you could use this knife against me," I said, tossing it on the sand near him. "Nice try, but I'm a pirate now. I'm one of you."

"If you were really a pirate, you'd never have given that back," Devlin said.

"I want the knife that belongs to me," I said. "Not this inferior toy you're using." And with that I began walking away.

"Sage!" Devlin cried.

I turned in time to see him hurl the knife at me. Instinctively I raised my sword, using the flat side of the blade to deflect the knife away. It shot to the right and landed in a patch of tall grass.

Devlin locked eyes with me and his smile darkened. "So you can use a sword after all. But you won't yet. What are you saving it for?"

I hesitated for just a moment before I said, "I am better than you, Devlin. And I'm saving this sword until it's time for everyone else to understand that too."

He let me leave, but I knew it wouldn't be long before I'd have to pay for those words.

· TWENTY-EIGHT ·

On my way back to the main part of camp, I spied Imogen near a clump of trees. She was kneeling on the ground planting a patch of daisies, and frowned when she looked up and saw me.

"You look upset," she said. "What happened down there?"

"Time is running out. For both of us."

She motioned me toward her and I sighed. I'd have preferred to be alone until I'd calmed down, but I never could refuse her requests, and especially not here.

"Someone might see us," I said, glancing around. There were others in the area, but at least nobody was nearby.

"Come here, then." I followed her down a small hill to where the trees and slope provided good protection from any casual observation. She pulled a raw potato from a pocket of her apron, and then gestured for me to sit beside her, which I did. "The burn from that branding iron can be painful."

I made a face. "A potato?"

"Hush. Show me your arm." I held out the arm that had been branded. Imogen supported the back of my hand and rotated my wrist so she could see the burn better. "Does it hurt?"

"I'm fine."

"Of course you are. They could break your bones in half and you'd tell me that's fine too." Then she let my arm rest in her lap while she cut away some of the peel from the potato.

Imogen next sliced the potato into thin strips and laid them over the burn. Almost instantly, they started to pull the heat from my arm. When she finished laying the strips down, she set the knife and the rest of the potato on the ground. She put one hand under my wrist and the other beneath my elbow, keeping the potato slices balanced.

We sat that way in silence for several minutes. I didn't want to speak and shatter our delicate peace. I'd either make things worse or finally convince her to leave. And I was ashamed to realize a part of me didn't want to succeed in making her go. There was a comfort in having someone on my side in this miserable place.

"I saw you and Devlin down on the beach," she finally said. "He was taunting you."

"It was a test."

"You're still here, so you must have passed."

"I didn't. I doubt there's any way to pass his tests."

Imogen began adjusting the strips, moving cooler ones onto the burn and dropping the others on the ground. "I thought you were going to fight him. Even from where I stood it was obvious you wanted to."

"Yes, I did." I still wanted to, in fact.

"You can't bring the pirates down, Jaron."

"I know."

"Which means our only choice is to escape this place. We can run from here tonight, you and me. There's no shame in that."

"Run?" Irritated, I shook the strips off my arm, then stood and picked up my sword. "Tell me why you knew I had another reason for leaving the castle last week. Do you recall that?"

A single tear rolled down Imogen's cheek before she answered. "It was because you don't run. Not even when it's the only logical thing to do."

"No," I snapped. "Never." And I started to walk away.

"Jaron, there's more." Before I had turned around, she stood and added, "I overheard Devlin talking. Roden's coming. He's expected sometime tomorrow."

I paused and closed my eyes before speaking. "Does he know about you?"

Imogen shook her head. "I also heard that he volunteered to come to Carthya that night. Not because he cared about the message he was supposed to give you, but because he wanted you to know about him. Don't you see how personal his attack on you was?"

I understood that very well. Enough to have carried that knowledge like a lead weight in my chest ever since I had last seen him.

I cocked my head. "You were not planning on telling me this?"

"I hoped the pirates would reject you and send you away, or that you'd see the foolishness of what you're doing and leave before I had to tell you." Forgetting the risk of anyone seeing us, she stepped closer to me. "Don't you see? He'll know it's you as soon as he hears the name Sage. Of any name you might've chosen here, couldn't you at least have thought that through better? Given yourself a name that wouldn't call him to you?"

I lowered my eyes and Imogen drew in a stilted breath. "Oh," she whispered. "That was the plan. You want him to find you. Please tell me I'm wrong."

I sighed. "You're not."

That made her angry. "Do you forget he nearly killed you last week? And now you've left the safety of your walls and your armies and your friends, and come here alone? How does that make anything better? Don't you know what you're up against?"

I locked my jaw forward and stared away from her, but she wasn't finished. "I know you're strong and you can handle a weapon, but they say that Roden hasn't set down his sword for a minute since the night you were crowned. And when he returns, it won't only be him you'll have to fight. It's all of the pirates. They'll be on his side and there's no chance you can win against all of them. None." She cupped her hands around my face so that I had to look at her. "Please. You've got to accept what I'm saying. No matter how angry you are at the pirates, or at Roden, you will lose here tomorrow."

"You have so little faith in me?"

"Faith cannot save a person from reality." Tears filled her

eyes as she added, "I know it's not in you to run. At any other time I'd admire that. But just this once, you must. Do it for me. Stay alive for me."

"Is that really who you want me to be? A person who cowers for the rest of my life, like some helpless prey?"

"I want you to be a person who chooses to live! That's what I care about, that you live! And if we return to Carthya by morning, you can prepare your armies against an attack from the pirates."

"Yes, and the vote for a steward is the day after that! I'll have no control over those armies." Gregor would have little trouble persuading the regents to make him the steward. Under our present threat of war, the regents would do anything he wanted, blindly following his commands.

I stumbled, suddenly dizzy, and aware of my heart pounding against the wall of my chest.

It's time I learned who is in command. That had been Roden's message. As much as the Avenian king wanted my land, or the pirates wanted my wealth, they had no control over me . . . yet. But there was someone within reach of my power.

Ask the right questions. Conner told me that. From nearly the moment after I left Conner's dungeon, something had bothered me about our conversation. But for as often as I'd run his words over in my mind, I hadn't known what questions I should be asking. Now I did.

Imogen touched my arm. "Jaron, are you all right?"

"No," I croaked. As if the threat stood right in front of me, my hand locked on to my sword. In that moment, I knew what I had missed in Conner's dungeon.

And I sank to my knees.

When I'd asked Conner where he had gotten the dervanis oil, Gregor had put his hand on his sword.

"Why would he do that?" I mumbled. "It was only a question. Why would Gregor reach for his sword?"

Imogen shook her head. "What are you talking about?"

Mott had told me that a month before my family's deaths, my father had become suspicious of the regents and begun requiring them to be searched before they entered the castle walls. Yet Conner got in with the vial of dervanis oil from the pirates.

Ask the right questions.

The question wasn't where he got the poison. It was how he got inside the castle with it.

Conner had needed help to kill my family. There was a second traitor in my castle.

Conner might not even have realized he had help. The pirates could have easily coordinated with someone else to let Conner pass through.

Only one man would have the authority to allow a regent to enter the castle without being searched. It was the same man who would have allowed the king of Avenia to enter my gates without identifying his attendants as pirates.

Gregor had reached for his sword in the dungeon because in that moment, he thought I knew he was the second traitor.

He had expected to need his sword. Against me.

Gregor had known I would be attacked in the gardens. He knew Roden's message was intended to frighten me into submission, and it allowed Gregor to make a case to the regents that I needed a steward.

And wherever Gregor wanted to send me into hiding, I was willing to wager the pirates knew about that place too.

The pirates didn't care about killing Conner. His connection to them was already exposed. But Gregor needed him dead, to protect his own involvement in my family's murders.

In two days, Gregor would have himself declared steward over Carthya. And all that stood between him and success was Tobias, who was, at that moment, pretending to be me. Tobias was in grave danger. And what of Amarinda, who'd be caught in the middle of them both?

I glanced up at Imogen, who looked half-panicked by then. "What's happening?" she asked.

After standing again, I said, "It's time to go. Meet me in the stables tonight. One hour after the last light goes out in the camp."

"Vigils guard the camp."

"Can you avoid them?"

"Yes." Imogen paused a moment, then wiped a fallen tear off her cheek. "Thank you, Jaron."

I nodded back at her and then closed my eyes, trying to piece together everything that would have to happen next. When I opened them again, Imogen was gone.

· TWENTY-NINE ·

Fink was already seated when I came to dinner that night. Erick sat across the table and several men down, but Fink scooted aside to make room for me. However, after an unenthusiastic hello, he pushed his bowl forward and laid his head on his hands.

"Sleepy?" I asked. "Didn't get your afternoon nap?"

"Hush." Fink's irritable tone took me by surprise. I thought we had firmly established as a rule of our friendship that I was the cranky one.

"Sit up or they'll ladle stew onto your head." He glared at me but obeyed. Then I asked, "What's the matter?"

Fink snuck a look around to see whether any of the nearby pirates were listening. As if their top priority was eavesdropping on a kid too young to even be considered for piracy. Then he leaned in to me and whispered, "I want to go home."

"What home? Back to the thieves?"

"Maybe. I don't like it here."

"Erick's staying," I said. "I doubt he'll ever go back."

"I know." Then he shrugged. "What about you?"

If I didn't go home, Tobias's deception would be revealed. Gregor would exact his revenge upon Tobias, and likely solidify his hold on both Amarinda and my kingdom before I could return and expose him. But if I left now, the pirates would bring war to Carthya and destroy everything.

"I don't know what I should do," I mumbled.

We fell silent as Serena, the dark-headed girl who had served me at other meals, came by to ladle food into our bowls. She put a hand on my shoulder and whispered, "You need a little extra. You're too thin."

I smiled back at her and appreciated the additional serving. Even though I wasn't particularly hungry, I planned to eat the entire bowl. I'd begun to notice the same thing about myself lately.

"Look at that." Fink pointed down the tables to Imogen, whose eyes narrowed as she stared at Serena. "I don't think she hates you after all. I think she's mad that the other girl just gave you extra. She's jealous."

I met Imogen's eye and subtly shook my head at her. She got the message and turned away from me.

From his place at another table, Devlin stood and his voice boomed, "I'm in the mood for some entertainment. We should have a sword match."

Everyone fell silent. Nobody considered standing at the other end of Devlin's sword as entertainment. Devlin withdrew his blade and began randomly pointing it at one man and then another. "Should I fight you? Or you?" My focus went to the bowl in front of me and my jaw tightened. Devlin continued, "Come now, are there no volunteers? No one who thinks he's better than me?" Then his eyes landed upon me like the glare of the sun. "Sage, you will fight."

It was not a request and there was no choice I could make and win. Either I lost my life to Devlin, or to his men after I defeated him. My stomach churned.

"Can we at least eat while the stew is warm?" I asked.

"I've eaten already, and the supper won't matter to you." Because I wouldn't live long enough to digest it.

I took another bite anyway. Devlin continued watching me as he left his place at the table and began walking in my direction. Finally, I forced myself to stand. The only thing I knew for certain was that one way or another, I was going to lose.

Then Devlin cried out in a rage, and for the first time I looked up. There was stew spilled down his front, gravy dripping off his right arm and chest.

"Forgive me, sir. I didn't see you coming." Imogen bowed low before Devlin, the empty pot of stew clutched in her hands.

"Clumsy servant girl!" Devlin raised a hand to strike her, and slowly lowered it. He glared at her, then at me, then cursed and stomped away.

I retreated back to the seat, though my hand was gripped so firmly around my sword it took a conscious effort to release it and reach again for my spoon. With the silent help of the other girls, Imogen collected what she could of the mess she had made, and hurried away. Low murmurs rumbled amongst the men, but no one wanted his voice to stand out. Across from me, Fink sat nearly frozen.

"Fink," I hissed. "Eat."

"He would've killed you just now."

"Eat."

But he only pushed his bowl away and leaned his head back on the table. I finally settled a debate inside my head that I'd been struggling with all evening. I dipped my spoon into my bowl and whispered, "One hour after the last light goes out tonight, meet me in the stables."

"Why?"

"Just be there. And make sure nobody follows you."

Fink was already gone when I got up about a half hour after lights-out. He'd made an excuse over an hour ago to visit the outhouse and never returned. Nobody had noticed.

I rose silently, then tousled the blanket so that it would appear I was still in my cot. If the devils were merciful tonight, nobody else in this room was awake. Especially not the person whose cot I was tiptoeing toward.

Erick was sleeping near the far end of the hut, in an unfavorable location where the cool sea breeze would first flow through. Because of that, he was bundled up tightly in his blanket, his head partially buried.

Every pirate had the area beneath his cot to use for personal storage. Most of the men had trunks or crates for their things.

However, since he was so new here, Erick had very few things and had only set below the cot whatever he wasn't comfortable sleeping with. His boots were there, and the sheath for his sword, which was empty. I guessed he was probably sleeping with his sword — most of the men did. I softly patted the ground until I found the item I wanted.

I picked up Harlowe's pocket watch, holding it tightly to diminish the constant sound of its ticking, and tucked it into my shirt. With silent movements, I then slipped out of the hut. The skies were dark and cloudy, which was a gift in that it allowed me to hide from any pirates who kept nighttime vigils. I made my way to the hut where Devlin slept and stood outside for a minute or two while I decided what to do. I could tell from here that I wouldn't be blessed with sneaking into the room of a snorer, as I had been with Conner. Devlin was likely to be a light sleeper, and somehow in the pitch blackness of his room, I would have only a few minutes to find my knife. It wasn't a good idea.

Still, I really wanted that knife. Or rather, I didn't want Devlin to have it.

I inched his door open, but only had one foot inside his hut before I stepped out again. Someone else was nearby. I swung around, hearing the soft crunch of sand behind me. Imogen stepped from the shadows with a finger pressed to her lips.

She put her mouth next to my ear and whispered, "What are you doing?"

"You need a weapon," I replied. "Just in case."

"You'll be there to protect me. Besides, I have this." Then she leaned away from me and withdrew a kitchen knife from her pocket.

I nodded in approval, but looked back at Devlin's door. "Wait for me." I started forward, but Imogen touched my arm and shook her head.

"No, Jaron," she said. "Please, let's just leave."

It wasn't what I wanted to hear, but she was right. It was foolish to risk so much by going in there. Imogen walked forward, urging me away with her. Finally, I gave in and followed. Keeping to the shadows, we hurried toward the stables.

"Do you know how many vigils keep watch overnight?" I asked.

"I'm not sure. All I can tell you is that one passes near our quarters every ten minutes or so."

That had been my experience when I'd helped the sailor escape. It wasn't much time.

We crouched behind some bushes near the stables. A vigil was walking through the center of them, looking in on the horses.

"We'll have to hurry once he leaves." I withdrew Harlowe's pocket watch from my shirt and pressed it into her hand.

"What's this?" she asked. Even after she recognized the object she still shook her head.

"Hide it," I whispered. "It's very important."

She angled away from me and when she turned back, the pocket watch was no longer in her hand. "Why —" she began, but I shushed her as the vigil left the gate and limped toward us. As he got nearer, I realized it was the same curly-haired boy who Devlin had beat with the switch yesterday. Mrs. Turbeldy had used a switch on me once at the orphanage, and I recognized the pained way he walked.

I held out my hand for Imogen's knife, but before she gave it to me, the boy stopped very near us. "Whoever's hiding there, come out," he said.

I put a hand on Imogen's shoulder, holding her down as I stood. Hopefully, he hadn't seen us both. He held a sword in one hand, and the tip was aimed low. This boy wasn't a swordsman.

He stepped even closer to me. "What are you doing out of bed?"

"I'd prefer if you didn't ask about that."

"There's someone else with you."

"I'd especially prefer if you didn't ask me that."

"Stand up," the boy ordered.

Slowly, Imogen stood. I noticed she'd pulled her braid loose, obviously suggesting that we had snuck out here for romantic reasons.

The boy shook his head. "Nobody touches the girls. It's part of the code."

"Let it pass this once, will you?" He didn't look convinced so I added, "We all make mistakes with the code. Maybe it's girls. Maybe it's failing to tie a prisoner's knots correctly."

His face fell. He obviously didn't like being reminded

that my intervention had saved him from a worse beating.

"I didn't see you here," he finally said. "But I'm not the only vigil so you'd better leave soon."

"That's definitely the plan," I said.

Once he was gone, Imogen and I ran into the stables. Mystic was housed in a center stall, and with Imogen's help, two minutes later he was saddled and ready to ride.

"Someone else is here," she said, backing into the shadows.

I glanced up and saw Fink hop into the stables from the top of the fence. "It's all right," I said, motioning Imogen forward. "He's leaving too."

"It was harder than I thought to get here," Fink said. "Sorry I'm late." He stopped briefly when he saw Imogen. "What's she doing here? I thought she hates you."

If she didn't now, she soon would. I helped Imogen onto Mystic's back, and then gestured for Fink to move closer.

"We can't take your horse," Fink said.

"I'll bet Mystic that you can," I said. "He's your horse now."

"Then we'll need a second horse for you," Imogen said, looking around.

"No." I shook my head firmly. "We don't."

"Mystic won't carry the three of us." Then Imogen's hopeful expression deflated. "Oh no. No! That's why you gave me the watch."

"It's for a noble in Libeth named Rulon Harlowe. Make sure he gets it."

"We agreed not to stay here," she said. "Please don't play these games."

My expression hardened, making it clear that this was no game. Then I handed her a letter, explaining the details of Gregor's deception. "You must place this in Mott's hand and no one else's. Destroy it if there is the risk of anyone else touching it. I won't be far behind."

"No, you must come with us," Imogen said, clutching the note.

I opened my hand, revealing the knife she had brought from the kitchens. She double-checked the pocket of her skirt where she had left it, despite the fact it was obviously not there. "Will you promise to leave now, or shall I give this to Fink, who will make sure you leave?"

Imogen pressed her lips together and stared forward. I handed Fink the rope Devlin had used to tie me up. "Tie her to you if necessary, but she does not leave your side until you're both safe and far from this place." Then I handed Fink the knife.

When Imogen did speak, the words were clipped and angry. "I planted the flowers for you, but they're already dying. You know why? Because they're in bad soil. They don't belong here and neither do you. Go look at them and you'll see your own future."

Maybe that was my future, but I was finished arguing with her. I only led Mystic forward, saying, "Mott is at the church in

Dichell. Fink, you must get her there. I want all three of you to get out of Avenia."

"What about you?" Imogen asked.

"If I leave, I'll meet you in Drylliad."

"What do you mean *if*?"

I frowned at her, then slapped Mystic's backside. Imogen turned back to look at me and said, "Jaron, please." But they were already leaving.

As they rode away, I heard Fink ask, "Who's Jaron?"

· THIRTY ·

The clanging of an alarm bell broke through the early morning peace. I was already awake, as I had been all night. It was one week since I had left Drylliad, and too much had happened in that time. But nothing worried me like what the next few hours might bring. Obviously, Imogen's absence had prompted the alarm.

Agor ran into our hut and yelled, "One of the serving girls is missing. We think she stole a horse."

Erick stood beside his bed, looking around. "Fink is missing too — the boy who came with me."

"It was your horse," Agor said to me.

"It's Fink's horse now," I said. "He won it last night in a bet. They can't have gone far, perhaps just gathering berries in the woods."

"Those places were checked already." Agor's eyes darkened. "Besides, they'd have still needed permission to leave. Devlin's convinced they got scared and ran. But where?"

"Fink would go back to Dichell," Erick said.

"But the serving girl wouldn't want to go there," I said.

"Last time I talked to her she was very clear on that."

"So far we can't find anything missing other than the horse." Agor called to everyone, "Get dressed. We're going to make a thorough search of the camp."

I began pulling my boots on. Erick already wore his and came to sit beside me.

"What do you think happened?" he asked. "Do you think Fink wanted to leave?"

"He didn't belong here," I said. "If he got away, you should be happy for him."

"Yeah." Disappointed, Erick clicked his tongue. "But I was getting used to having him underfoot."

Once I was ready, we joined in the search around camp. It was an entirely useless act, not only because it was obvious they had left, but because so many of us had been ordered to look for them we nearly tripped over one another in the effort.

I'd gone first to the stables, ensuring nothing had been left behind to incriminate me. Then I traced each of our steps back as far as I could, but everything was clean. Eventually, Agor came to the only conclusion he could: Imogen and Fink had run away.

With that, the pirates began gathering to the tables for breakfast. Unfortunately, the serving girls had been questioned about Imogen all morning, so nothing was ready. Everyone was already irritable at having their morning taken up in a vain search for two people who really didn't matter here anyway. Hunger wasn't helping the situation.

I started down the hill toward the beach, putting myself as far as possible from everyone else. Time was running out and I needed a place to think.

"Someone's coming!" a vigil yelled from up at the main part of camp. "The girl and the boy are back."

My head whipped around, and I scrambled up near him and some other men to where I could get a better view. How dare she? It was hard enough to get her safely away the first time. There was no chance I could do it again, and even if I could, not before it was too late. But from where I stood, I still couldn't see her.

"They are not alone," the vigil continued. "They're prisoners."

"Whose prisoners?" Agor yanked the scope from the vigil's hands and pressed it to his eye.

"Who is it?" Devlin demanded.

Agor returned the scope to the vigil and called back, "It looks like that Carthyan soldier, the one who helped Vargan get our men into Drylliad. What was his name?"

Devlin pulled out his sword and his tone went sour. "Gregor Breslan."

I shrank against the nearby tree, my heart pounding wildly. Gregor had come to Tarblade Bay. And Imogen was his prisoner.

I was carefully hidden from Gregor as he rode into camp towing Imogen and Fink on Mystic's back, yet from where I stood I still had a good view of everything. Imogen and Fink were tied together with the rope I'd given Fink, and both looked terrified.

My mind raced to decide what to do next. Neither Imogen nor Fink was a pirate, so they weren't bound by the code. Not officially anyway. I figured they'd be taken to the jail unharmed, where they'd remain until I could sneak down there and get them out.

With that settled, I turned my attention to Gregor's arrival at camp. From the grumbles I heard, nobody was happy to see him here. But nothing they felt could've matched my distress. I couldn't ignore the possibility that he'd already discovered Tobias and knew I was here. If so, then he'd come to expose me.

Just as Erick and I had done when we came, Gregor entered camp with his sword held high, blade down.

Agor was the first to approach him. "Master Breslan, weren't you warned not to come here uninvited? The plan was for us to wait until after a steward was in place, when Jaron was less visible."

"I knew that I couldn't come without reason," Gregor responded. "But I have that. First, allow me to present you with two of your runaways, as a gift."

Fink must have told him they came from here. Imogen never would have.

"Where did you find them?" Agor asked.

"Miles from here. On the road to Dichell."

I quietly groaned. Maybe they figured it would be harder

to track their escape if they kept to the roads, but staying off any trail would have been better.

Erick crept up beside me, apparently unaware that I had no interest in petty conversation. He tapped my shoulder and said, "What do you think, Sage? What will they do to Fink and the flower girl?"

I shrugged in answer while Agor stepped closer to Gregor's prisoners. "Whose idea was it to leave?"

"It was mine," Imogen said. "I convinced the boy to come with me in case I needed help along the way."

"That's not true," Fink said. "We both wanted to leave. We were scared."

"Of course you were," Agor said. "But you should have gone to Devlin and asked to be dismissed. To run under the cover of darkness looks very suspicious."

"You should be suspicious," Gregor said. "I don't know the boy, but this is no ordinary girl. She was instrumental in bringing King Jaron back to the throne of Carthya. Everyone knows they are the closest of friends."

This caught Devlin's attention. He stepped forward and ordered a couple of pirates to pull Fink and Imogen off the horse. Fink was dragged off first. They set him on his knees and told him if he moved an inch they'd cut off his legs. Fink's eyes were wide, and he didn't blink once. He wasn't going anywhere.

Next, Imogen was brought to face Devlin. She stood tall, but even from here I could sense her fear.

"How does a girl go from a friendship with the king of

Carthya to coming into service for Avenian pirates?" Devlin asked.

"Gregor is wrong. Jaron isn't my friend." Imogen spoke so confidently I wondered whether she believed it. "He sent me away, as far from his castle as I could go. Even Gregor can vouch for that fact. I needed a living, so I came here."

"Still, that's a most amazing coincidence. Surely you know of our history with your king." Devlin laughed darkly. "Gregor, tell her."

"Conner hired these same pirates to kill Jaron four years ago," Gregor said. "I'm sure in all your many conversations he must have mentioned that." Then Gregor turned his attention to Devlin. "And it's why I came. The regents have agreed to give you Bevin Conner. That fool was arrogant enough to believe he killed the royal family without help, that he alone had ties to you. I'm glad to be rid of him."

"Conner's death was always your desire, not ours," Devlin said. "We agreed to kill him so he wouldn't accidentally expose your connection to us, but our interest is with Jaron. What about him?"

Gregor nodded. "I tried to send him to the southern border where you'd have easy access to him, but against my wishes he returned to Drylliad. However, he's all but barricaded himself inside his quarters. He's afraid and paranoid and weak, but it won't be long before he recovers and tries to regain control. The pirates have wanted Jaron for years, and there is no better time to take him than now. Upon my return home, the regents will select me as the steward of Carthya. I'll have total command of our armies and will grant you safe passage. This agreement will cement the friendship between us."

Erick looked at me. "I think we'll have that Carthyan treasure of yours soon, but not in the way we planned."

"No," I muttered. "This wasn't my plan either." I was glad that Gregor remained unaware of Tobias impersonating me in the castle, but based upon his invitation to the pirates just now, there was no cause for celebration.

Devlin and Agor stood together, privately discussing what Gregor had said. Fink remained motionless on his knees but he wisely kept calm. Imogen stood alone near the center of the group, obviously terrified but trying not to show it. In a show of arrogance, Gregor arched his neck as he waited for their verdict. It appeared that he had failed to recognize Mystic. He'd captured them in the darkness. Perhaps it hadn't occurred to him to check the horse more carefully since then.

After a few minutes, Devlin pointed to Fink and Imogen. "We'll deal with these two first. Under pirate law, there's no official violation we can accuse them of, but their leaving cannot go unpunished either. Take them to the jail until we figure out what to do."

"But there was a crime," Gregor said. "By this girl."

Even from my hiding place, I heard Devlin's impatient sigh. "What is it?"

Gregor pulled a pocket watch from his coat. Harlowe's pocket watch. "She was hiding this in her skirt. It's a man's watch, so she must have stolen it."

Erick patted his pockets. Until now, in all the commotion he hadn't thought about it being missing. He darted up from his position and ran into the courtyard. "That's mine!"

"When did you last have it?" Agor asked.

"Last night. I put it under my cot before bed."

"The girl couldn't have gotten there to steal it, but Fink slept nearby." Agor looked at the two of them. "One of you had better confess, and save your companion from your punishment."

Fink and Imogen looked at each other, eyes wide with horror. But it was Imogen who spoke. "I took the watch. Fink didn't even know I had it."

"Move the boy aside," Devlin said. "We have some business with the girl." He walked closer to her, and she seemed to shrink in his shadow. "According to pirate code, we never touch the girls in our service. But if one of them conducts a crime against us, her punishment is no less severe. Bring me a whip!"

Gregor stepped forward. "Let me take her instead. We can use her as insurance against Jaron fighting back. He will hand over all of Carthya to protect her. I can guarantee that."

A whip was passed to Devlin. He ran his hands along the cable and said, "Our punishment first. Then you may have her for whatever purpose you desire. First and foremost, my pirates must be taught that we do not steal from one another! Turn the girl around."

"She didn't steal that watch." All eyes went to me as I stepped into the courtyard, slightly out of breath from hurrying so fast. "I did."

· THIRTY-ONE ·

In any other circumstance, there would have been a certain amount of comedy associated with my entrance. Although the rest of the pirates only saw Sage walking forward, Gregor actually stumbled back in shock. It's too bad he didn't trip and injure himself.

My sword was in my hand, and I held it ready as I looked at Devlin. "Did you hear me? That pocket watch was my crime. For that matter, so was their running away. I made them leave last night. If you raise that whip against her, I promise to strike you down before it has a second to fly."

Devlin grinned. "You took the pocket watch because you're a thief, but I thought we had agreed you're no swordsman, Sage."

By now, Gregor had recovered. "Sage? Devlin, forgive my accusation, but you are a fool. Don't you know who this is?"

Devlin didn't appear to forgive the accusation. With a sneer on his face, he folded his arms and said, "Enlighten me."

Gregor looked at me and frowned. "He can perform the Avenian accent as well as his own Carthyan tongue. And although he has the reputation for being able to steal the white off of snow if he chooses to, this boy is far from being a mere thief. Devlin, you are facing the boy who has haunted the pirates for the past four years. This is Jaron, the lost prince of Carthya."

Again, the comedic value of this moment could not be denied, except that no one, not even I, was laughing. But Devlin nearly dropped the whip and his mouth hung open in total disbelief. Because of the sword in my hand, nobody advanced on me yet, nor would they until Devlin ordered them to.

Near the front of the crowd of pirates, Erick was shaking his head. I truly regretted having misled him into bringing me here, largely because he was in great danger now. Next to him, a red-faced Agor appeared to already be plotting his death.

Or I could be wrong. It was more likely that Agor was thinking about my death, at least as his first priority. Erick would be next.

"Is this true?" Devlin asked me. "You're Prince Jaron?"

"*King* Jaron, actually. News must travel slower amongst the illiterate." I glared at Gregor with every inch of disdain I felt. "Shouldn't you be groveling to me or bowing or something?"

Gregor smiled. "I think before I have the chance, you will already be dead."

"Ah. So much for all your toasts to my long life."

"Take comfort in knowing you'll join the rest of your family soon." Then Gregor furrowed his dark brows. "If you're here, who's back at the castle?"

I cocked my head. "Tell me your secrets and I'll tell you mine." My attention returned to Devlin. "Anything that happens now is between you and me. Fink and Imogen are distractions. Release them."

"And then what?" Devlin asked.

"Then the pirates surrender to me and I leave in peace." I tilted my head toward Gregor. "In exchange, you can have him."

"But that would deny me the greatest unfinished job the pirates have had in our history," Devlin said. "Some of us have never gotten over the disappointment of failing to kill you."

"There are several people who share your same disappointment," I said. "Frankly, I don't think it's fair that you get to kill me when there were others who wanted to do it first."

Devlin barked out a bitter laugh. "Lock the kid in that room above the beach. We don't need him here. And take Gregor to the jail."

"What?" Gregor snarled and began to withdraw his sword, but four pirates were beside him before he had the chance.

"Until this moment, all we had was the chance to kill Jaron." Devlin's tone was equally nasty. "But now we have him, and the steward of Carthya too." He nodded at some of his men. "Take them away."

Pirates grabbed Fink and yanked him to his feet. Several more surrounded Gregor, disarmed him, and led them both away. Gregor's strange combination of threats and pleas for mercy could be heard for some distance. It wasn't his finest moment.

Next, Devlin cocked his head at Imogen. "We have no need

of Gregor to get what we want from Carthya. Because we have her."

I moved closer to Imogen, blocking her body with mine. "Lock her in the room with Fink. Anything you want from her you can get from me."

Devlin smiled at me. "Actually, I think the opposite is true. Anything I want from you, I can get by using her." He raised a hand to his men. "You know what to do."

Like bees to a hive, pirates swarmed me. I struck where I could, and gave out a fair share of wounds, but I took a few too. Even Erick was working with them, but although I had the chance to give him a hit, I turned elsewhere. It didn't matter where I fought, because there were pirates advancing from every direction, and the fight was over far too quickly. They got my sword, which someone used to club me in the back and send me to the ground. Once I was down, they pulled my arms behind me and tied them, then dropped both Imogen and me at Devlin's feet.

I pressed the side of my body against hers in a lame attempt to offer some comfort. But she knew how few options remained. There was little comfort for that.

"Valiant effort, young king, but you must have known you never had a chance against us. So you came here promising to reveal the location of the Carthyan treasury, and you will. Frankly, I was skeptical of that promise at first, but I should have been more trusting. Obviously, you know exactly where it is. Show me."

Agor already had the map of Carthya spread on the ground beside me. Then he arched an eyebrow, waiting to see what I'd do.

I ignored the map and said nothing. Devlin was clearly enjoying hearing himself speak, so I didn't think he really expected me to add to the conversation. Especially because I wasn't inclined to do anything he wanted.

Devlin began pacing a line in front of us and spoke for all his pirates to hear, "I knew that someday we'd play a role in the downfall of Carthya, but I had thought it would unfold under orders from the king of Avenia. That changes now. By the end of this day there will be no Jaron. I will be king of Carthya."

"You wouldn't want to be king of my country," I said.

"Why is that?"

"Well, you're rather fat. I doubt you'd fit onto my throne."

He laughed. "I appreciate your concern, but it will do until a new throne can be made for me. Now, if I'm not mistaken, there's a young princess in Carthya who is obligated to marry whoever wears the crown. I hear she's very pretty."

"And you're very ugly," I said. "Have mercy on your children. Even the princess's beauty won't compensate for you."

"That's a risk I'm willing to take."

"Then what now?" I cocked my head, the only defiance I could offer from this position. "Because you should know that I will never give up my country, and certainly not to a pig like you."

"And next you'll say that I'll have to kill you to do it, right?"

Devlin grinned. "Let me save you the words. I have no intention of killing you . . . yet. Jaron, you will give me the location of that cave, and you will give up the throne, or I will kill that girl kneeling beside you."

At the nod of his head, two pirates lifted Imogen to her feet. She screamed in terror and looked back at me.

I tried to stand but pirates were on either side of me, clamping me down. "You are still bound by your code," I yelled. "She's committed no crime. You can't touch her!"

"She lied to me when she came," he said. "That negates the code. Prepare her."

I continued to struggle. "You are the ultimate coward. Deal with me, Devlin. Not her!"

"Gregor was right," Devlin said, looping the whip again. "You'd do anything for this girl."

Pirates tied each of Imogen's hands on opposite ends of a wide board they had lowered from a tree. Slots were carved into each end for her wrists. They'd prevent her from moving too much as they whipped her.

By this time I had worked a hand free of the ropes behind my back. I stretched out a foot to trip a pirate behind me and rose up to hit another in the jaw. I ducked the attempt of a third man to grab me and tried for his sword. But before I could reach it, several more pirates had me again. One punched me in the back, forcing the air from my lungs. Before I could recover, another two got my arms pinched behind me.

"Devlin, I challenge you." I still gasped for air and my voice was dry and hoarse. "I challenge you as king of the pirates."

Devlin shook his head. "You have no right to a challenge. You lied to me to come here."

Technically, I hadn't lied, but this was no time for the fine points of that debate. I pulled one arm free long enough to reveal the pirate branding. "Whatever I did to get here, I am a pirate. I have every right to challenge you, and you are obligated by the code to answer it."

"All right," Devlin said, finally lowering his whip. "Give this boy-king his sword. I accept your challenge. Prepare to die."

· THIRTY-TWO ·

The fact is that I wasn't prepared to die. Not only would I be dead, but even worse, it would prove everyone right who had called me a fool for coming here. Besides, it would give Gregor the last laugh, and I had no intention of dying and allowing him that satisfaction. However, I assumed that Devlin probably had no plans to die either. One of us would have to lose. I hoped it was him.

The pirates formed a rowdy and uneven circle around us. Imogen was left outside the circle, but I preferred that. If things did go badly, I didn't want her to have to see it. I mumbled my wish for the devils to use their mischief against Devlin, rather than me. It was a fair request. The devils had spent a lot of time on me lately.

Agor tossed my sword into the ring, requiring me to dive close to Devlin to retrieve it. I leapt at it and quickly rolled away from him. He stabbed at the ground and caught the back of my shirt, which snagged for a second before I tore free.

Devlin had punched his sword so deeply into the ground that he needed both hands to tug it out. I used that opportunity to slash his ankle. He yelped and brought his sword up at me as it came loose. I blocked it with my sword, though I had to roll on my back to do it. When he reared up for a second swipe, I kicked hard at his knees, knocking him backward.

Around us, the crowd was cheering for Devlin. I didn't detect anyone calling my name, at least, not without some wish for my death attached to it. No big surprise there.

While Devlin stumbled away, I jumped to my feet and ran for him. He recovered and we locked swords. It was obvious that he was far stronger than I. I could block his blows but only with considerable effort, and mine seemed to have little more impact than if I'd tossed feathers at him.

However, I had the advantage of being a smaller target and was much quicker on my feet, so it was easier to dodge his hits and swipes. I was also younger, so I decided to make him move as much as possible, to tire him. Gradually, that seemed to be working. His sword still struck mine ferociously, but his reaction time was slowing. I used the gaps to work in extra hits.

He attacked to my right, which I blocked, but it knocked me off balance. He used the moment to switch hands, and so I charged forward, piercing his shoulder. Devlin cried out and fell back. With his weaker arm and with his injury bleeding profusely, I finally gained the advantage.

I increased the speed of my sword, forcing him back against the crowd, which had now largely fallen silent. They gave him no leeway and for the first time it occurred to me that there might be several who liked the idea of losing Devlin as their king. However, that didn't mean any of them wanted me to have the job.

Devlin dropped his sword and I exhaled, relieved that this fight was about to be over. But his other hand swung at me from behind his back, and I ducked when I realized what he was holding.

"That's my knife!" I scowled, insulted that he had attempted to kill me using my own weapon. I hammered his arm with the flat edge of my blade. His reflexes reacted and the knife fell. He started toward it but I kicked his thigh, knocking him to the ground.

Devlin put an arm in the air for mercy and slowly rose to his knees. I kept my sword at his neck as I crouched low enough to pick up my knife. "Thanks for not making me steal this. That was going to be a lot of work."

Devlin bowed his head. "Sage . . . Jaron, spare my life, I beg you."

"If you want to live, then release Imogen first."

"Devlin has no authority to release her, even to save his own life," Agor said, stepping forward. "She still must answer for violating the pirate code."

"But I can save you, Jaron," Devlin grunted, and held his wounded shoulder. "If you kill me, my pirates will never accept you as their king. From the instant I fall, your rule will be challenged by one pirate after another until your strength eventually fails. So if you give me my life, I'll give you yours. I'll let you go free, and the pirates will never come against you again."

"If this is a sincere offer, tell me the names of anyone else in my court with any connection to you."

Devlin growled, but I kept the point of my blade at his neck. To encourage the conversation, I gave him a scratch and he said, "There's no one else. After Conner's failure, Gregor was our only remaining connection to your court."

I withdrew the blade slightly. "And do I have your word on this?"

"Yes." He looked up at me. "Please."

"Then I accept your offer. With one exception. If I can trade one life for yours, then it must be Imogen's. Let her go. Assure me she has safe passage away from here."

Devlin blinked in disbelief. "And what happens to you?"

"You have me. But she walks free."

"Then release her yourself." Devlin grunted at the men behind us, "You heard this fool's bargain. Move aside!"

The crowd parted, revealing Imogen behind them. Tears stained her cheeks and new drops fell again when she saw me. I reached for the ropes around her wrists and began untying them.

"This can't happen," Imogen said. "There must be another way. If you finished it with Devlin —"

"He was right. If I took his place as king right now, they'd kill me first and then come for you. At least this way, one of us walks free."

"Then let it be you," Imogen said. "You must save your kingdom."

"You will save it. You must return to Drylliad and expose Gregor's treachery."

"No, Jaron. They're going to kill you!"

Getting killed wasn't in my plans, although admittedly, the outlook wasn't presently as good as I would've liked. But Devlin still needed me to find that cave. I had some time.

I glanced back at the pirates. Several were tending to Devlin's shoulder but many more looked my way with fisted hands, waiting for the order to take me. I knew what would happen when they did, and it terrified me. But I didn't want Imogen to see, didn't want her to know. The thought of it made my own hands shake, and I had trouble loosening the rest of the rope.

Panicked, Imogen touched my cheek with her free hand. "A king would give his life for his country. But I'm asking you to save it, and not just for me. If you fall, all of Carthya falls."

Unable to loosen the knot on her right hand with my trembling fingers, I used my knife to slice through the rope. She pulled free, then wrapped her arms around me and said, "If there's any friendship between us, then you must do what I ask. There has to be a way for you to leave. Find that, and come with me, please. It's not too late."

Forcing myself to concentrate, I leaned closer to her and whispered in her ear, "This isn't over. I didn't come here to fail."

"And I didn't come here to lose you!" Her fingers dug into my shoulders with the desperation she felt. "All that's left is for you to run. If you won't do that for me, then do it for your people. Don't they matter to you?"

"Of course they do." It hurt that she'd suggest otherwise. I closed my eyes, almost too full of emotion to breathe. But when I opened them again my voice was firm. "Take Mystic and get to Drylliad. Do not come back here. Ever."

Before she could respond, several pirates grabbed me from behind. They removed my sword and took the knife. Again. I didn't resist, except for what it took to watch Imogen as she ran to Mystic and leapt on his back. She paused when she saw me and looked for a moment like she might try fighting Devlin herself.

"Go!" I yelled at her.

With tears streaming down her face, Imogen nodded, then kicked at Mystic's side and disappeared into the woods.

By this time, Devlin had been given a chair and his shoulder was wrapped in a bandage. He'd need better care soon, but it would do for now. They brought me to face him and forced me to my knees at his feet. Refusing to kneel, I shifted my legs into a sitting position. That only amused him temporarily.

"You made an oath to me," Devlin said. "Can we agree that you violated it?"

Not by my definitions, but again, Devlin wasn't the type to debate the subtleties of word meanings. And possibly even then I had violated it.

"Any chance we can bypass the cruelest method of death and settle this over a game of cards?" I asked.

Devlin chuckled lightly. "Are you afraid?"

Afraid didn't even begin to describe the terror I felt. Pinched behind me, my hands still shook. But I was angry with myself too. Because for all my good intentions, it was obvious that I had been wrong to come here. There were so many who would pay for my mistakes.

Devlin leaned in toward me. "You should be afraid. Because I still have my whip and my map of Carthya. I'll give you as many lashes as it takes until you're ready to disclose the location of that cave."

He nodded at whoever was holding me. They yanked me to my feet and dragged me to the same post where Imogen had been tied only moments ago. Dried blood stained the wrist holds of the post. I briefly wondered whose it was and what they'd done to earn a place here. Whoever it had been, the blood had probably come from them trying to pull their hands free. The pirates would let me get to the same point of desperation, I was sure of that. I was equally certain that when they finally did decide to kill me, I'd be grateful for it.

As they began to tie me, I wanted to yell out, to release some of my fear that way, but I held it in. Imogen wouldn't be that far from here yet, and I didn't want her to know what was about to happen. If it was possible to scream on the inside, though, I was, and the sound of it was deafening.

· THIRTY-THREE ·

My shirt was already in rags, so it was an easy thing for them to tear the rest of it away. Devlin remained in his chair where he could watch me, but Agor held the whip and I could tell by the fierceness of his expression that he relished the opportunity to use it.

"Who are you to make me look like such a fool?" he sneered.

I thought the answer to that had been more than adequately covered, so I didn't bother to respond.

"You may have defeated Devlin, but in a real fight I could still beat you," Agor said.

That was unlikely. Agor was too predictable to be very dangerous. But telling him that would only make him angrier than he already was, and since he held the whip, I opted for silence.

With my shirt off, Agor walked a full circle around me, surveying exactly where he wanted to begin. I took deep breaths and tried to prepare for what was coming. It hadn't been that long since Mott and Cregan whipped me in Conner's dungeon. And as horrible as that had been, Conner's strap had been thick, intended to bruise me rather than to leave the deep cuts Agor's whip would inflict. Mott's whipping had come as a punishment, and I'd known the torture would end if I just endured it. But Agor wanted something from me. He'd continue until I gave them the location of the cave, or until I was dead.

"Come see him," Agor said to Devlin, still looking at me. "This is not the body you'd expect of a king."

Irritated at being treated like a show exhibit, I rolled my eyes, but again I held my tongue. If nothing else, it bought me another minute or two.

Curious, Devlin rose from his chair and walked behind me as well. From where he'd sat, he would already have seen the slash across my stomach from Erick's thief, and the cut from Roden on my arm. But I was far too thin for someone who was literally given the king's feast each meal. I was also covered in bruises from my sword match with Agor, I had numerous scrapes from my fight with the pirates just now, and I had the two scars on my back from Farthenwood.

Devlin walked back to face me, but I couldn't read his expression. It wasn't quite a look of respect, but it wasn't anger either.

"I thought you were from a civilized country," he said. "How have you come to look more like Carthya's whipping boy than its king?"

"I have a habit of irritating some of our less civilized people," I answered. "But you seem like a civilized . . . pirate. I'd much prefer it if you didn't have me whipped."

"And why shouldn't I?"

With some effort, I forced a smile to my face. "Because it will hurt."

"I hope so." Devlin held his shoulder as he returned to his chair. "You'll get enough lashes to learn some humility, then we'll have a talk about that cave."

"That's a waste of your time," I said. "It's not in me to become humble, nor to reveal secrets to my enemies."

Agor unwound his whip and snapped it once in the air. I cringed when I heard it and gritted my teeth together. It would be impossible to keep myself from crying out, even to save Imogen from hearing, and a part of me worried that no matter what I had said, eventually I would give in to anything Devlin wanted.

Agor grunted as he reared his arm back in his first move to strike me, only the whip didn't fly.

"What?" Agor looked behind him, confused.

I looked as well. Roden was standing at the edge of the crowd of pirates who had gathered to watch. In his hand was the end of the whip. He'd wound it around his wrist and continued to wind it, pulling it from Agor's grip. In all that time, he never took his eyes off me. I could almost feel them boring into me.

Roden had stopped my whipping for now — which I greatly appreciated, but there was a total lack of sympathy in his expression, and that concerned me.

"How dare you," Agor said.

"Roden! What's the meaning of this?" Devlin asked.

Roden finished winding the whip and then tossed it to the ground. Addressing me, he said, "A message came ordering me back early. It said that a boy named Sage was with the pirates, promising some sort of treasure. But I told myself it couldn't be you."

"It's not the first time you've been wrong about me," I said.

Roden raised his voice. "Devlin, you promised that any action involving the king of Carthya would be my privilege."

"That all changed when your king got himself made one of my pirates."

Roden turned to me, genuinely surprised. He noticed the branding on my forearm and his mouth dropped open. Our eyes met again and I smiled, a little embarrassed at how stupid it sounded when Devlin said it aloud.

"Him?" Roden shook his head fiercely as if the movement would help his understanding. "The king of Carthya is a pirate?"

"We didn't know who he really was."

"You should have known!" Roden's face darkened. "I told you about him. I warned you."

Even bound and ready to be whipped, I couldn't help but feel a little honored that the pirates had to be warned about me.

"You told us about Jaron," Devlin said. "The name of Sage was never mentioned."

Roden looked at me and his eyes narrowed. "Whatever his name, I'm here now and he's mine. Release him."

Devlin shook his head. "He just bargained away his life to me, saving a girl named Imogen."

Roden shot a glare at me. This time I looked away. I didn't want any questions about her involvement here.

Roden turned back to Devlin. "You've already made a bargain with me."

Devlin had begun to bleed through the bandage on his shoulder, yet he still made the effort to stand and face Roden. "We agreed that when the pirates attacked Carthya, you would have the king as your reward. But this is different. Jaron came here on his own."

Roden stepped closer to Devlin, clearly angry. "The plan was just to kill Jaron, and let Avenia take both the blame and the spoils. If you kill him here, Carthya will want revenge on us."

"I've heard his reputation," Devlin said. "Carthya won't fight for him."

"Yes, they will," Roden said firmly. "If he's the boy I knew at Farthenwood, then his people will follow him to the devil's lair and back."

I cocked my head at that. Was I still the boy Roden had known at Farthenwood? I wished I could talk with him in private. There was so much anger in Roden's eyes, but was that because of me or Devlin?

Roden folded his arms. "So what are your intentions with him?"

"Somewhere in Carthya is a cave full of the wealth of the royals. I'll do whatever it takes until he reveals that location, then it'll be my decision what to do with him after that."

"No," Roden insisted. "I want him. Now."

Devlin ignored Roden. "Agor, give Roden's king twenty lashes to start, then we'll ask him about the cave." To Roden he said, "I'll make you this deal. After I have Carthya's treasure, you can take whatever's left of Jaron. I don't wish to deprive you of your revenge."

My head snapped up then. Roden wanted revenge because I had taken the throne of Carthya and he had not. But he'd already given me a rather painful cut on the arm. We were more than even. Despite the disadvantage of my current position, I felt justifiably angry.

"This bargaining will stop at once!" I yelled. "Devlin, you're a coward and a pig. Give me whatever punishment you want. I will never, *never* reveal the location of that cave. And, Roden, you know my name. You know that throne always belonged to me. Nothing you can do will ever change that fact. It will only make you a traitor, a lower form of life than Devlin, if that's possible."

Without waiting for an order, Agor grabbed the whip and moved to strike me with it. I had closed my eyes in anticipation of the sting, so I didn't see the speed of Roden's movement. All I knew was that before the whip touched me, Agor's angry cry turned to a grunt of pain and he fell to the ground. When I looked, Roden stood behind him, his sword red with blood.

"Stop him," Devlin shouted.

Just as he had with my vigils at the castle, Roden cut through the pirates like they were little more than soft butter. It didn't take long before the rest of them backed away. And once they saw where he was going, they stopped fighting him entirely.

Devlin stood behind the rest of his men, not because they were protecting him but because he was using them to hide. He had withdrawn his sword but held it limply in his good arm.

"I am the king of these pirates," Devlin said. "Roden, you have violated the oath —"

"And you violated our bargain," Roden said. "Drop your sword."

"Never." Devlin raised his sword to attack, but in a single move, Roden deflected his thrust and stabbed Devlin just below the chest. Devlin was dead the instant he hit the ground.

There was a long moment while everyone stared at their king's body, as if it was impossible that after so many years he could be gone so quickly, and with surprisingly little effort on Roden's part.

Roden stared at him too. Of course, Devlin had made the first strike, but I didn't think Roden had intended to kill him. Now that he had, Roden was more than just a pirate here. And he knew it.

"You have a new king," Roden announced. "You will follow my orders now." The others looked up at him, not sure what to expect next. Then he nodded at me. "Get Jaron down from there and someone find him a shirt. Put him in the jail until I decide what to do with him next."

"My traitorous captain of the guard is in the jail," I said. "One of us is bound to kill the other in there, so if you want access to us both, I'd suggest taking me elsewhere."

Roden glanced at a pirate next to me who said, "I'll put him with a boy we just locked away. I think they came here together."

"Is it secure?" Roden asked.

"Probably more so than the jail. Nobody's ever escaped it."

"Fine."

The ropes were cut away from my hands and pirates grabbed me on either side. Roden never looked up as they led me away. I said nothing to him either, mostly because I didn't know the words. Roden hadn't saved me from the pirates. He'd only delayed what now seemed inevitable.

· THIRTY-FOUR ·

As the pirate had told Roden, the room where they took me did seem far more secure than the jail where I'd been yesterday. The jail was nearly at ground level, so if a prisoner could get past the vigil, he could be on the run in seconds.

In contrast, this room was midway up the cliff, above the living quarters, and it took the men considerable time to unlock the door to put me inside, so it would likely be nearly impossible to pick the lock from within the room. Even if someone could do it, the stairs down would take him past several well-armed pirates, and there were no stairs up to the top of the cliff. It was obvious why nobody had ever escaped from here. I doubted many people had even tried.

Fink reacted with an excited yelp and a high jump when the locked door opened and he saw me on the other side.

"I didn't think I'd see you again," he said. "No offense, but I really didn't."

I smiled tiredly. "No offense."

My escorts thrust me into the room, which was furnished

only with a small table and a single chair. One who had been particularly unkind in the way he held my arm said to Fink, "He's not out of trouble yet, boy, so don't get too attached."

They tossed a shirt into the room, which, surprisingly, was in better condition than the one I'd worn before. Then they locked the door behind us and left the room.

"No vigil?" I asked Fink, pulling the shirt over my head.

"I asked for one, just to have someone to talk to. They said one wasn't needed here, and besides, I'm not much of a threat to anyone."

"You're not," I agreed. "But I'm glad you're here."

"Where's Imogen?"

"She left. I hope."

"Oh. That's good." Fink sat on the table and stared at me. "She said your name is Jaron, that you're the king of Carthya."

I sat beside him on the table, looking at nothing in particular. "She's right."

He scratched his nose and continued to stare. "You don't look like a king. Or act like one."

"Often I don't feel like a king either."

"She said you came here to destroy the pirates, and that it was the worst idea anyone's ever had."

"It's hard to argue with that kind of logic."

"And she said that you're the biggest fool of a king that Carthya has ever seen, and that it's stupid for you to let yourself get killed because you're probably the only person capable of saving your country."

I grinned. "Maybe you shouldn't tell me anything else she said. I don't think I can handle hearing any more of her opinions."

Fink smiled back at me. "Yeah. I didn't even get to the really mean things." He yawned. "But I liked you when you were Sage. I guess even though you're a king, we can still be friends, right?"

"Sure." I stood and began pacing the room. How long would Roden let me stay in here? What would he do when he finally did come for me?

There was a small window at the far end of the room, opposite the door. Standing beneath it I still couldn't see the top of the cliff, but I had a good idea of how far above the ground we were. Then I continued my pacing.

"I'm hungry," Fink eventually said. "You?"

"Yeah, I am too." The last I'd eaten was only a little at supper the night before, and it was entering the afternoon now. But distracting myself from the hunger pangs wasn't difficult. Not when the distraction was figuring out how to keep Roden from killing me before I'd had my chance with him.

I turned to Fink. "Listen, there's a new pirate king and his name is Roden. The only reason I'm still here is that Roden has a grudge from our past and he wants to take his time with me. So when he comes, I don't want you to be my friend, I don't want you to defend me or try to help me in any way. That would only make things worse for you."

Fink shrugged. "I'm not afraid."

I grabbed his arm to force him to look at me. "This is serious, Fink. I could've said all sorts of horrible things just now to make you genuinely hate me. Believe me, I know how to do that. But I'm trying to do this differently. I have to trust you to do this. You must make Roden think you want to get away from me. Say anything you have to say. *Do* anything you have to do, even if you think it'll hurt me. It's the only way you'll survive."

Fink frowned, then opened his mouth to speak. He was stopped by the sound of a key in the locked door.

I stood, ready for whoever was about to come through the door, then glanced at Fink. "Anything you have to do," I repeated.

Erick was pushed into the room first, then shoved to the floor by the men behind him. His right eye was bruised and swollen and he had a bloody lip, but he was walking evenly, so I hoped the worst was over for him. Unfortunately, it probably wasn't.

The intensity of Erick's glare when he caught my eye was murderous. I would've apologized right there except that it would have sounded ridiculous and insulting. Besides, Erick wasn't alone.

Two large men followed him into the room, while at least three or four others guarded the doorway. The two who entered carried chains in their arms with manacles linked to each set. Presumably for me.

I attempted to do this the peaceful way and held out my arms to show I wouldn't fight. The pirates shoved me hard against the wall anyway, so I felt justified in kicking them back. If they weren't playing nice, I didn't see why I should have to.

Fink and Erick stood at the opposite end of the room. Fear was evident on Fink's face, but Erick looked a little smug. If he was happy to see me get some of what I deserved, then I couldn't blame him.

They wrapped the chain around a post in the corner of the room, then the pirates clamped the manacles firmly around my wrists and ankles. I adjusted my feet to keep my balance, which one pirate interpreted as an aggressive move. He landed a merciless fist into my gut. I doubled over, choking on my own breath.

In the background I heard Fink say, "Now give him one for me."

I smiled slightly but remained bent over. There was too strong a possibility that if I stood up straight again, the pirates would only honor Fink's request.

A pirate leaned over and snarled, "You think you were in trouble when Devlin was king? I just heard what the new king has planned for you. I'd suggest you ask the devils to take you now, before he gets here."

It wasn't a bad suggestion, except that the devils were clearly on Roden's side.

· THIRTY-FIVE ·

As soon as the pirates left, Fink started toward me but Erick grabbed his shoulder and held him back.

"He's not a friend," Erick said coldly. "Not mine or yours."

Fink looked at me, and I very slightly shook my head. I'd told him that he had to convince Roden of his dislike for me. His eyes darkened as he realized he had to convince everyone else of that too.

"I just wanted to hurt him myself," Fink said. It wouldn't have mattered if he did, because I doubted Fink could hit hard enough to compare with anything else I'd faced today, but I was glad to see him back off anyway.

"For what it's worth, Erick, I'm sorry." I said the words slowly, because my stomach still ached.

"It's worth nothing!" Erick shouted. "You lied about who you are and lied about the treasure! Anything that happens now is better than you deserve. I put my own life on the line to bring you here. When they're done with you they'll kill me, probably Fink too."

"Things didn't go the way I'd planned." Not that it would make any difference to him, or to me, but it needed to be said.

Erick stepped forward. I hoped he didn't intend to hit me too. Or that if he did, he would choose one of the few spots on my body not already bruised. "There's one thing that's been bothering me," he said. "When we went to that noble's house in Libeth and you chased after that man, did you really kill him?"

"I never claimed to have," I said. "That was your assumption. And no, I never touched him. He was my friend."

"You say that as if he no longer is."

"He'll serve me for as long as I'm king." I paused, thinking of how much frustration I must have caused Mott over the past several days. "But I doubt that I have any friends left."

"Not here you don't." With that, Erick sat heavily on the chair in the room and folded his arms.

Fink climbed onto the table beside him, sat cross-legged, and rested his head in his hands. Neither of them looked at me.

I shifted my weight so that I could lean into the corner of the room and then closed my eyes. If nothing else, at least I could get a little sleep.

Whether I slept for two minutes or two hours, I couldn't be sure. But I awoke to loud voices, and the sound of a key turning in the locked door. My eyes opened slowly, reluctantly. I glanced at Erick and Fink, who were still sitting in their same places as before.

Erick cocked his head, hearing the key as well. "Are you ready for whoever's on the other side?" he asked.

"No," I muttered. And I wasn't.

When the door opened, Erick and Fink jumped to their feet and backed against the far wall. I still felt groggy and was slower to straighten up. In fact, it was difficult to summon any energy whatsoever. The strain of the last several days had finally caught up to me.

This time it was Roden who entered. The same two pirates who had chained me up came with him, and as before, several others waited in the doorway.

Roden folded his arms and stared icily at me. It was nothing new to have someone look at me with expressions of anger or dislike. But I didn't like it coming from Roden. Back at Farthenwood, we had formed what I thought was a decent friendship. Then he became manipulated by Conner's servant Cregan, to fulfill Cregan's dark ambitions. Perhaps it was my own arrogance at work, but I found it hard to believe that Roden could hate me so much, just because I had the crown and he didn't. In light of this, I thought it best to let him speak first, so I waited, eyes lowered.

He spoke first to Fink. "Erick claims he didn't know who Sage was before. Did you?"

Fink shook his head, then said, "But I didn't think he was a regular thief either. He was just different from the rest."

Moving his attention to Erick, Roden narrowed his eyes. "Even the boy knew something was wrong. Neither of you leaves this room alive."

The obvious exception to his words was me, which I found

less than comforting. Whatever Roden wanted me left alive for, it wasn't going to be good.

"Please," Fink said, sniffing. I looked over and the kid was actually crying. "Please don't hurt me. I'm only a child."

"Stop that."

"Please, sir." Large tears rolled down Fink's face. It was impressive, really.

Roden rolled his eyes, but the tears did their job and he softened. "I'll think about it, all right? Just stop!"

"If you keep us alive, we can still prove ourselves."

Roden cocked an eyebrow. "Yeah? How?"

"We'll take care of Jaron for you." Recovering a bit too quickly, Fink wiped his eyes and said, "Erick and I have a score to settle with him now."

I nearly laughed. It was a good attempt by Fink to sound hateful toward me, but he didn't pull it off well. Roden only shook his head at him. "Thanks, but I have my own plans for him."

Which, unfortunately, I had already suspected.

Now Roden turned to me. "You ignored my threat last week."

"Looks that way."

"Did you think I wasn't serious? That I couldn't do everything I told you I would?"

"I knew you were serious," I replied. "That's why I had to come."

"But you were looking for me before that. You sent Mott and Tobias all over Carthya to find me. Why?"

"I didn't like the way things ended in that tunnel." Roden and I had fought in a narrow passage beneath the castle on the night I returned there. If he had defeated me, he would have entered the castle and tried to claim the throne as Jaron. But it wouldn't have worked. Roden never would've gotten far with Kerwyn and the fraud would have been exposed. At one point during our fight I had backed off when I could have killed Roden. There was a moment when I thought he had also backed off, though I had never been sure of that.

Roden chuckled. "You didn't like how things ended? And how is that, with me alive?" His tone darkened. "I suppose you think you were merciful that night, allowing me to run. But you weren't. You cursed me. Where else was I supposed to go to get away from you?"

"It would've been nice if you had chosen somewhere less dangerous," I said. "You're an even worse pirate than I am."

In an instant, Roden's face hardened and he backhanded me across the face. "We're equals now, so you can't talk to me like that. I'm as much of a king as you are."

"Hardly," I scoffed. "There's no honor in being the king of the pirates. No glory, and no reward other than an eventual death at the hands of your own men."

"Then I wonder why you'd take the trouble to come all this way and join us," he said.

"You didn't leave me much of a choice."

"Or maybe you want to finish what we started in your gardens." When I held my gaze on him he added, "I was there because you cheated before, that night you were crowned. You cheated to win that duel and cheated me out of the throne!"

When Roden and I fought that night, I had pretended to fall and lose my sword. But what I'd done wasn't a cheat. It was a trick, yes, but Roden had no one to blame for falling for it except himself. Especially because I had warned him earlier it's what I would do.

"Everything about you is a lie," Roden said. "It always was. Do you know what it was like the next morning in Drylliad? Everywhere I turned, it was celebration and talk of a new day for Carthya, and all for who? You?"

"Yeah, it was for me. I am Jaron. Maybe you don't like that fact, but nothing you can do will change it."

"Whatever your name is, you don't deserve the throne." Roden's voice grew louder, sharper. "It was supposed to be given to whoever won in that tunnel. It was supposed to be me!"

"Then give me a sword and we'll fight again," I suggested. "If you win, you have me for whatever revenge you want. And if I win, I get what I want."

"Another sword fight is pointless because I already have you." Roden's eyes narrowed. "And I know what you want: You thought by coming here you could somehow stop the pirates from invading Carthya."

I nodded. "That's still my intention, by the way."

"Well, I'm their king now. And you're out of time to stop me from doing anything. Tonight I've ordered a feast in celebration of my becoming king. Afterward, in front of everyone, *I'm* going to be the one to end *your* life, to show what happens to anyone who crosses me. I'll use your death to solidify my reign."

He hadn't intended to be funny, but I laughed at him anyway. "I'm very glad you said that. Because until hearing you speak just now, I had thought I was the most ridiculous ruler in these lands."

Roden raised his hand to strike me again, but this time I would not flinch and he slowly lowered it.

"Let's go," he told the pirates with him. "There's a lot to do before tonight."

"You can't leave him like this," the larger of the pirates said. "You were the one who told us the stories about him."

"He got out of rope before," Roden said. "Not chains. He won't get through these."

Actually, I would. The pin Imogen had snuck to me was still in my boot. It'd easily pick the lock on these chains.

"But if he did get free, he could climb out that window."

Roden faced me. "I can't deny that possibility."

Neither could I. In fact, that was my plan.

Roden grabbed a club from a pirate in the doorway and walked closer to me. He swung it once in the air, testing its weight. Something turned in my gut, a warning perhaps. But Roden wanted me alive for tonight, so I hoped he only meant to threaten me with it.

"Sorry about this," Roden said. And as he swung the club back over his shoulder, I saw what he intended.

"Don't!" I yelled. "Roden, don't!"

But he did. The club crashed into my lower right leg like I'd been hit with a cannonball. Lightning ripped through every nerve of my body and escaped through my screams. I knew immediately that the bone was broken, though with so much pain, I couldn't tell how badly.

Held upright only by the manacles, I collapsed to one side and vomited, my head swimming in a dense fog.

"He won't escape those chains now," Roden said. "But if he does, he's not going anywhere."

I wished I could've had some clever response to that, but my world was quickly fading. Reeling from a toxic combination of pain, hunger, and exhaustion, I slumped forward and let the darkness take over.

· THIRTY-SIX ·

It was the pain that eventually awoke me. The shock of Roden's strike had sent me into unconsciousness, but that had gradually evolved into a restless and unproductive sleep. The chains around my wrists were too high on the wall to allow me to sit on the ground, so when I tried to balance on my injured leg and adjust my weight, a bolt of pain tore through me. My eyes flew open and I cried out. When I focused on Erick and Fink, I saw them standing on their end of the room, staring at me in horror.

"How long was I out?" I mumbled. Neither of them responded so I focused directly on Fink. "How long?"

"A couple of hours maybe."

It wasn't quite dark yet. From the angle of the sun coming through the window, I guessed there were still another two or three hours until sundown. Not much time.

"How does it feel?" Fink asked.

"Like butterfly kisses, what do you think?" I leaned my head back to stretch out the muscles, but it did little good. My neck had been in one position for so long, it was now angrily protesting my attempts to use it.

"Why did you talk to Roden like that?" Erick asked, clearly still upset with me.

"I made a mistake." My hope had been that if I got Roden angry enough, he would challenge me to another sword fight. Clearly, that plan hadn't worked.

"Here's what I don't understand," Erick said. "You were a king, you had everything. Now you've sunk to our level and you'll lose everything. Not only your life, but he'll come for your kingdom too."

"You're wrong on all counts," I said. "I'm still a king. My title isn't determined by my crown; it's in my blood. Gregor is imprisoned here, so at least for now, my kingdom is safe." Then I looked directly at Erick. "And my stature never sank when I joined you. You may be a thief, but there is far more good in you than bad. I'm better off for knowing you."

Erick's eyes fluttered and he finally looked down, silent.

I turned my attention to the more immediate problem. Roden wasn't clear about when the supper would begin tonight, but without question I was running out of time.

The complication was that Imogen's pin was in the boot of my leg that Roden had broken. I made a vain attempt to wiggle the foot, even though I knew it would hurt and would be useless in helping to remove the boot. I couldn't get my hands down as far as my feet to pull it off, and even if I could, the manacle around my ankle made the boot tighter than usual.

I nodded at Fink, calling him to come. He hesitated and I said, "Don't make me beg for help. Come here."

Fink glanced at Erick, who didn't acknowledge him, then crossed the room to me.

"As gently as you can, you've got to get this boot off my foot." I winced as I spoke and Fink paled. To encourage him, I added, "They're a little big on me anyway, so they should slide easily. Just go slow."

Fink knelt beside the injured leg. I couldn't do anything to lift it for him, and when he raised it slightly and tugged at the heel, I cried out and told him to stop.

"New plan," I said between shallow breaths. "Try rolling the leather down."

Fink touched the top of my boot. He pulled at the sides, and the pain flared inside me, but this time it was him who gave up. "I think that'd be worse than just pulling it off," he said.

Still on his side of the room, Erick muttered something to himself, then stood. Without looking at me, he reached into his own boot and pulled out a small folding knife. "Back off," he ordered Fink, who quickly obeyed. Then he went down on one knee and began cutting the leather down its side. It was a slow process since the knife was so small, and every time he moved my leg even by a hair, I gasped and tried not to pass out again.

When he reached the sole, it was a comparatively easy thing to lift the rest of the boot free from my foot.

"There's a pin in it," I said between breaths. "Give it to me."

"Let me do it," Fink said. "You can't reach the lock on those chains anyway."

Fink widened the pin to its full length, then slid one end into the manacles locked around my wrists. He toyed with it until he found the lever he was seeking. With one careful push, there was a clicking sound and the manacles pulled apart. He next went to work on the ankle manacles, and when they unlocked he was very careful in removing them.

Free from the chains, I crumpled to the ground. It hurt to fall, but my good leg was too tired to lower me more carefully.

"What now?" Fink asked. "The lock is on the other side of the door. We're still stuck in this room."

I glanced up at the window, grateful for the first time that I had recently become so thin. Erick stared at me, incredulous. "Do you know where we are? More than a stone's throw above the beach and nearly the same below the cliff top. There's nowhere to go."

Fink pressed close to Erick's side and whispered to him, "Roden said he could climb."

"Up a cliff?" Erick shook his head. "Maybe with two good legs, but not one."

"Punch out the glass," I said to Fink. "Then pray there's no one below us."

Fink held out his hand for Erick's knife. Erick sighed loudly before handing it over. Then Fink grabbed the chair from the corner to stand on while he broke out the glass. We waited in silence for the sound of footsteps outside the door, but none came. Roden would want a big dinner. I was sure he was keeping everyone occupied.

When the window was cleared, I gestured to the chair on which Fink had stood. "Now break that. Don't split the longer pieces."

"A leg brace," Erick muttered. "Yeah, that'll make all the difference." But he went to the chair anyway and began hitting it against the wall.

While he did, I asked Fink to remove his shirt and rip it into the longest lengths he could. Then I laid my head flat on the floor and closed my eyes. Roden was going to regret having done this to me; I'd make sure of it.

With one final hit, the last joints of the chair fell apart. Most of it came to pieces in unusable sections, but Erick was able to break away enough to end up with one straight piece of wood nearly as long as my entire leg. I told him to break it even more. I needed to bend my knee if I was going to keep my balance.

They did the rest of the work without any further instructions. Fink held a piece of wood both on the inside and outside of my leg while Erick tied the strips from the shirt as tightly as he could. I hated that I needed their help, all the while knowing this would've been impossible to do on my own. My leg still pulsed with pain, but once it was braced with the wood, it was more manageable than before. I stood and tested my stance on the floor. I made no effort to put weight on my injured leg, thankful that years of climbing and walking on narrow ledges had given me good balance and strength.

"Now scoot the table beneath the window," I said.

"You've got no chance on that cliff," Erick said.

"I'd rather fall from that cliff than wait here to be killed!" The fear I felt came out sounding like anger. "Now help me. Please!"

"You're a complete fool," Erick said.

"So I've been told." I stared at each of them a moment and said, "I think I'll be discovered before anyone comes here looking for me. But in case I'm wrong about that, you should come up with a story to explain how I escaped here on my own."

"I knew I'd hate you before this was over," Erick said.

"I'm sorry you do. You're one of only a few people who I'd have preferred to like me."

Erick looked down at his knife, sighed heavily, then held it out to me. "Take it."

But I shook my head. "It's your last defense. I've taken enough from you already."

I sat on the table, then got to a standing position. I clamped my fingers around the windowsill, but there was no traction on the wall for my foot. Erick sighed again and pushed the table away, using his own strength to lift me until I angled my way through the window.

I paused to sit on the windowsill, with everything but my legs already on the outside. A cool breeze washed up from the sea below us, and I took that in with a deep breath. Erick had underestimated the distance, both to the ground and the cliff above me, yet the texture of the cliff wall was better than I'd hoped for. Vines and plants grew dense and well rooted, and there were many rocks and missing chunks of earth. I didn't know whether I could make it to the top on one leg or not, but I thought it was a great day to try.

· THIRTY-SEVEN ·

It only took me a short distance of climbing to willingly admit this had been a terrible idea. I hadn't accounted for the added strain it would put on my shoulders and arms to compensate for my useless leg, and my leg that did work was screaming for relief.

Every inch I rose required a series of steps. First was to visually locate my next hold. Generally speaking, this wasn't too difficult, and I planned ahead to be sure I wouldn't find myself in trouble farther up. The second step was to reach for it with my lead hand, the stronger one that would keep a steady grip even if everything else failed. Then I used both hands to dig into the wall while I jumped to the next hold with my good foot. I found that I could use my injured leg temporarily for the jump. It hurt like the devils themselves had come to torture me, but as long as I moved quickly, it kept me balanced for the final step of moving my second hand into the new position.

A climb like this normally would've taken me only a half hour, but I was moving considerably slower than usual. The sunlight was inching away and with it, any hope I might have to survive the night. I heard the sounds of pirates moving above me, but luckily, none of them thought to look over the cliff wall for anyone. Most of them seemed fairly busy anyway, probably still in preparation for Roden's dinner.

After an hour I was more than halfway up. Every muscle in my body ached and I was soaked in sweat, but I knew now that it was possible to succeed. So I forced myself to continue upward, letting thoughts of those I cared for most spur my strength.

I had to live. There were so many people I needed to apologize to, so many people I hoped to see again. Beyond that, it was strange to realize that I wanted to see Drylliad again, to gaze at the white walls of my castle and walk through its doors, where I belonged.

And so I continued to climb. There came a point when the anticipation of pain no longer deterred me from using my hurt leg. I still couldn't put weight on it, but every other muscle now hurt so much I was willing to use it more for balance and stability. Besides, I had to hurry. If I was still here when it got dark, I had no chance of reaching the top.

The sun was only minutes from setting when my lead hand grabbed a rock lodged into the surface of the cliff. I hesitated a moment to be sure I was alone. By this time, the dinner seemed to have already started, so nobody was around. Apparently, Roden wouldn't send someone to get me until after the meal ended. I hoped they had many courses left to eat.

With a final hoist, I rolled to the top of the cliff, where I lay breathless for several minutes before it occurred to me to continue moving. When it did, I could do nothing more than scoot beneath a bush. Every part of me hurt, with some muscles on my shoulders competing against the pain in my broken leg.

Then I glanced to the side and smiled.

Soon after I came to Mrs. Turbeldy's orphanage, there had been one night when I took a beating after stopping one boy from kicking a much younger boy for stealing food. Afterward, Mrs. Turbeldy showed me an aravac plant in her yard, a dense, dark green bush with narrow leaves and bright purple flowers, and told me how chewing on its leaves helped numb pain.

I had just rolled beneath an aravac plant.

I gripped a branch tightly and ran my hand down it to strip the leaves free, then stuffed several in my mouth. The taste was awful, but the numbing effects began to work almost immediately.

When I'd gotten all the use from them that I could, I spat them out, then stripped another branch and began chewing on those. They didn't stop my pain, but they did ease it a bit. As I chewed, I tightened the fabric around my leg brace, which also helped with the pain there.

Moving forward again was an act of pure willpower on my part, but I told myself that it would only get worse the longer I waited. Still, I couldn't move until I pictured Roden walking up to me, seeing that I had made it here, but no farther. I could almost hear his laughter, mocking my failed effort to reach him.

All I could do to move was lie on the ground, pushing my

body forward with my good leg while my injured one dragged uselessly along behind me. Though I was alone, I felt pathetic to have to travel this way, no better than a slithering snake. Even Fink's rat walked with more dignity than this. Maybe this was what I'd come to. Was it possible for a king to run so far from his identity that he ceased to be anyone special? Because I had never felt lower, or less worthy of my title.

By the roars of laughter in the distance, it was easy to know where the pirates were eating. They weren't far from me now. I passed the arena where Agor and I had dueled. The thin wooden swords were still hanging from the tree. Slowly I got to my feet, then grabbed two of them to use as crutches. They weren't much better, forcing me to stoop over like a hunchback, gritting my teeth with every halted step I took, but at least I wasn't crawling. About halfway to the pirates, one of them broke and I collapsed again onto the ground.

Once more, my abject position brought a smile to my face. A patch of Imogen's flowers was right in front of me. It was hard to miss them. They seemed to be everywhere I was, or at least, every place where I might find myself in trouble. Imogen said she planted them for me, as constant reminders of the danger I was in.

Then I groaned as I finally understood. No, Imogen planted them *because* of the danger. They were *for* me. I dug beneath the flowers with my fingers and very quickly felt something hard beneath them. After a little more digging I pulled out a knife. Undoubtedly one of the many knives Agor had said were missing from the kitchen. Imogen must have buried them all over this camp. For me.

When I got up again, I hid the knife in my boot, then tossed the broken sword away. It had splintered into long, jagged edges that were completely unusable. I continued to use the other sword. If I let the wood carry my weight, I could hop forward while using my injured leg only when necessary for balance. I felt entirely useless, and I had never needed more determination than with each hop I took toward Roden.

A sweet smell filled the air as I got closer, and I guessed some sort of hot pudding was being served. On the outskirts of the camp, someone had left a pile of used dishes. Probably the serving girls who had to haul them back and forth from the kitchen. I quietly went through them in search of food, anything that was edible. Much of what I ate was nothing but gristle carved off the side of a roast, yet I took all I could get.

"Oh."

I swerved around, too anxious and hungry to care how humiliating this was. Serena had spotted me. She faced me, frozen in her steps. I put a finger to my lips, a silent plea for her help. Her eyes darted in every direction before she walked over to some dishes farther away from me. She picked up a load and carried them to where I was hiding, setting them down in front of me. There wasn't much more food on them, but every morsel was a boost to my strength.

With the food in my stomach and the effects of the aravac

plant soothing the aches and pains, there was no point in waiting any longer. I was as ready as I'd ever be tonight.

I stood and used the sword to hobble my way into the dinner. The tables were arranged in a large square and Roden sat at the head of them all. The pirates were so engrossed in their conversations and eating, it took a while before they noticed me. When they did, it immediately became quieter than a chapel.

Roden stood and his mouth hung open. His eyes went from my bound leg to the wooden sword in my hand. "You can't be serious."

"Let's finish what was begun in my gardens," I said in the strongest voice I could muster. "Roden, I've come to challenge you as king of the pirates."

· THIRTY-EIGHT ·

Most of the pirates kept their seats as they waited to see what Roden would do next. He chuckled for a moment as if he was sure I must be joking, then when he saw I wasn't, he nodded. "All right." In a louder voice he ordered the tables to be moved so that a battle ring could be formed.

"I need a sword first," I said. "People here keep taking mine."

Roden chuckled again as he walked toward me. He gestured to the one I'd been using as a crutch. "You have one."

"Made of wood. How am I supposed to stab you? It's not even pointed at the end."

Roden scratched his chin and smiled wickedly. "I wouldn't have chosen that one either. But sometimes we have to live with the consequences of our choices. What did you think would happen when you came here?"

"The same thing I think now. Any pirate who doesn't swear loyalty to me is going to die tonight. And you're going to return home with me to Carthya." I studied his reaction carefully to see if my words were having any impact. But I couldn't tell, at least not yet. "I want you at my side, Roden. I need a captain of the guard I can trust."

Along with several of the pirates who had overheard, Roden laughed out loud at that. "You've gone mad. Haven't you noticed? I'm your worst enemy."

"You don't have to be. I'm convinced you'd be a far better friend than enemy."

"I just broke your leg, and by the end of this night I plan to kill you."

"Well, if you ask nicely, I might let you apologize for that." I gestured around us. "This place isn't for you. It's Carthyan blood that runs in your veins."

"That means nothing."

"It means we don't have to fight." I lowered my sword to emphasize my point. "In fact, I'd genuinely prefer not to. I need you, Roden. War is coming."

He shook his head in disbelief. "Yes, I know. I'm bringing you that war."

With a grin, I said, "Then you can see my logic for coming here."

A pirate approached Roden. "The tables are ready. A space has been cleared for you."

Roden looked over at me. "If you back out now, I promise to make your death quick. It's the best that I can do."

"No, the best thing you can do is leave this place."

"Make me," Roden taunted.

"As you wish." Planting my good leg as solidly as possible on the ground, I raised my sword again. "Your time as a pirate ends tonight. Either you will come with me as the loyal captain of my guard, or I will kill you here."

Roden scoffed. "On one leg?"

"It's hard to defeat you unless I use at least one," I said, smiling. "Come with me instead. Make that choice."

Roden pulled his sword from his scabbard and swung it in a full circle around him. He handled his weapon with an ease that lifelong warriors would envy. "I won't give you another choice, Jaron. Unless you surrender now, I will kill you."

And the fight began.

Walking wasn't an option for me, so I had to use what was available. I nearly fell over in smashing the wooden sword against a large rock on the ground. It splintered just as the other sword had, leaving me with an end much sharper than the point of a blade, even though it was still made of wood and an inferior weapon.

Roden's objective was clearly to knock me off balance, but I ducked most of his harder swings and held steady with only slight help from my injured leg. When he caught onto my strategy, he swung lower, forcing me to block him with the wooden sword, near the hilt where it was strongest. Each time he did, though, he had to raise his sword back again, and I used the moment to scratch him with the shards of my broken blade. I never got him deeply, but all of the longer tips had blood on them, so for now, I was still keeping up.

"Roden, this isn't what you want," I said.

"I'm a king here."

"You're a lion ruling a nest of maggots. There's no glory in that, no honor. You are better than this."

"You're only trying to trick me," Roden said. "You've become so desperate that this offer is your last hope."

"When I'm desperate I'll ask Tobias for help. This is no trick."

He swung again for my chest. I ducked but it cost me my balance. Roden used the chance to push me to the ground. The fall sent tremors of pain through me, and gave him time to put a foot on my sword, crushing it.

"Now, see that move?" I said. "It was brilliant. You'd be an excellent captain."

He didn't even smile, but instead swung his blade harder at me. I dodged it and then kicked him with my good leg. He stumbled back a step before he raised his sword again. I leaned forward and grabbed his legs. He tumbled beside me and his blade grazed my shoulder.

I reached for the knife from Imogen and stabbed Roden's thigh. He yelped and leapt away. "Those leg wounds hurt, don't you think?" I said.

Roden caught me on the jaw with his fist, but as I fell back I kicked him in the neck. And because I thought his punch was a dirty trick, I kicked him extra hard again. This time, as Roden reacted, his grip on his sword loosened. I dove for it, but he recovered and scooted away, then stood.

"Get up," he said, heaving gasps of air. "This is a sword fight, not a wrestling match."

I held up a hand while I caught my own breath. Roden lowered his sword and took my arm, helping me up.

"Why me?" Roden asked. "There're others you can choose, men of experience, warriors."

"Anyone fierce enough to threaten an attack on Carthya is fierce enough to defend it."

"But how could you ever trust me?" Roden asked. "After everything between us."

"Because you could've killed me just now." I locked eyes with him. "I know everything about how to make an enemy but very little about friendship. Still, I think we were friends back at Farthenwood, until Cregan poisoned your mind."

"Cregan only wanted me to become the prince."

"But that's the problem. If you accept that you never had a chance to become the prince — never — then you can start to look at everything you *could* become."

"You always were Jaron," Roden mumbled, as if this was the first time it had occurred to him.

"And you are Jaron's friend. I have so few friends I don't say that lightly. You don't belong here. You never did." Roden looked at me and something changed in his eyes. I wasn't sure what he was thinking, but at least he was listening and not trying to stab me. I continued, "You want to be someone who matters to this world. If you want to make a difference, then let it be a difference for good. In Carthya, you will stand at my side and we will fight together. And that matters."

Roden faltered a moment, then called out, "He needs a sword. I can't defeat him honorably unless he's armed."

Someone tossed a sword into the ring, far from where I stood. I cocked my head toward it and arched a brow. "That doesn't count as my being armed. Not if it's over there."

Roden groaned, then walked to get the sword for me. The instant it was in my hands, he struck again.

With a real sword I could fight in a more traditional style, minus the obvious complication of a broken leg. I kept my right foot touched to the ground to steady my weight and grimaced each time I needed to use it. Roden's hits were harder than mine, but I was faster. Except Roden had figured out that all he had to do was rotate a little, which slowed me down, so our blades held each other in a sort of dance.

In their enthusiasm, the crowd of pirates gradually tightened around us, condensing our circle. This seemed to frustrate Roden, who could have used the space to increase the leverage and strength of his swings. It was an advantage to me since the less movement I made, the better. My leg screamed in protest of each step, and it was getting harder every second to ignore it.

I edged Roden toward the thicker part of the crowd. Because of its size, it was slower to react and had the effect of cornering him until the space gradually widened again.

Our blades clashed and parted, then I raised my sword for an attack. He put his blade in position to stop me and got an inadvertent shove from someone too close behind him. He turned his head, very briefly, to yell at everyone to get back.

I swung my blade onto his hand rather than his sword. He yelped as blood trickled down his arm. He tried to swing again, but with the injury to his hand his grip failed and he dropped his sword. I grabbed Roden's shirt, using his weight for balance as I pressed my blade to his neck.

"Let go of your anger," I said to Roden. "I became who I was meant to be and you should do the same. You can be so much more than this."

The hard expression on Roden's face did not change.

I inched the sword away from his neck and added, "You are not meant to be a king. But you are meant to lead the king's armies. You are my choice, my guardian, and my protector. Roden, I need you as my friend."

Something flickered in his eyes again. Roden opened his mouth to say something. Whatever it would have been, he didn't get the chance. I heard only the hard footsteps of a pirate behind me as he jumped into the circle. Before I had the chance to turn to him, he thrust out a foot and kicked me directly on the calf of my wounded leg. I screamed and fell forward, my entire body consumed in pain. My sword fell far out of my reach, and I landed face-first on the ground.

All around me, the pirates laughed and congratulated their comrade. But with his sword in his hands again, Roden widened the circle and yelled, "Stop it! How dare you interfere with my fight?"

The pirates fell silent. The man who had kicked me snarled, "He was about to kill you."

"If he was, then it was a fair win. I'm not fit to rule anyway if I needed your help to defeat a one-legged opponent."

Roden glanced down at me. I'd managed to roll to one side, but the pain in my leg suffocated me with nausea and dizziness. My vision had blurred so that I couldn't tell for certain whether Roden was standing crookedly, or whether the ground where I lay had somehow tilted.

"Get your sword," Roden said. "Get your sword and fight me."

My eyes flitted up to him, then I laid my head back on my arm. There was no point in continuing to fight. Before, I could at least use my broken leg for balance. But I wouldn't even be able to stand now. It was all I could do to remain conscious.

Roden walked toward me. "Get your weapon," he said. "You started this fight and you will finish it."

He would finish it.

I closed my eyes a moment, then finally made the decision that if I was about to die, I would do it with a sword in my hand. Digging my fingers into the dirt, I clawed my way toward the fallen sword. My injured leg dragged uselessly behind me, with my good leg little more helpful in pushing me forward.

Roden stood back as I passed him, the point of his sword dangling somewhere above me. I reached the sword by my fingertips and inched it into my hand. Using my other hand to prop myself up, I raised the sword and forced a slight smile to my face. "This is your last chance to surrender," I said, my words barely audible to my own ears, much less his.

"I have no choice, then." Roden raised his sword, and I closed my eyes, as prepared as I ever could be for his blade to pierce me and finish off the pain. But he slammed the tip of his sword into the dirt beside me and fell on his knees. "Obviously, I must surrender, or lose this battle."

I opened my eyes and saw Roden's crooked grin as he stared back at me. Then he nudged his head, clearly exasperated that I was slow in catching the meaning of his words. Finally, I held out my sword, with no more strength in my hand than had I been a small child. But my voice was strong as I said, "Swear loyalty to me, Roden, and renounce the pirates."

Roden bowed his head. "Jaron, you have defeated me in battle. Therefore, I renounce my position and swear loyalty to you, as King of Carthya, King of the Avenian Pirates, and my King always, wherever in this world you go." When I motioned for him to stand, he turned to the pirates still surrounding us and said, "You heard me. Jaron won this battle and he commands us now."

It was the last thing I heard before I blacked out.

· THIRTY-NINE ·

When I regained consciousness, I was in an actual bed and was covered in blankets. Three or four lit candles were in the room, or hut, where I guessed I was. Although I'd figured out that much, it wasn't clear *why* I might be here. Maybe it was a dream. A slight shift in position sent waves of pain through me and I gasped. Definitely not a dream, then.

"Shh." Serena appeared beside me and helped me lie back down. She glanced behind her. "Roden, he's awake."

She moved aside and Roden filled the frame of my blurred vision. "I don't think I ever could've killed you," he said. "Not when it came down to it."

"You couldn't have told me that in the gardens?"

"I didn't know it myself, not until the end. As proof of that, I let you win. I went easy on you the whole time."

"Then I demand a rematch." I smiled sleepily. "But not today." In a whisper I added, "Where will you be when I'm ready?"

"At your side, Jaron, as captain of your guard." My smile widened and I closed my eyes to return to sleep.

When Roden woke me it was light again. Serena was in her chair with a bowl of something that was steaming, but the thought of eating made my stomach turn.

"Are you hurting much?" Roden asked.

I squinted at him. "Is that a joke? How many pieces do you suppose my leg is in right now?"

He rolled his eyes. "I forgot what a baby you can be when you're injured."

I eyed a cup sitting beside my bed. If it wouldn't have been so difficult, I'd have thrown it at him.

Roden sat beside me and smiled sympathetically. "There's no one here who can fix that leg."

"You should've thought of that before you broke it."

"There was no need to fix the leg of a dead man."

"Ah. How's your leg where I stabbed you?"

"It hurts."

"Good." I closed my eyes again, wanting more sleep, but Roden shook my arm. I shrank from his touch and directed my attention to Serena. "Get me some aravac leaves, all you can find."

When she left, Roden said, "They'll help the pain but won't fix your leg."

"Prepare a cart to take us to Libeth," I said. "A noble named Rulon Harlowe lives there. That's where we're going, if he'll have me."

"I don't think you're strong enough to travel. You don't look so good."

"I don't feel so good. But I doubt I'm the most popular person here. My odds are better on the road to Libeth."

"And what are you going to do about the pirates?"

"That's your decision." Then I remembered that Roden had given me the win. I was the pirate king now. "Send for that man, Erick." I was still tired and my words were slurring. "Fink too. Bring them."

Roden stood and immediately I fell back asleep. I awoke some time later when the door creaked open and Erick walked in, with Fink at his heels.

Erick shook his head in disbelief when he saw me. "I kept watching at the window, waiting to see your body fall. When I didn't see it, I figured you'd fallen in another place. It never occurred to me you were still alive."

Fink rushed forward but I held up a hand to stop him. Even that movement hurt. "If you touch me, I'll have you hanged," I warned. He probably wasn't going to, but I was feeling particularly cautious.

"I heard you won the sword fight," Erick said.

Above me, Roden gave a cough. I looked from his annoyed expression back to Erick. "That debate hasn't been settled. But I am king here now."

Roden managed a half smile at my words, then cursed under his breath.

Erick went on as if he hadn't noticed. "To your credit, everyone's talking about what you did. Nobody likes you, but they respect you."

I nodded. That was good enough.

"What are your plans now?" he asked.

I tried to shrug but gave up the effort and instead just said, "I have to go home. But someone needs to be in charge while I'm gone."

"And you've chosen Roden to lead us." Obviously, the latest gossip hadn't reached Erick's locked room.

"Don't be ridiculous. He just lost to a one-legged opponent, who I might add was mostly unconscious by the end. No, Erick, you're in charge now." Erick's eyes widened but I quickly added, "On two conditions. The first is that you must return that pocket watch to me. I'm tired of trying to steal it from you."

Erick groaned and pulled the watch from his shirt, then held it out to me. "It doesn't keep good time."

"That's not why I want it," I said, clutching it in my hand. "The second condition is that you remind the pirates of their oath to the pirate king, to me. But I'm also the Carthyan king, so to cause harm to any citizen of Carthya, or to our land or property, is to harm me. From now on, there will be an oath of peace between us. All pirates must renew their oaths or be expelled."

Erick shook his head in protest. "They'll never agree."

"You'll make them agree. Tell them if they get bored, then they can always disturb the peace of my enemies. Now go, Erick, get me their oaths."

He stood to leave, then hesitated and said, "Gregor wants to see you."

"But I don't want to see him." Even the thought of it was nauseating.

"He said to remind you that despite his crimes, he did keep your princess safe and he thinks that's worth a few minutes of your time."

I closed my eyes to rest them and mumbled, "Very well, then."

When Erick left, I looked over to Fink. "What do you want? Not to stay here, I'd guess."

Fink thought for a moment, and then said, "Can I come with you?"

"I'm not sure. You're pretty annoying." Then I raised a corner of my mouth. "Yes, I want you to come to Drylliad with me. But you'll have to give up your plans of being a thief and get a proper education."

Fink wrinkled his nose. "Education?"

"Yes. And learn a few manners. I can't decide which you need more. My friend Tobias will teach you, and if you give him any trouble, I'll order him to be twice as boring as usual. Trust me, he can do it."

"Can I bring my rat?"

"No." He tilted his head, but I tightened my stare at him. "No."

Reluctantly, Fink agreed; then, with heavy eyes, I looked at Roden. "Am I safe under your watch?"

"You're safe," Roden assured me as I drifted off.

I didn't sleep as well after that. A new pain had formed in

my leg and I lay half-awake and half-submerged in nightmares that kept the pain fresh. Still, I preferred that to being awoken some time later with the news that Erick had brought Gregor to see me.

Roden helped me into a sitting position, which made my head swim with dizziness. I knew I looked bad, but I refused to look like an invalid.

Erick escorted Gregor in, his hands tied behind him and his clothing stripped of decoration. He gave me a quick appraisal, then began, "Jaron —"

"You'll address me by my title," I said sharply. "And bow until your pointed chin scrapes the floor."

"Yes, Your Majesty." He didn't quite make it to the floor, but did put in a fair effort.

"If you hope to convince me of your innocence, then you're wasting my time."

"No, Your Majesty. I ask only for the same mercy you extended to Master Conner. Please take me back to Drylliad with you. The pirates —"

"The pirates can't be that bad. After all, you were happy to ask their help in killing me."

Gregor's teeth were gritted so tightly together I wondered if his jaw had stopped working. "I had my reasons."

"Such as?"

For the first time since he entered, he looked directly at me. "You missed important meals, made jokes about the regents, and ignored your father's future plans. I genuinely felt I'd do a better job as king. But now I confess that perhaps you were right. It seems there is a threat against Carthya after all."

It wasn't anywhere near as interesting an excuse as I'd expected. "Well, I'd bring you back, except it would require me to look at you during the ride and I'm already feeling sick enough. No, you'll stay here and face whatever consequences the pirates intend for you."

"You're their king too."

I nodded toward Erick. "But it's his decision now. Use your poisonous tongue to beg mercy from him. Now go away."

Erick stepped forward and lifted Gregor by his bound hands. "The night before you left, you asked if I thought you wanted to run." Gregor's tone was somewhere between panicked and furious now. "I did think that. I thought you were the worst of cowards and it justified my belief that I should be named steward."

Despite the pain it caused, I leaned forward and in a soft whisper said, "There was something you failed to understand about me." He tilted his head and in my strongest voice I added, "I never run!"

Gregor's eyes widened, then his face paled as Erick dragged him away, handing him off to pirates who had been waiting outside.

"The oaths?" I asked Erick when he turned back to me.

"Nobody's happy about it," he said. "But I pointed out that we'd never get you to leave unless they made the oath. Besides, we figure if you stayed, there's not a lot more that the pirates could do to you. The oath is secure. The pirates are officially at peace with Carthya."

With relief, I said, "Very good."

"It's not all good," Erick continued. "It won't be long before the king of Avenia learns that you've stolen the pirates' loyalty from him. He won't be happy about this."

"Well, I'm not happy with him either." He had conspired with the pirates in trying to overthrow me. It was unlikely that he and I would sit down for tea together anytime soon. I used the last of my energy to say, "No matter what comes, you'll see that the pirates keep their oath to me. If there is a fight, they will fight for me."

"You are our king," Erick said.

I nodded, then said to Roden, "It's time to leave. I want to go home."

· FORTY ·

The ride to Libeth was a study in the art of torture. Roden drove a cart led by his horse and mine, and I yelled more than once that I was certain he was deliberately driving into every bump or pothole. He said he was going as fast as he could, which wasn't exactly a denial. I cursed back at him until Fink told me he was learning words even the pirates didn't use. I told him to be quiet and let me try to rest. Before long I began shivering. Fink pushed blankets close around my body, but it didn't do much good because the cold wasn't outside. It was in me, like ice water had filled my veins. The nausea returned, and with it a sort of dizziness that only got worse when I closed my eyes. But sleep was impossible and with every mile I felt considerably worse. Eventually, Fink faded into the background, melting away like characters often did in my dreams.

It was late at night when the cart finally stopped. I was aware of Roden talking to me and pressing my neck for a pulse, but when I tried to explain what I wanted he just stared at me as if he didn't understand.

A moment later, Harlowe's face was leaning over mine. He barked orders at people I couldn't see and then picked me up to carry me into his home. I tried to talk to him, but he told me to hush and that everything was going to be all right. I understood that already. Wasn't that why I'd come to the pirates in the first place, to fix things? I was just so tired and nothing anyone did or said made any sense.

Harlowe laid me on a bed in a room I didn't recognize and covered me in blankets. I kept pushing them off and fighting whoever was nearby until I got the item from my shirt that I wanted.

"Harlowe," I mumbled. He appeared and said something about having already sent for a surgeon. That didn't matter. I could hardly feel my leg anymore. All I wanted was to give him the pocket watch, which I pressed into his hand. "Forgive me," I whispered. I wasn't sure whether he understood me or not, but he brushed my sweat-dampened hair off my face and told me to go to sleep. This time, I obeyed.

I awoke next to a sensation in my leg so fierce that I shot up in bed and screamed. My hand went for my knife, but as had been common lately, it wasn't there. So I kicked forward with my good leg and connected with someone who grunted and fell backward.

Hands pressed me down, and somewhere in the room Roden's voice said it was only the surgeon setting my leg and to stay calm. I wondered if that was who I'd just kicked. If so, he deserved it for hurting me so badly.

The worst of the pain passed and eventually the hands released me. Someone tried to give me something to drink, but it was hot in my mouth and I spat it out.

I heard someone say Imogen's name. And I lost consciousness again.

The next time I awoke, things were beginning to make more sense. The curtains in the room were shut, but narrow slits of light peeked through them. I groaned as I tried to roll over, and the next face I saw was Imogen's. She radiated with a glimmer of light on her skin, which made me wonder whether the devils were playing a joke on me, and if she wasn't really here.

"Drink this." She helped me sit up enough to swallow a honey tea that both warmed and soothed my dry throat. Until then, I hadn't realized how thirsty I was.

"Where did you come from?" I asked.

"Harlowe's messenger caught up to Mott and me as we were leaving Dichell. We were on our way to the pirates, to come after you."

"I told you not to go back to the pirates."

"Yes, but you didn't tell Mott, and unfortunately he was my ride."

I smiled until it took too much effort. "You're starting to sound like me. That's not good."

Rather than answer, Imogen offered me more to drink. I took it, then asked, "Are we at Harlowe's?"

"Yes. He asked to see you as soon as you were coherent again."

"I remember being confused," I said. "But only because nobody could understand me."

"Your body was in shock. The surgeon was surprised you survived the trip here."

"Me too. Roden's a terrible driver."

"He had to travel fast. He knew the danger you were in."

A door behind me opened and Imogen looked up and then motioned at whoever was there to enter. When Harlowe came around my bed, he bowed low. Imogen invited him to take her chair and said she'd return in a few minutes.

Harlowe sat, smiled grimly at me, then leaned forward with his arms resting on his legs.

"The thieves were going to rob someone." It was important to make him understand that before anything else was spoken. "If I didn't bring them here —"

"Then they'd have gone somewhere else and caused actual damage. I know. Mott explained after you left."

"Mott didn't know. I never told him."

"But he knows you, and so he explained."

"I'm sorry, Harlowe. I frightened Nila."

"Nila was afraid *for* you, not of you."

"How is she?"

"She's adjusting, but she misses her parents."

"I'm sorry for that too. I didn't know the raids were happening."

After clearing his throat, Harlowe said, "I tried to talk to the king — your father — not long ago. He referred me to his prime regent, Master Veldergrath."

My stomach tightened. My contempt for Veldergrath was lower than my opinion of rats, if the one could be distinguished from the other. "He was dismissed as a regent last month," I said. "But someone should've listened when you came." It was hard to ask the next question, but I needed to know the answer. "Did my father know what was happening here?"

He frowned at me. "I don't know. We tried to get messages to him, but I don't know if he ever received them."

It probably didn't matter. I doubted my father would've had the will to stop Avenia if he did know. I laid my head back on the pillow and rested. After a moment I said, "That day I brought Nila here, you asked me to stay the night. Was that a sincere offer?"

"Of course it was."

"Because of what I'd done for her?"

"Because you looked like someone who needed a place to stay."

"And why did you give me your son's watch?"

He hesitated, then said, "I didn't know why you'd joined up with the thieves, but I knew you weren't like them. I hoped the watch would help you remember your way back, maybe keep you from getting lost in their world."

My eyes had become heavy again. Harlowe made a move to leave, but I asked him to wait. When he sat again I said, "You prefer to avoid the politics in Drylliad. Honestly, so do I. But Carthya needs you and I need a prime regent."

Harlowe sat up straight. "Prime? That's a title given for seniority amongst your regents. There are many others —"

"They're all idiots. We both know that. Please, Harlowe, will you come to Drylliad?"

There was no hesitation. "As you wish, Your Majesty."

"I'm Jaron." My words were beginning to slur and I knew more sleep wasn't far off. "That's my name."

· FORTY-ONE ·

When Imogen had cared for me at Farthenwood, she was still a servant herself and subject to Conner's orders. But now we were in Harlowe's home, and it quickly became apparent that she was in control of every aspect of my care.

She forced food and water into me until I refused to open my mouth, tended to the cuts and scrapes on my chest and back, and stayed with me constantly unless someone else was there to visit. Through all that we said little to each other. I don't think either of us knew the right words.

For the most part, I let her manage things without complaining. I did tell her later that same afternoon that it was time to return to Drylliad. I asked her to arrange for a messenger who would notify Amarinda and Tobias to find an excuse to leave and meet me in Farthenwood. There we could set everything straight before I returned to the castle.

"Don't you think they'll notice the king returning to Drylliad with a broken leg?" she asked, smiling.

"I might not be king anymore," I replied. Even without

Gregor, perhaps the vote on the steward had taken place.

Her response was interrupted by a knock on the door, and Mott was admitted into my room. Imogen again made an excuse to leave and he sat in her chair.

It was difficult to know where to begin with him. I knew he'd be respectful because of my title and the extent of my injuries, but I wanted more than that. I needed to know what it would take for him to consider me a friend again, if anything could. Apparently, he felt awkward too, because he spent more effort studying the floor than actually looking at me.

Finally, I said it. "I won't apologize for what I've done. But I must apologize for how difficult my actions must have been for you."

"Fair enough." Then he added, "But for the record, I won't apologize for my anger about your leaving. I'm glad that everything turned out as it did, but it was still far too reckless."

"Agreed." I paused, then said, "Although in the same circumstances, I'd do it again. Except for the part about making Roden angry enough to break my leg."

We were quiet a moment, and then, in a much sadder voice, Mott added, "Why didn't you let me come with you? I could have protected you."

I looked at him. "But that's just the problem. You would have protected me, which would have risked both our lives. And it had to be me who went. I knew at some point that I'd have to face Roden. He wouldn't have returned with anyone else."

"After the way he threatened you, I thought you'd have to kill him."

"Only if there was no other choice. My hope was always to get him back on my side again."

"He's better off here with us."

"And we're better off with him," I said. "He's a dangerous enemy but a fierce friend. Carthya needs him on our side."

"But how can you trust him? After all he's done to you?"

"When we fought that last time, he could've easily ended things by striking at my leg. He never did, not once. If he wanted me dead, I would be."

Mott nodded. "Then I'll learn to trust him too. You do have friends, Jaron. We will always stand by you."

I understood that better now. I pointed to his forearm, still bandaged tightly. "I'm sorry about your arm, outside Harlowe's office."

"I'd only arrived a little earlier that night. Harlowe was doing his best to deny having seen you, but it was obvious he had." The corner of Mott's mouth lifted. "He thought you were a runaway servant, probably owned by a noble in Drylliad."

For some reason, that struck me as funny. I chuckled only until it hurt, then said, "Harlowe's a good man. I asked him to be my prime regent."

Mott's eyebrows rose. "Prime? That's going to upset your other regents. Some of them have been there longer than you've been alive."

"They were ready to give control of Carthya to a traitor. Once Gregor's treachery is known, they'll be a lot humbler. Harlowe is the right man to lead them."

"He'll serve you well." Mott pressed his lips together and then said, "He couldn't understand how a king could abandon everything to join up with thieves and pirates. He worried that you had forgotten yourself."

"I never forgot myself, not once," I mumbled. "That was the hardest part." Then I looked up at Mott. "Nor can I ever forgive myself, if you won't forgive me."

"For this?" He tilted his head. "There's nothing to forgive."

"No, not for what I've done." I lowered my gaze and fingered a loose thread on the blanket. "I ask you to forgive who I am. It will never be easy to serve with me."

Mott's eyes moistened. "I am certain of that. But I will serve you anyway."

With that, I laid my head back on my pillow and rested. When Mott began speaking again, I opened my eyes but only stared forward.

"I should know better than to ever doubt you." Mott placed a hand on my arm. "Today you live because of everything you've done right in your life. You did well."

I smiled and returned to sleep. There was nothing kinder he could have said.

Imogen was there when I awoke. I must have slept through the night because it was a morning sun warming the room. This time she helped me sit up and placed a tray of food on my lap.

"You look like yourself again," she said. "Whoever that is."

I blinked a few times to put her in better focus. "An invalid? That's the real me?"

"Of course not. But —" Short on words, she only shrugged. "You look . . . content. It suits you."

I chuckled. "No, it doesn't."

"I suppose not." She grew quiet for a moment, then said, "I shouldn't have gone to the pirates, even on Amarinda's orders."

"Agreed."

"We hoped that I could help. The hairpin, the flowers, they were meant to save you."

"No, Imogen," I said. "It's you who saves me. And not just from the pirates. I need you. When we get back to the castle — "

"I'm not going back." She exhaled slowly, as if hoping to silently express the worst news. "Jaron, please understand. I can't be there anymore."

"Why not?" Of course she'd come with me. How else would things return to normal? There was an edge to my tone now. "Is it the servants, or the princess —"

"It's you. I can't go back and be near you." Her brows pressed together and a small line formed between them. "Things are different now. Can't you feel it?"

In that moment, most of what I felt was frustration. When I'd dismissed her from the castle, I'd known that I had hurt her, but surely she understood my reasons by now. I said, "The night I sent you away, that was only —"

"It was the right thing to do and we both know it. Devlin would have used me to take the kingdom from you."

I shook my head. "Yes, he tried. But it didn't work."

"What if he hadn't let you fight him? Would you have told him about the cave to keep him from whipping me?"

She had made her point. Whatever my options, I could never have allowed him to harm her. Yet this was no solution. Finally, I mumbled, "You have to come back. It's only a friendship, Imogen."

Tears welled in her eyes. "No, Jaron, it's not. Maybe it never was. Don't you see that it hurts me to be close to you?"

Hurt — that was the effect I seemed to have on those closest to me. Maybe what I'd done over the past several days had been necessary for Carthya, but there was always a price for my actions. This time, it had cost me the dearest friendship I had.

Imogen brushed at an escaped tear with the tips of her fingers. "Besides, if I go back, I'll be in the way of you and Amarinda."

"That's what's bothering you? I can make everything work out there."

She frowned, and even through tears her tone became brusque. "How is that? Will you choose me and humiliate the princess? Destroy the relationship with her country, our only ally?" She shook her head. "The people love her, Jaron, and they should. Choose me, and you would lose your people."

Choose? I was so taken aback, I could only stammer, "I'm not choosing anyone!"

"You don't have to. I'm making the choice." Imogen's eyes darted away, then she added, "Harlowe offered me a position to stay and watch after Nila, and I'm going to accept it. You must return to Drylliad and learn to trust Amarinda. Learn to need *her.*"

With a scoff, I turned away. After having come so far, I was back exactly where I had started. Imogen sat and touched my arm. "Jaron, she's on your side; she always was."

"She's friends with a traitor."

"She's *your* friend, which you'd know if you had ever given her the chance to show it. How is it that you can see your enemies so clearly and never your friends?" Imogen closed her eyes, very briefly, to steady her emotions. "You are a king, and she is meant to become your queen. You'll marry her one day."

This time, I caught a tremor in her voice and wondered if I'd been mistaken before. Perhaps Imogen hadn't been saying we were no longer friends. Maybe her message was that we were no longer *only* friends.

It was impossible to look directly at her as I mumbled, "Imogen, do you love me?"

My heart pounded while I awaited her response. With every endless second that passed, I felt increasingly certain that I never should have attempted such a question. I understood the concept of love but had long doubted anyone's ability to feel that way for me. All I dared hope to ask of Imogen was friendship, and now it seemed even that was failing.

After a long, horrible silence, she shook her head and whispered, "I don't belong in your world, Jaron. You have the princess. Win *her* heart. Be *hers*."

I searched Imogen's face for any sign that she might be hiding her true emotions. After all, I had concealed the truth of my feelings behind the terrible things I'd said to her the night I sent her from the castle. A jumble of emotions collided within me, and I wondered if this was the way I had made Imogen feel that night, as though her entire world was splitting apart. She was masking her pain; I knew her well enough to see that. But for reasons I still couldn't understand, I was the cause of it.

Yet in the end, the reasons didn't matter. She was right. Whatever either of us felt, she could never belong to me. My future had but one path, and that was with the betrothed princess.

I nodded silently back at her, and with that, she stood and made herself busy in the room. "You should be ready to leave shortly. Harlowe's having a bed made up for you in a wagon."

As if I cared about that. "No more beds," I grunted. "I'll go in a carriage."

"All right. If you're up to it."

She wouldn't even face me now, which was awful. But I suspected it would be far worse to look in her eyes and see nothing but indifference in them.

I tried one last time, hoping to make her understand me. "Wherever our lives lead us, one thing is certain. You and I will always be connected. You might be able to deny that, but I can't. Even I am not that good a liar."

Imogen nodded, then turned to me only long enough to lower herself into a deep, respectful curtsy. "Please excuse me . . . Your Highness. We are not likely to ever see each other again. Be happy in your life." And she left.

· FORTY-TWO ·

Mott and Roden drove the carriage back to Farthenwood. Harlowe rode beside me and Fink sat across from him. It still hurt to sit up but not too much. My leg was propped up on the seat across from me and padded with what I guessed was possibly every spare blanket in all of Libeth. An earthquake could shake Carthya to its core but even then, it'd barely jar my leg.

For the most part we traveled in silence. I liked that about Harlowe. He made no attempts at meaningless chatter or wit and was often content just to listen and watch the world around him. In contrast, Fink appeared to be fighting the urge to speak, just to release the energy trapped inside him. But someone must have threatened him, because whenever he looked at me and opened his mouth, he closed it again and returned to looking out the window.

It was dark when we arrived at Farthenwood. Fink had slept for most of the ride and remained asleep even after the carriage stopped. The royal carriage was already there.

Tobias came out to greet us almost immediately. He drew

in a sharp breath when I emerged with a battle-bruised face and my leg in a splint, but he made a valiant attempt at a convincing smile. And he eyed Roden suspiciously, but I supposed Roden would have to deal with that for a while. Besides, Tobias would get over it once everything was explained to him.

"You're going to be a teacher after all," I said to Tobias as we passed by. "Your first student is asleep in the carriage. I wish you the best of luck."

Tobias furrowed his brow and glanced doubtfully at the carriage.

"If that wasn't enough trouble, I have another request," I said. "I still need one more regent. Please accept, Tobias."

His eyes widened. "Are you offering that to me? Really?"

"Thank me now. Because you won't spend much time with those fools before you'll regret accepting."

"Then I will thank you, Your Majesty." Tobias kissed the king's ring, then handed it to me and said, "I brought a change of clothes so that I can just be myself again. There's another set for you too, though I'm not sure how you'll fit the pants over your leg."

"I'll figure something out. What about the princess? Is she here?"

Tobias nodded. "She said that if you want to talk, she'll meet wherever you ask." I started forward and he added, "I spent a lot of time with her this week. She is sincere about caring for you."

"If someone can find something to eat, I'm really hungry,"

I said, bypassing his evaluation of her. "It'll take a while to change clothes, but will you ask her to join me when I'm finished?"

It was nearly an hour later before I was dressed and ready for her to enter the small dining room. I wouldn't allow Tobias to escort her in until my leg was already propped under the table. Yet she must have known about my condition because the first thing she looked at was the chair across from me. And she sat in the chair Tobias pulled out for her before I would have had time to stand and greet her properly, if I could have done that, of course.

Her clothing tonight was simple, a blue cotton bodice and blue-striped skirt over a white chemise. Her warm brown hair fell like a waterfall down her back and was tied with a white ribbon. Whatever she was to me, I couldn't deny her beauty. She'd turn heads even wearing sackcloth.

Amarinda began the conversation. "What have you done to your hair?"

It struck me as odd that even though I was covered in cuts and bruises, not to mention an obvious injury to my leg, my hair was the one thing she chose to comment on. Then I realized that was probably her intention, to make it clear she was seeing me without calling attention to how bad I looked. So I grinned. "I wanted to give the castle hairdresser a challenge."

"It's thoughtful of you to always find ways to entertain your servants."

"That's just the kind of good person he is," Tobias said.

Amarinda smiled at him. "You'd be proud of Tobias. He did an admirable job in your absence. On the day the regents were supposed to vote on the stewardship, he sent them a ten-page paper explaining in great detail how, with only eighteen regents, their vote had no binding authority. He was brilliant!"

"Thank you, my lady," Tobias said.

"So the vote will be delayed?" I asked.

She shook her head. "There will be no vote. You alone are the ruler of Carthya."

I closed my eyes as feelings of relief coursed through me. Then, glancing at Tobias, I asked, "How can I repay you?"

"Just promise never to do that to me again. No offense, Jaron, but I don't want your life. Even locked away behind closed doors I got a taste for how awful it can be."

"Did anyone try to kill you while I was gone?"

"No."

"Then you didn't even get a taste. Will you leave us now?"

After Tobias bowed and left, I turned to Amarinda. "You sent Imogen to the pirates."

A lock of the princess's hair fell forward as she slowly nodded. "We talked for a very long time before she left the castle. I told her what you had said to me about the attack. Imogen was sure you would go to the pirates. She offered to go there too, certain that if anyone could change your mind, she could. Or if not, at least she could keep you safe."

"You should have forbidden her from going."

"I could also command the sun not to rise and yet it would. She would have gone anyway, Jaron."

"And what about you? I left you in a terrible position."

"Not really." Her long eyelashes fluttered, then she said, "My part in this was insignificant."

"Nothing was more significant than to have someone to carry on for Carthya. Besides that, I put you at risk. Mott has already ridden on ahead to inform Kerwyn of Gregor's treachery." For that part, I barely looked at her. Gregor had been her closest friend. "My biggest worry was what would happen to you if I didn't return."

"If there was any threat, Gregor would have protected me. Whatever his intentions with you, he'd still have made sure I was safe." She lowered her eyes. "I think he believed that once he sat on the throne, he'd have me for a wife."

"Was he correct?"

She frowned. "Under no circumstances would I ever have accepted him. Did you think I could spend so much time with him and not see what he was?"

"Then you knew?"

"Not exactly. But I was suspicious. After your family's deaths, I realized there had been small hints of his disloyalty. I made the decision to form a friendship with Gregor, hoping that in a closer relationship I could find some evidence against him. The only reason I brought Conner that dinner was because Gregor had suggested it. I think that was his way of testing me against you."

"His test nearly worked. I was ready to declare you a trai-tor." The thought of how things could have turned out so much worse made me shudder. I added, "You risked so much. Why didn't you just tell me?"

She straightened her back. "I could barely tell you the time of day without you cutting off our conversation. Besides, he was your captain. I didn't want to come to you with accusations that I couldn't prove. Then everything happened so fast after the assassination attempt. I tried to talk with you late that night, but the vigils at your door told me you had snuck out and nobody knew where you were. Then you were gone so quickly the next morning."

I leaned back in my chair and chuckled at that. With a curious tilt of her head, she said, "I just confessed to keeping a secret that nearly got you killed. I thought you'd be angry, not amused."

"I'm only angry with myself." I sighed. "Mott was right all along. I am a fool. I knew of your friendship with Gregor. Because of that, I wouldn't talk to you either. If I had, every-thing might have been so much simpler."

"Oh." Amarinda smiled shyly. "It's a wonder you and I found anything at all to talk about."

"We didn't, not really. Imogen kept asking me to make things right with you, but I wouldn't. Any failure between us is entirely my fault."

Amarinda pressed her lips together, then said, "I heard that Imogen stayed behind, in Libeth."

"Yes."

"Do you hate me, because I'm not her, because you'll have to marry me one day?"

I stared at her a moment before I snorted out another impolite laugh. She flashed a glare that too quickly turned to pain. "Forgive me," I said. "It's just that those were nearly the words I've wanted to say to you all this time, and never dared." Before she could speak, I added, "Do you hate me? Because I'm not my brother and because you'll have to marry me one day?"

A very slow smile crossed her face and she gave an understanding nod and gestured with her hand. It brushed against mine. She started to pull it back but I took hers and held it, in a sign of our partnership, that from now on we would stand together. Her hand was closed in a fist at first, but she slowly relaxed and folded it into mine. I'd never held someone's hand before, not like this. It was both wonderful and frightening.

"I'm letting her go," I said. "And I'm asking you to let him go too."

She nodded slowly. "Are we friends, Jaron?"

"We are."

With her other hand, Amarinda brushed my forearm where the mark of the pirates was branded into my skin. The burn was still red and tender, but somehow it didn't hurt the way she touched it.

"It might fade eventually," I said, "but it will never go away."

"It shouldn't go away. It's part of your history now. What you've done is a part of Carthya's history."

"Still, I'll try to keep it hidden whenever possible."

Amarinda's grip tightened. "It's not necessary for you to hide that. Nor to hide anything from me."

There was silence again, but less awkward than before. Her hand felt soft and I wondered if mine was too rough to be comfortable for her. I hoped that *I* had not become too rough for her.

Finally, I grinned and said, "I won't eat meat if it's been overcooked." She glanced up at me, confused, and I added, "I thought you should know that, since we're going to be friends now."

Amarinda's smile widened. "I think it's unfair that women aren't allowed to wear trousers. They seem far more comfortable than dresses."

I chuckled. "They're not. Every year I think fashion invents one more piece I have to add to my wardrobe."

"And one more layer to my skirts." She thought for a moment, then said, "I think it's funny when you're rude to the cook. I shouldn't admit that, but his face turns all sorts of colors when you are and there's nothing he can do about it."

"He can overcook my meat."

This time she laughed and even gave my hand a squeeze. We fell silent. After a while I said, "I won't rule as my father did, and you can never expect me to be my brother. But I'll rule the best way I can and hope it will be enough to make you a proud queen one day."

"What about this day?" When she smiled at me, it was obvious that something had changed between us. She added, "Jaron, I'm proud of what you did for Carthya, proud that you trusted me to rule while you were gone. And I'm proud to be sitting beside you now. There are great things ahead for us."

And for the first time since becoming king, I believed her.

· FORTY-THREE ·

It was late evening when we rode into Drylliad. Even then, the streets seemed quieter than usual and many of the homes were dark. Perhaps the time was much later than I had thought. Still tired, I laid my head against the seat as we entered through the castle gates. Fink parted the curtained windows of the carriage and tried to talk to me, but Harlowe firmly shushed him and told him to give me some silence.

So much had changed since I had left nearly two weeks ago. Some things were for the better. Carthya was safe from Gregor and a pirate attack, both Roden and Amarinda were with me, and the threat of a steward had passed. But not everything was how I wanted it. I vaguely wondered if my father would approve of what I'd done. Probably not, but I could accept that.

"Are you ready for this?" I asked Harlowe as our carriage stopped. "With all apologies, you'll soon see what it means to be associated with me." Whatever the people thought of me, I hoped they'd give Harlowe the respect he deserved.

Harlowe smiled back warmly. "A better question, Your Majesty, is if *you* are ready."

He stepped out first, and I realized my courtyard was much better lit than it usually was at night. Then Harlowe held out a hand for Amarinda. When she exited the carriage, I began to hear noises outside, murmurs and the shuffling of feet.

Then Harlowe leaned in. "You'll want help out of this carriage, sire."

Angrily, I shook my head. "How many servants have gathered for this exhibition? I'll do it myself before I have them laugh at my helplessness."

Harlowe held out his hand to me. "Take my arm, *please*. Trust me."

So I scooted closer to the door and he widened it for me. At first all I could see was the courtyard lined with torches, so bright I had to squint against the light. Then as I took my first steps onto the ground, a cheer thundered throughout the yard.

I hesitated at first, and without Harlowe to balance me I might have fallen. Was it possible that cheer had been for me? Smiling, Harlowe said, "So this is what you warned me about? What it means to be associated with you?"

I shook my head, not understanding. Then somewhere above me, I heard Kerwyn's voice echo, "Hail His Majesty. Jaron, the Ascendant King of Carthya." And more cheers followed.

At my side, Amarinda said, "Jaron the Ascendant. I like that. See your people welcome you home."

Harlowe led me forward, to where the light wasn't so harsh and I could have a better look. As far as I could see, the courtyard was packed with people. My people. Then slowly, almost reverently, they went to their knees and all fell silent.

Together, Mott and Kerwyn walked up to me. They bowed, and Kerwyn wiped tears from his eyes as he stood again. He shook his head as he stared at me.

"I know how I look," I said.

But he only raised a corner of his mouth and replied, "No, I don't think you have any idea what we all see in you."

I was still confused. "Did you order the people to come?"

"They came on their own," Kerwyn said. "After they heard what you've done for them."

"But how —" Then my eyes narrowed. "Mott?"

"I might have mentioned it to a few people." He chuckled as he spoke, clearly pleased with himself.

I looked over the crowd again, completely overwhelmed. Conner had told me I was king only by blood, not because it was what the people wanted. But that wasn't true anymore. Tears welled in my eyes, bringing to the surface an emotion that I had always thought would forever linger out of my reach. I was at peace. Another battle, far greater than anything I'd faced with the pirates, was over.

A smile rose from my heart and widened across my face. I raised both arms and with a new strength to my voice, said, "My people, my friends. We are Carthya!"

I stayed that way while they cheered again, then I lowered

my arms and turned to Mott, exhaustion finally winning the battle. "Will you help me to my room?"

He dipped his head at me. "Yes, my king." And more cheering followed my exit from the courtyard.

———

For the next two months everything was calm. When necessary, Amarinda and I appeared in public together, though because of my leg there were fewer events than usual. More often, she joined me for private dinners in the evening. Other people were sometimes included, but whatever our group, it was a good time.

After eight weeks, the physician allowed me to remove the wrap around my leg and encouraged me to begin using it as much as possible. No encouragement was necessary. It was the height of our warm season and I was desperate to be outside. I set a routine of running as long as I could each morning and evening, usually until Mott found me with the stern reminder that my leg hadn't fully healed yet. I reminded him I'd likely always have some pain in the leg, so it was better I get used to it now.

It was on one of those evenings when I noticed Mott coming toward me on the lawn. Normally, I'd have kept running and let him do the work to get my attention. But he wasn't alone that night. Kerwyn and Amarinda were with him, and all three had strained looks on their faces.

The groomsman attending me ran up with a towel when

he saw I'd stopped. I hung it around my shoulders, then dismissed him.

"What's happened?" My question was addressed to no one specifically.

Kerwyn answered. "It's bad, Jaron. Last night the Avenian army crossed our borders. Libeth is destroyed."

For a long moment, I could not breathe, could not comprehend the violence of such an act. I had known something was coming soon, but not this. Nothing like this. I faltered for words but looked at Mott for answers. He said, "Nila escaped with one of Harlowe's servants. That's who brought us word of the attack. Harlowe's with them now."

"Imogen?"

Amarinda gently shook her head. "They took her. Harlowe's servant believes the Avenians were in Libeth for that purpose. To get at her."

To get at me.

"We'll find her." Mott's hand already gripped the handle of his sword.

"But it's worse," Kerwyn said. "We have also just received word that Gelyn and Mendenwal are advancing from the north and east. This was a coordinated attack and we are surrounded. Jaron, the war has begun."

· ACKNOWLEDGMENTS ·

*The process of bringing a book from concept all the way
into readers' hands is a journey that requires the time
and talents of many dedicated people, from publicity,
marketing, and art direction to conferences, sales, and
beyond. I cannot acknowledge everyone by name here,
but I hope they will know that I am grateful for
their efforts and their enthusiasm.*

*Specifically, I must begin with expressing my love
and gratitude to my husband, who has never failed
in his support of both me and my career. I am grateful
to my children as well, who without complaint have
encouraged me to pursue my writing dreams. Many
thanks to my wonderful agent, Ammi-Joan Paquette,
whose sharp eye and thoughtful analysis of this story
made all the difference in the most crucial moments.
I must also express appreciation to David Levithan*

for his brilliant input on this series, and for his

continual support of my writing.

I saved one name for last, that of my editor,

Lisa Sandell. Thanks to her patience, guidance,

and keen intelligence, this book has come a long way

from its early drafts. If there is any praise given to this

series, then she is a vital and significant partner in these

pages and fully deserves to share in the honors. Beyond

that, she has become a valuable part of my life, and I'm

honored to call her my friend.

· ABOUT THE AUTHOR ·

JENNIFER A. NIELSEN is the author of *The False Prince*, the first book in The Ascendance Trilogy. She collects old books, loves good theater, and thinks that a quiet afternoon in the mountains is a nearly perfect moment.

A major influence for Sage's story came from the music of Eddie Vedder and one of his greatest songs, "Guaranteed." From his line "I knew all the rules, but the rules did not know me," Sage was born. Sage's personality is his own, but Jennifer did borrow two of his traits from a couple of students she once taught in a high school debate class. One of them was popular, brilliant, and relentlessly mischievous. He could steal the watch off a person's wrist without their knowing and would return it to them later, usually to their embarrassment. The other student had a broad spectrum of impressive talents, not the least of which was his ability to roll a coin over his knuckles. If he had wanted to, he'd have made a fine pickpocket. As it was, he went on to become a lawyer. Go figure.

Jennifer lives in northern Utah with her husband, their three children, and a perpetually muddy dog.